ABOUT THE AUTHOR

Narcissism for Beginners is Martine McDonagh's third novel. Martine worked for thirty years as an artist manager in the music industry and is currently programme leader on the Creative Writing & Publishing MA at West Dean College in Sussex.

BY THE SAME AUTHOR

'Told with passion and real skill… a disturbing but rewarding read that makes a virtue of brevity and a narrow focus.'   —*The Bookbag*

'This novel manages to combine the nightmare of post environmental apocalypse with a psychological thriller… McDonagh's novel is a fine example of the spec fiction genre, the changed world she has created seems eerily real.'   —*Gaskella*

'Evocative and intriguing, this novel deserves an audience.'
—*The Argus*

'The novel is both poignant and terrifying. The world created here is so vivid and real, it would be hard not to be moved by it.'
—Post-Apocalyptic Book Club

'Martine McDonagh has worked in the rock industry for a long time and her writing still works to this tempo, to these dynamics – physical, sensual and nerve-racking.'
—Jean-Daniel Beauvallet, *Les Inrockuptibles*

'The writing touches subconscious strata; the mystery unfolds hypnotically; the reader is drawn into a parallel universe all too frighteningly real.'
—Lenny Kaye, author of *Waylon* and *You Call It Madness*

'This book certainly got under my skin – if you like your books dark and more than a little disturbing, this one is for you.'
—Mick Jackson,
Man Booker shortlisted author of *The Widow's Tale*

PRAISE FOR *After Phoenix*

'Martine McDonagh writes simply, sparingly, intelligently and unsentimentally about both big and small things.'
—Stephen May, Costa Prize shortlisted author of *Life! Death! Prizes!*

'A great read.'   —Araminta Hall, author of *Dot*

'A raw, emotive portrayal of a family pushed to its limits by grief.'
—Lizzie Enfeld, author of *Living with It*

'Given that the book's subject is grief, and that grief is a dulling, leaden, grey and tedious feeling, it's amazing how vital, entertaining and even funny *After Phoenix* is, without in any way shortchanging the reality of the experience.' —*Caustic Cover Critic*

'In this moving portrait of not only what comes after loss but what comes after that, McDonagh demonstrates more finesse on the subject than anyone in recent memory.'
—Alex Green, author of *Emergency Anthems*

'Heart-wrenching and life-affirming in equal measure, the author has managed to give real insight whilst still being entertaining and making you want to turn the pages – your heart will ache but it will also laugh.' —*Lizlovesbooks*

'Despite beginning with a tragedy, this book is never entirely without hope and is a powerful portrait of grief and how time heals. Powerful stuff.' —*Annabel's House of Books*

'It's not as tough a read as it sounds. The silliness and amiable chaos of family life is a strong part of the narrative, even as the remaining trio battle their way through grief. But it's as good an evocation of the abysmal sting of sudden death as I can remember reading.'
—*Booksquawk*

'An intelligent, well observed account of how the same event can impact different people. Incredibly moving yet often still very funny, it deals with the most difficult of subjects but is never bleak. The family members have a sense of warmth and love about them, even as their lives fall apart. I loved every minute of it.' —*A Sense Sublime*

'A heart-warming tale of family unity and the conquering of grief.'
—*Northern Soul*

Dear Reader,

The book you are holding came about in a rather different way to most others. It was funded directly by readers through a new website: Unbound. Unbound is the creation of three writers. We started the company because we believed there had to be a better deal for both writers and readers. On the Unbound website, authors share the ideas for the books they want to write directly with readers. If enough of you support the book by pledging for it in advance, we produce a beautifully bound special subscribers' edition and distribute a regular edition and e-book wherever books are sold, in shops and online.

This new way of publishing is actually a very old idea (Samuel Johnson funded his dictionary this way). We're just using the internet to build each writer a network of patrons. Here, at the back of this book, you'll find the names of all the people who made it happen. Publishing in this way means readers are no longer just passive consumers of the books they buy, and authors are free to write the books they really want. They get a much fairer return too – half the profits their books generate, rather than a tiny percentage of the cover price.

If you're not yet a subscriber, we hope that you'll want to join our publishing revolution and have your name listed in one of our books in the future. To get you started, here is a £5 discount on your first pledge. Just visit unbound.com, make your pledge and type **beginners** in the promo code box when you check out.

Thank you for your support,

Dan, Justin and John
Founders, Unbound

This edition first published in 2017

Unbound

6th Floor Mutual House, 70 Conduit Street, London W1S 2GF

www.unbound.com

Text Design by PDQ

Art direction by Mark Ecob

A CIP record for this book is available from the British Library

ISBN 978-1-78352-344-3 (trade hbk)
ISBN 978-1-78352-345-0 (ebook)
ISBN 978-1-78352-346-7 (limited edition)

Printed in Great Britain by Clays Ltd, St Ives Plc

1 3 5 7 9 8 6 4 2

NARCISSISM FOR BEGINNERS

Martine McDonagh

unbound

And you measure for wealth by the things you can hold
And you measure for love by the sweet things you're told
And you live in the past or a dream that you're in
And your selfishness is your cardinal sin

And you want to be held with highest regard
It delights you so much, if he's trying so hard
And you try to conceal your ordinary way
With a smile or a shrug
Or some stolen cliché

But don't you understand, and don't you look about
I'm trying to take nothing from you
So why should you act so put out
For me

'Cause emotionally you're the same basic trip
And you know that I know of the times that you've slipped
So don't try to impress me, you're just pins and paint
And don't try to charm me with things that you ain't

And don't try to enchant me with your manner of dress
'Cause a monkey in silk is a monkey no less
So measure for measure reflect on my said
And when I won't see ya
Then measure it dead.

'Like Janis', Sixto Rodriguez

For Ben

The Making of Me

Turning twenty-one, not much about me changed, physically speaking. I didn't grow any taller. I didn't grow any fatter. Pinch me and you'll find no additional flesh on these bones. Even if we were the sole survivors of a plane wreck, you wouldn't eat me for dinner.

But nothing stayed the same either. My name grew longer, officially at least, and my bank balance got bigger – MUCH bigger. I have a bona fide Brit passport now and I'm not so sure where home is any more.

Who am I? Good question. I started out as Sonny Anderson. Now my official name is Sonny Anderson Agelaste-Bim, but I still go by Sonny Anderson. Your son. Twenty-one-year-old recovering addict and multi-millionaire. Pleased to (not) meet you.

Almost exactly one month ago, I hit the big Two-One. Back then – because man, it already feels like a lifetime ago – home was Redondo Beach, aka RB, Southern California, SoCal, where, as you know already, I lived since age eleven under the guardianship of one Thomas Hardiker. The word *guardian* puts me in mind of those sentry guys at the gates of Buckingham Palace, staring into the middle distance from under the weight of a big bearskin hat. Keeping the real world out while thinking about pizza or football, or measuring time by the movement of the sun. Whatever. Maybe they really are doing those things. From an outsider's point of view, they look like one man trying to keep a whole world of crap away just by standing still, and that's a massive job, right? Well, that's the job Thomas took on when he took charge of me. You still need to thank him for that.

At school, nobody knew Thomas wasn't my dad, mainly because no one ever cared to ask, even though we were a grown man and a young boy with completely different names, living together under one roof. If they *had* asked, I probably would have said, to maintain the enigma and to keep the story short, that Anderson is my mom's name, which is the truth anyway, right? If they then asked about you directly, which of course they never did – about why you weren't around – my story was that you died when I was small; I figured that would be a great conversation-stopper, which it was until this girlfriend at USC, my *alma mater* – we'll call her Anna – wanted to know everything, all the time, all the stuff I didn't even know myself. The only way to stop the questions was to dump her.

My twenty-first was never going to be your regular limo-riding fake-ID-burning drunken barhopping orgy. I indulged in all that shit way back and already outgrew it. Not so for the majority of my dishonourable collegiate peers, however. Senior year at USC was one protracted twenty-first birthday party, one after the other after the other, paid for by the *guilty *nostalgic *overindulgent (*delete as appropriate) parents of my self-entitled co-equals.

In one of his books, Gladwell (you know who I mean, right?) talks about October-born kids doing better in school than kids born later in the academic year. He gives various explanations for this phenomenon that I don't remember now (my memory is shot), but I do have a theory of my own that he missed. My theory is this: those kids, the September-October babies, also do better because they get all that woohoo jazzhands 'I'm legal' crap over and done with right at the start of Senior year. By Thanksgiving they're so bored of it all they elect to sit out the ongoing mayhem, thereby maintaining maximum brain functionality through their final semester and performing well at the appropriate time. Any time, Malcolm, any time.

My birthday (as you may or may not recall) is June 6th, which means I didn't turn twenty-one until after graduation, so according to Gladwell's theory I should score about as far off the high-achieving-

October-baby list as it gets, but I was the anomaly: I'd come out the other side of the whole NA thing by then, and sat out the shenanigans with the high-achievers. And as a result I did okay. I'm proud of my GPA, naturally, but I won't say what I got because that would be bragging and unBritish.

Personal background info. Loud noises make me flinch, and many, many much quieter ones, like kissy sucky mouth-noises, make me want to punch the wall, or the faces emitting the above-mentioned noises. Strangers at the door make me nervous. Random conversation in the street makes me suspicious. Even the smallest change to my routine needs to be – maybe I should say need*ed* to be because I like to think that recent revelations have transformed me – introduced slowly, over days, weeks, or ideally, never. Thomas, aforementioned guardian, knows better than anyone how much I hate change in general and surprises in particular. But even Thomas and his imaginary bearskin hat couldn't hold back the revolutionary tsunami that crashed through the walls of my existence on the day I turned twenty-one. *Au contraire*, it was Thomas who set it in motion.

On that momentous day, my alarm call as usual was the smell of bacon grilling in the pan. I rolled out of bed in my T-shirt and shorts, and fake-zombie-staggered into the kitchen. It's not so far to stagger. Our house is small and all on one level, a clapboard bungalow, wood not nasty vinyl – as Thomas calls the siding on our neighbour's house – facing the ocean. We don't own our home, it's a rental, but we've lived there so long the owner probably forgot it's theirs or else he or she died and nobody figured to tell us. Anyway, alive or dead we haven't heard from him or her in, like, eight years. We've never had to do the whole termite tent thing, but when a chunk of wood breaks off a window frame, or the roof springs a leak on a rainy day, Thomas puts on his worker apparel, patches it up and deducts what it cost from the monthly rental payment. Thomas probably paid for the house three times over already, so it should be ours by now anyway, or at least his. That might be an exaggeration; back then I had no idea how much houses cost. (When I say 'back then', we're only talking a month, right? Just to be clear.) Now I know how much everything costs.

Unlike you, we don't actually have an ocean view from our house, but walk two blocks west and there's the Pacific. On a quiet, breezy night we can sit out on our side deck and listen to the bells clanking and the seals honking as the waves rock the buoys out by the harbour wall around the pier. Thomas pronounces buoy *boy* (I guess you do too). I say *booey*, same as everyone else in RB, mainly to piss Thomas off. Even though he swears he won't ever cross the Atlantic again, Thomas works hard to conserve our British English, even if only at home. Upspeak is banned in our house. The most dangerous threat Thomas has made in years is to put a sign over our door saying *Thou Shalt Not Upspeak In This House of Reformation*.

I'm drifting.

Back to the revelations. That morning of my twenty-first, the whole place smelled of bacon on the griddle, and the man at the cooker flipping the pork (does that sound obscene to you?), his meetings-consultations-and-special-occasions apparel protected from the grease by a floral pinny loaned by Milly-Anna next door and never returned, was that same Thomas Hardiker. Guardian and principal player. Where he led, I followed, as did the Great Dudini, our dog, who was sat by the door, with one nostril on the bacon and the other on the alert for skunk.

'You are definitely gay,' I said to Thomas. We aren't super-nice to each other all the time like you're expected to be in SoCal. We say things to each other at home we wouldn't dare say in public. And despite your choice of name for me I am not sunny. We are not sunny. Thomas says that's because we're Brits. We like a nice dark cloud overhead from time to time. Which is just as well because there've been a few, metaphorically speaking.

But even those metaphorical clouds parted a little on my twenty-first birthday.

'Good morning and happy birthday,' Thomas said, making a big deal of tapping the clock on the range with the greasy flipper thing, 'what's left of it.' The hands on that clock haven't moved from the twenty 'til eight position since we moved here. It's always morning in the kitchen of the House of Reformation. Or evening. Because even a stopped clock is right twice a day, as Thomas says, twice a day. Ha ha. He hates that clock, it bugs the shit out of him that he can't fix it, and believe me he's tried.

There was no birthday plan. Plans change, are changeable. Fungible. The House of Reformation prefers ritual and unchanging routine. The birthday ritual being: brunch at twelve – bacon avocado tomato butties, no mayo (*butty* being a word for use inside the home only); a movie of the birthday person's choice (mine is always *Shaun of the Dead*), which runs while brunch is being eaten and gifts are being opened; a hike, in the location (Topanga Canyon) of the birthday person's choice; and dinner, at the most isolated table available – because of the kissy sucky mouth-noise problem I mentioned earlier – in the restaurant (Nelson's) of the birthday person's choice. My choices this year were the same as last year, and the year before that. Before that, I was incapable of choosing anything. My choices now are not fungible; they do not funge.

On a regular birthday, gift-opening is over and done with pronto, with minimal ceremony – materialistic values are not upheld in the House of Reformation – and I'm usually done by the time Shaun's crossed the street to Nelson's store the first time. (Seriously, if you haven't seen *Shaun of the Dead* – aka *SOTD*, pronounced *SOD*; the T is silent – you probably should watch it now, because I'll be referring to it a lot.)

The only clue pertaining to this being an irregular birthday was that Thomas's battered old bright-yellow Amoeba Records shopper was able to stand unsupported on the kitchen table, instead of hanging semi-deflated from the chair, indicating a more substantial load of gifts than on previous years. I estimated that this year's gift-opening might take at least until Ed tells Shaun there's a girl stumbling around in their back yard. (By the way, Amoeba is mine and T's favourite store in the whole of LA. We have a game we play when we go there, you might want to try it next time you're in the neighbourhood – I guess they have a religious section: 1. select a musical genre; 2. go to the appropriate clearance bins for said genre; 3. select three vinyls with artwork you like – they must cost no more than five bucks each; 4. buy them and take them home; 5. listen to the first, third and fifth track of each one, and 6. toss the vinyls you don't like, keep the ones you do. This much chance I can handle: organised chance. Mostly the music is lame, but occasionally you'll find something sweet, even if it's just the cover art. I have a couple of the coolest covers stuck to my bedroom wall back in RB, *The Boys from Brazil* – guess why – and *Jonathan Livingston Seagull*, because that was the first book Thomas gave me after we moved to RB.)

Besides ownership of the Key to the Universe transferring to my care there was no real reason this birthday should be any different from a regular birthday. Twenty-one is just another number, right? But pretty soon the whole day was thrown off. Let's just say that Shaun didn't step out of his house for a Cornetto and soda until well after eight p.m. In fact, the day was thrown so far off I never even got to finish my bacon butty, never mind the hike and dinner at Nelson's.

I don't know what Thomas did all those hours I was in my room. It wasn't like me disappearing into my room for several hours was such an unusual occurrence. Probably he changed out of his meetings-consultations-and-special-occasions apparel and into his worker apparel to mow the grass or pull imaginary weeds from his vegetable garden. Unlike your regular RB residents, we don't approve of the hire of cheap immigrant labour. 'Slavery was abolished in 1833,' says Thomas. 'I will be nobody's Great White Master. We can do our own gardening.' Or maybe he sat out front reading a book with the Great Dudini at his feet, or went out back to chat over the wall with our neighbours Milly-Anna (it's pronounced Millionaire, by the way – only in SoCal, right?) and her husband Silent Ike. He definitely would have walked the Great Dudini, at least once, probably twice. As I said, ritual and routine. Whatever, he would have gone on as usual until he figured it was time to try the pizza test. The Thomas Hardiker equivalent of smoking a skunk out of its hole. The smell of baking pizza dough will usually raise me from my gloom. When it doesn't, he knows something is seriously wrong.

Thomas is one of those people who *knows* stuff. He's been through a LOT. Back then I didn't know even half of it, probably still don't even now. It was Thomas who suggested I major in creative writing in college. 'It'll give you a place to go that isn't depression,' he said. I guess he knew way before I turned twenty-one that I still had it coming.

So, back to MY BIRTHDAY. (In case you forgot, I TURNED TWENTY-ONE. Okay, enough with the upper case, or *majuscules* as the French call them, a way cooler name.) What caused the kerfuffle (you can thank Thomas for my interesting vocabulary by the way) that sent me running to my bed? The stuff in the Amoeba Records bag, obviously, so let's go back to that.

Thomas was at the 'arranging tomatoes, grown by him in his garden, atop the bacon and avocado' stage in his sandwich construction, so I opened the fridge to grab the ketchup. 'What's in there?' I said, trying to be casual, referring to the Amoeba Records bag, but – wait for it – sarky TH joke alert…

'It's where we keep the food. It's called a fridge.'

Right.

Even the real clouds had dissolved and it was one of those sparkling SoCal mornings – actually quite rare in June, which is known for its gloomy tendencies and so would by default be our favourite month of the year, birthday or no birthday – so Thomas suggested we break with tradition and go eat our breakfast on the deck out back. It was a risky call, what with *SOTD* being all lined up and ready to go, but he must have picked up that I was in a pretty good mood, relaxed, chilled, unpuckered, and I can see now that he was testing the water. I'd seen the bag, got the measure of it, was confident I knew what was coming (books, I presumed) so I let him have his variation.

I'd like to be able to use this occasion as an example of how, if you allow one tiny regime change to slip through the filter, life snowballs out of control, but this variation from our usual routine had no influence at all on what came after; it would have happened anyway.

The Great Dudini followed us out into the yard, snuffling the ground behind us in hopes of a dropped crumb or two, and when Thomas went back inside for the bag of gifts and the ketchup I snuck him a tiny piece of birthday bacon. Not the regular ketchup, by the way, in case you're thinking I made a continuity slip: *his* ketchup, the bottle of brown stuff he drives all the way to Burbank to buy from the Brit store for like ten times the price of regular ketchup. Looks like barbecue sauce but tastes like salad dressing made of nothing but vinegar and black pepper. Thomas 'enhances the flavour' of anything he categorises as junk food with this stuff: bacon, fries, pizza. To be clear, fish and chips isn't junk food, because it's British. In company he draws the line at splashing it over ice-cream, but I bet when I'm not around even his favourite organic Madagascan vanilla gets a good shake of the brown stuff over it. Everyone needs things they do in secret, right?

There was a Y in the day of the week so Milly-Anna was in their back yard working out to the *Grease* movie soundtrack. (I actually used to like this movie when I was a kid – you must've seen it – Milly-Anna and I used to watch it together when she came to hang out while Thomas was out at his meetings.) We couldn't see her from our deck because of the wall separating our yards, but we could hear her singing along, loud and well off-key, her breathing all jerky because of the moves she was busting. One time – before we knew them properly, so it must have been real soon after we moved to Redondo – I climbed up on a garden chair to sneak a look over at what she was doing and wobbled right off again from laughing so hard. (And I'd seen some weird shit by then, right?) It's not any regular workout she does, it's the actual routine from the movie, right down to the simulated cigarette-butt stamp-out. Sometimes she yells at Silent Ike to come join her on the part where he has to follow her up the porch steps, crawl across and down the other side behind her, and unless it's her birthday he mostly pretends he can't hear her yelling over the loud music. I'm not saying we don't still snicker into our hands from time to time, but we're so accustomed to it now that it's blended into our own routine.

So, as I was saying, Thomas went inside to get his special ketchup. When he came back, I put down my sandwich and dipped my hand into the gift bag. (Did you know that, in German, *gift* means *poison*?)

The bag was loaded so that Thomas's gift came out first. It was obviously a book, which reassured me that my assumption about it all being books was correct. Never assume, right? He passed me a napkin to wipe my hands before I opened it because this wasn't just any book, it was a 1944 first edition hardcover copy of my favourite book ever, *Cannery Row*, by John Steinbeck. Signed by the author. Shipped all the way from a bookstore in Paris called *Shakespeare & Company*, the store all the famous writers who lived in Paris in the 1920s and '30s used to go to – Hemingway and that gang. Hemingway even writes about it in *A Moveable Feast*. Maybe he sold his copy of *Cannery Row* for booze money and now it's mine.

'Someone in West Hollywood was selling a copy too,' said Thomas, 'but I thought you'd like the one from Paris better.' Damn straight! It had a card inside the front cover with the store's Shakespeare's head logo stamped on it and, stapled to that, a cheque for three thousand dollars, signed by Thomas Hardiker.

'What?' I said, flabbergasted.

'The cheque is just symbolic,' he said. 'I'll give you the cash. I thought you might want to take that trip to London you've always talked about, to see where *SOTD* was filmed.'

Let's get things straight. I do not wish to appear ungrateful. I was not raised with the same ugly entitlement complex my aforementioned collegiate peers had – the absolute opposite, in fact. There could be no greater surprise, no more treasured gift than a *Cannery Row* first edition and the possibility of a trip to London, and yes, there should have been hugs and high-fives. In my defence – and to put my response, or non-response to be more accurate, in perspective – the shock of it would normally have been enough to send me rushing to my bed for at least the rest of the day, but when I woke up that morning I turned twenty-one I'd decided it was probably time to man up, grow some *cojones*. So instead of scuttling off to my room I sat back, took a couple deep breaths and a couple more bites from my butty (do you think about me biting someone's ass when I say that? I do) to get back in balance, to overthrow old habits, and then I dove my hand right back into the bag and pulled out the next gift. Which was an envelope. A plain old brown envelope. (How harmful, right?)

The sender's address was in Zurich, Switzerland. I didn't know anyone there, and to be completely honest I barely knew where *there* is. I knew it was in Europe, but exactly where, I couldn't have said. Despite Thomas's best efforts, I've become an American. I did look it up later, while I was lying on my bed trying to figure out my situation. Switzerland is about a quarter the size of California and has like half the population of the Greater Los Angeles area. In America it would be a ski resort, but over there, it's a country.

Inside the envelope were two sheets of paper clipped together. The top sheet was a letter from a lawyer's office, *Binggeli, Birchmeier & Geisert*, signed by Herr Philipp Binggeli. It was actually addressed to me using my dad's family name, Mr Sonny Anderson Agelaste-

Bim – which in the light of the above suddenly doesn't seem quite so ridiculous – even though I've never gone by that name, even when I lived with my dad.

Transfer of Estate Agelaste-Bim.

I stared at the words on the page but nothing was going in. I passed it to Thomas. He read it and turned the page. '*Shit*,' he said, and looked at me as if he'd never seen me before in his life.

'What?'

He held the second sheet of paper in front of my face and pointed to the bottom of the page. It was all set out like a bank statement and at the bottom, beside the words *Total Estate Value*, were two numbers, one prefixed by USD, the other by SF. There were so many numbers with so many points and commas all over the place that my brain froze and my eyesight fuzzed. I could see it was a LOT, in both currencies, but I still didn't get it. So Thomas spelled it out – it was more than a lot, it was millions of dollars, and they were all mine because I, little old Sonny Anderson Agelaste-Bim, represent the end of the Agelaste-Bim family line.

'Welcome to Trustafaria,' said Thomas.

Thomas is also a Trustafarian. I had no clue what that meant until Thomas explained that a Trustafarian is a guy – or a girl, I guess, but usually a guy because the kinds of people who have *old money* still believe in male supremacy – who lives on the proceeds of an inheritance, trust fund, whatever. Dictionary definition: a rich young person who adopts a bohemian lifestyle and lives in a non-affluent area. I should say Thomas *was* a Trustafarian because he stopped drawing on his fund years ago. As far as I knew back then, Thomas had worked for every cent he made and spent. And we didn't live like non-affluent bohemians; we lived like non-affluent ordinary people with issues. Which makes his gift cheque even more generous, right?

Looking back, I guess Thomas had known all along there would be money coming my way, but the expression on his face when it arrived – like he'd been waiting for a bus but got a gold-plated limo flown in by pterodactyls – gave a pretty clear indication that he'd been clueless as to just how swanky my lot on Planet Trustafaria was actually going to be. And that's when I caved and went to my room, leaving my transition to manhood incomplete. Thomas told me later he was in so much shock he didn't even register the Great Dudini gobbling up what was left of both our butties, proving he'd had no idea how much money was coming to me – because only an idiot gifts three thousand bucks to a multi-millionaire, right? Though even when we'd both recovered he refused to take his gift back. 'You might want to make the London trip first and then decide what to do about your inheritance,' he said. He was right, as usual. I might choose to reject it (I still haven't decided, but that's none of your business), like I believed he'd rejected his.

A couple days later, Thomas reminded me there was still stuff in the bag to be opened. This all turned out to be not gifts so much as shit I'd never seen before that now belonged to me. 'No rush,' he said, 'it's not going anywhere.'

It took another couple days for me to pick up the bag and take it into my room, where I sat staring into it like it was a mountain pool into which I'd been told to plunge my naked body in midwinter. Common wisdom says it's always safest to test the water with your extremities, so I dipped my hand in first and pushed it all the way down. Down in the depths was a box, about the size of a kiddie shoebox. To the side of that was one of those plastic pocket folders that female sophomores use to submit papers to the professors they want to sleep with, only theirs are generally pink and this one was white. Inside was a bunch more envelopes. I picked one that had my real name on the front, Sonny Anderson, which made it less scary, plus it had already been opened, so I knew Thomas had seen what was inside and that also made it feel safer. Seriously, I've developed a fear of envelopes, envelophobia; don't ever ask me to present an Oscar. I took out the sheet of paper. My birth certificate – over there they call it an *Extract*, 'over there' being Scotland. I already knew I was born in Scotland, Thomas had told me that years earlier, and obviously I knew I had a mother and a father even if I didn't remember them particularly fondly (my dad). Or at all (you).

Father's Name: Unknown. (Known Names: Robin Agelaste-Bim, aka, Agelaste Bim, aka, Guru Bim.) Father's Occupation: Unknown. (Known Occupation: Guru.) Father's Dwelling Place: Unknown. (Known Dwelling Place: Hell – that's a guess.) Mother's Name: Sarah Anderson. Mother's Occupation: Housewife. Mother's Dwelling

Place: Drongnock.

It was kind of exciting to see it all written down. Suddenly it was like you really existed, which meant that I really existed too – officially, I mean; I wasn't *that* much of a fuck-up – and if we both really existed then it was possible we might meet one day, right?

I had no idea then where Drongnock is. If it had said Nowheresville that would have been great too, maybe even greater, because it would have made you seem even more ordinary, even more *housewifely* and *motherly*.

I summoned the courage to open another envelope. A list of names and addresses, all in the UK. I took it through to Thomas, who played it right down, said they were all people who had known either you or my dad or both, and who would be pleased to see me if I made my trip or would help out if I hit any trouble. Marsha Ray I remembered from Brazil and I told Thomas she was the last person I'd call on if I needed help. 'Okay, fair enough,' he said, 'maybe one of the others,' and told me who they all were: Andrew Harrison, the guy you were living with when I was born; and Ruth Williams, who knew you better than she knew my dad, but she knew you both; and Doris Henry, who looked after my dad when he was a boy. And an address with no name next to it, which Thomas said was the house they stayed in before we went to Brazil. 'We weren't there long so it's not important but I thought you might want to stop off and see it if you're on your way to Scotland to see Andrew.'

Okay, backing up.

Before Thomas and I came to RB, ten, eleven years ago, a bunch of us lived in Brazil: me, Thomas, my dad and Marsha Ray. Back then, I had no memories of my life before Brazil.

'Wait, so you're saying you think I should go meet all these people?'

'It's up to you. They'd all love to see you.'

'Even Marsha Ray?'

Thomas shrugged, then nodded apologetically.

I knew what he was getting at. Thomas says the past is important. Without the past we have no present and without memory we have no past. I knew why he thought I should go. I've been through a lot, have tried to forget it all and am (was) stuck. I was at a crossroads; we didn't need to discuss it but obviously it's important to know where you come from, who made you what you are. I was like Shaun in *SOTD* when Liz dumps him and Pete yells at him, 'SORT YOUR FUCKING LIFE OUT, MATE.'

I pulled a bunch of photos out of the folder. Twenty years ago, when I was a baby, people still paid for prints of every photograph they took; it was the only way to get to see them. Even the shit ones, which I guess you paid for, laughed at, separated from the good ones and tossed in the trash like you would a two-legged carrot at the market. (Although for Thomas a two-legged carrot would be a prized possession, especially if he grew it himself. I don't think he has a photograph collection but if he does, I never want to see it.) A couple of the pictures in the folder I'd seen before, but I couldn't say when. The one of my dad in his pink guru apparel, sitting cross-legged in the garden in Olinda, I've seen, like, a million times since.

A guru is someone who follows nobody on Twitter but has thousands of social media suckers following him. Go figure.

There was a photo of baby me I'd never seen before. At least, Thomas said it was me but I guess it could have been anybody. There was no one else in the picture to validate his claim, and, even if there had been, how would I have known who *they* were? Another one of me, a couple years later, with way more hair, black like mine, and wearing real kid clothes and sitting in a wheelbarrow. This kid did look like me now and there was even a hint of another person present, in the form of two hands, gripping the handles of the wheelbarrow. But whoever those hands and forearms belonged to had had them amputated at the elbow by whoever was holding the camera.

One picture still creeps me out, I don't know why but it does. First time I saw it, I looked at it for a while and then I had to go lie down on my bed for a longer while to think about it. It's of a man and a woman standing side by side. The guy is my dad in his guru clothes and a beard, and the other, I guess, is you. You can't see your face because you're looking down at his hand, which is spread flat against your belly, and where your face should be is a shining drape of black hair. He is staring right into the camera and smiling. Not happy and joyful smiling, smug and self-important smiling. *I'm a guru smiling for the camera* smiling. The only kind of smiling I ever saw him do.

When I imagined reaching into the picture and sweeping your hair away from your face, my imagination put my own face where yours should be. And I wasn't even high.

That was enough of the bag for a while.

Eventually I got up from my bed and life went on for a few more days. I continued my post-graduation break like nothing happened. Except that I had intended to look for a summer job, but what with being a multi-millionaire and all I didn't know if I needed to do that any more. I just had to complete a couple forms to claim my inheritance and avoid ever needing a job.

I didn't complete the forms. I didn't look for a job. Instead I did things I hadn't done in years, like ride my bike. Most days I cycled to Santa Monica and back on the Marvin Braude, a thirty-mile round trip. I watched movies. Okay, I watched *a* movie, *Shaun of the Dead*. I scoffed Trader Joe's non-pareils by the tubful. I avoided all the Big Subjects. Thomas went on as usual, routine-ritual-routine, but I could sense him watching and thinking and wondering how long until I'd be ready to talk. Thomas was always ready to talk and as usual I was keeping him waiting. Or maybe all he was thinking about was whether the Great Dudini would prefer to turn left instead of right on the street for his walk that day. Now I've read his letters, though, I'm pretty sure that he was avoiding the Big Subjects too; they were too big even for him.

I'm going too fast again.

One night at dinner we were talking about my ride that day and I showed Thomas the videos I'd shot on my phone. The regular stuff: a pelican kamikazeing into the ocean by the pier; a dolphin, hanging with the surfer dudes, looping the waves real close to the beach at Hermosa; two palm trees by LAX that, if you got the angle right, looked like they were on a tiny desert island; the fat silver underbelly of the plane that took off right over my head while I was lining up the picture of the two palm trees. Man, that was loud.

It was the plane that did it – let Thomas in.

'Have you had any more thoughts about going to England?' he said.

I actually hadn't thought about it at all, but said, 'Yes. I think I will.' And that was the decision made, right there. Even though I knew Thomas wouldn't be coming with me like I'd always assumed he would. Since Brazil, I'd never been anywhere outside the state of California and I'd hardly even travelled to school alone until I started at USC. 'Do I even have a passport?' I said.

Turned out I did. Thomas had ordered it from the UK five years before, just in case I needed it, using my birth certificate and a photo from the bunch we had taken for my Junior High ID. Man, I look grim in that picture. You know how sometimes you can look at a picture of your younger self and know exactly what you were thinking at the exact moment the picture was taken? You know it but can't articulate it; you remember having the thought but not the words that describe the thought. I guess that's probably classified as a feeling, then, right? If I were the immigration official processing that application I'd have refused it. At sixteen I was into my fourth year of getting wasted and the thoughts in my head at the time that picture was taken were the exact opposite of SoCal Positivity. But I guess I don't look so different now, just a little healthier. Like I said, no more flesh on these bones.

I lifted the final item, the box, out of the bag and put it on the table. Thomas pushed the salt and pepper and guacamole out of the way, already gone brown and unappetising because he forgot to leave the avo stone in, and I opened the box right there among the pizza crusts and soggy salad leaves. 'It's your father's autobiography,' said Thomas when I flipped the lid back. Not a book, not even a manuscript, but a bunch of small tapes with their own special machine to play them on, about the size of an old-school cellphone. 'Your father always said writing wasn't his medium,' said Thomas. 'I haven't listened to them.'

Writing isn't my medium? Who the fuck says that?

So, to summarise, Thomas put all that shit together for my birthday so I could go to the UK and discover my lost past and move on unburdened into adulthood. Despite our pretence about it being a *Shaun of the Dead* zombie pilgrimage, in my heart of hearts I knew I was going to look for you, and in his heart of hearts Thomas knew that too; we just couldn't admit it openly. I assumed his silence on the subject was to avoid sending me into such a panic that I wouldn't go.

Like I said, never assume.

Next thing I know, I'm on the plane to London, my backpack loaded with the important stuff Thomas gave me inside a plastic sleeve: the list of names and addresses, the photos, and a list of all the SOTD location addresses in London, printed off the IMDb website as back-up in case I lose my phone or my tablet. Also, weighing me down, the whole damn box of my dad's tapes because I didn't have the cojones to listen to them before I left or the wherewithal to just leave them behind.

Milly-Anna cried when we said goodbye, even though she knew for like a week that I was leaving and would only be gone for a couple weeks – or so we thought back then. She gave me a tub of non-pareils for sustenance because 'those flight meals are so icky', and Silent Ike gave me a dictionary of British slang and shook my hand. Kind of an ironic gift from a man who never speaks, so it was pretty obvious the dictionary had been Thomas's idea and he was way more interested in it than I was, at least until it disappointed him. According to him, The Man Who Hasn't Set Foot on British Territory for Twenty Years, it was out of date. So we watched SOTD together for the last time and we shouted 'nincompoop' and 'bloody bugger' over all the 21st-century cursewords. Definitely out of date.

Then we were driving me to LAX like it was part of our daily routine and for a moment my brain got confused and thought we were headed for my NA meeting at Hermosa even though it was the wrong time of day and I hadn't been there for three years. But we kept on going up PCH, through Hermosa, through Manhattan and El Segundo.

Thomas looked kind of nervous too as we entered the terminal and I remembered he hadn't flown anywhere in years either and was probably suffering vicarious anxiety. By the time we hit the departure gate though he relaxed enough to throw me a high-five as if saying goodbye at the airport was the kind of thing we did all the time. 'Oh, that Sonny,' an onlooker might say, 'where's he headed *this* time?'

I guess I've grown since I last sat on a plane; I need more physical space than my seat provides. But I luck out when the guy at the other end of our row gets upgraded and I score all three seats to myself. The woman across the aisle seems to think I should have offered my good fortune up to her and squints her curses in my direction. If I weren't so scared of losing my privilege I'd tell her and her sense of entitlement to go swivel. Instead I send her a creepy SoCal smile as if to say, 'Hey, lady, be happy for me, and next time it might be you!' and settle back to explore the movie channel.

I watch three movies one after the other: one about a guy who likes to tie women up in his basement and make them cry by playing Whitney Houston CDs; one in black and white about a cute girl in New York who isn't much good at anything but works it all out in the end; then next up, from the classics selection, ladies and gentlemen, it's *Shaun of the Dead*. (A message from the Universe, right?) In a few hours, I tell myself as I stretch out across all three seats, those same streets and sidewalks will be right there under my feet.

Somewhere in the middle of the first movie, my meal arrives and it's not at all icky because Thomas knew to advance-order the Asian vegan option. I opt for non-pareils instead of rehydrated melon for dessert and then all the lights go out and the plane is in total darkness, except for all the little rectangles of blue light flashing on to people's faces, and I'm actually quite cosy. I doze off right after Philip has died, just like I do at home.

When the attendant wakes me for breakfast the plane is all lit up again. My whole body feels empty, like all the blood's been sucked out of my veins, a not completely unfamiliar sensation. I flip open my breakfast box and eat, gorming like a zombie at the little plane on the moving map as it jerks its way towards London at five hundred and something miles per hour. One hour till landing.

It's cool watching the numbers wind down to zero as the cartoon plane's nose hits the black spot of London. When the wheels of the real plane hit the runway, some guy in the row behind me starts clapping. Thomas warned me this might happen. In addition to kissy sucky mouth-noises I also can't stand the sound of palms smacking together, be they dry, sweaty or otherwise. I cover my ears but the noise gets louder because other people join in, probably so the first

guy – I'm guessing only a guy or a monkey would applaud a routine
landing – won't be embarrassed. I feel like Shaun at the beginning of
SOTD, on a bus where all the other passengers are indistinguishable
from zombies, and Oh My Gosh, I'm in London.

London airport is on the west side of the city. My hotel is on the west
side too, but closer in to downtown, in the Bayswater neighbourhood,
right by Hyde Park. The train from the airport brings me to Paddington
station and from there it's ten blocks or so to the hotel. Even though
my backpack is dragging on my shoulders and my head feels like it's
detached from the rest of my body, and even though I can now afford
to ride everywhere by taxi, I walk, because I want to feel the London
sidewalk under my shoes, to test it out, see if it feels like home.

Man, London is alive-alive-o. So many people out walking on the
street. It makes RB look like one of those ghost towns out in the desert
where the only residents are starving kitties and the only vegetation
is tumbleweed. People walk in RB too, of course. When they need
to get from their car to the store. Or from their car to the boardwalk.
Maybe every couple blocks you'll see someone with a dog leash or
three attached to one hand and a baggie of doggie poop swinging
from the other. In RB walking is exercise, to be done as little or as
often as your level of obsession, or the number of doggies in your
care, demands. In London, a pair of legs is a means of transportation.

This morning most people around me are rushing along, their
faces screwed up from stress or lack of sleep, going about important
business. You hardly notice the others, the shopping zombies,
daydreaming along in amongst them. I'm with them, shuffling along,
enchanted, excluded like the main character in a movie about a
man who falls asleep on a beach in SoCal and wakes up as a multi-
millionaire wandering the streets in a mankini in a strange but
familiar city six thousand miles from home.

Across the street, a couple blocks from my hotel, is a mom and
pop's store like the one where Shaun buys a can of soda for himself
and a Cornetto for Ed, and I get my second rush of excitement. I have
a secondary SOTD mission that I call the Cornetto Challenge.

Did you watch SOTD yet? The first time I watched it Thomas
had to translate what Ed was saying because he says Cornetto without

pronouncing the 't's, but that has nothing to do with my Challenge.

In the movie, Shaun walks home from the store, and sits on the sofa to channel-surf and chat to Ed, who's stood looking out of the window. Then they go out into their back yard and try to kill zombie one, go back inside the house, kill zombie two, then outside again to kill zombies one and three. No big deal, right, BUT, all this happens BEFORE Ed sits down to eat his Cornetto. It's at least ten minutes since the ice-cream left the store, in movie time, which is probably more like thirty minutes in real time. This is ice-cream we're talking about. It melts, right? So, while I am eager to eat my first Cornetto, the Cornetto Challenge has to take precedence. Trivial as it may seem to you, it's important to me to know if a Cornetto is still edible ten minutes after coming out of the freezer.

To the store.

It's tiny, about one-eightieth the size of our local drugstore but with the same amount of stuff for sale. The guy at the register points at a freezer rammed into the corner between the magazine display and the shelf of potato chips and I almost clear the shelves of produce when I try to manocuvre my backpack in the limited space available. I'd care more if I wasn't about to buy my first two Cornettos ever. (*Two?* you say. What, you think I'm gonna *wait* ten minutes? Obviously I need one to eat as soon as I leave the store.) In a frenzy of cinematic authenticity I grab a can of soda I don't really want and head for the register. The guy scans my stuff without asking me how I am today, or smiling, or making eye contact. Even when I say, 'Thank you, Nelson,' to drop him a clue he shows no recognition of what we're doing here and just throws my three purchases into a blue plastic bag. Thomas would shudder at the casual use of plastic, start muttering about the fish in the ocean, I feel like a criminal just touching the bag.

A combination of ice-cream ecstasy and looking in the wrong direction to cross the street almost gets me killed. Fortunately the taxi driver sees me first and presses his whole body weight against his horn. The headline flashes into my mind: *World's Youngest Multi-Millionaire Walks Into Traffic, Dies Enjoying First Ever Cornetto. It's What He Would Have Wanted, Says Tearful Guardian.*

I figure the hotel wouldn't appreciate me dripping ice-cream

juice all over the lobby before I've even checked in so I cross over
to the park and dump my backpack on to the first bench I see, in the
shade of a big old tree. Not a palm tree – there are no palm trees here
– a real tree, with thick green leaves as big as hands.

On the bench opposite, a guy in a grey suit so shiny it might
actually be made of silver is reading a pink newspaper and talking
on his phone. A steady stream of joggers and cyclists runs between
us. The clock on my phone tells me I have another five minutes to
wait before the Challenge is up so I spread the empty wrapper of
my F.E.C. on the ground and take a photo of it to send to Thomas.
Meanwhile the guy opposite has folded his pink paper and stood up
to leave. 'I hope you're going to pick that up again,' he says as he skips
between two bikes. Fuck off, asshole, I say. In my head.

When the ten minutes is up my Cornetto Challenge Cornetto is
too soft to eat, but I eat-slash-drink it anyway and message the result
with the photo to Thomas and he writes back right away. *So the idea
of people coming back to life as zombies to eat the living is entirely
plausible, but an ice-cream not having melted in ten minutes is an
insurmountable problem?* Thomas never abbreviates his text messages,
spells out every word in full. It's three a.m. in RB; he must have stayed
awake waiting for me to message him. I imagine him there on the
sofa, a bearskin hat covering the top half of his face.

Man, I'm tired.

I wake up in the middle of the night when my phone whistles in a
new message from Thomas. *Your challenge is null and void. There's
a jump cut. Watch it again. A hundred dollars says Shaun put the
Cornetto in the freezer.*

Motherflipper. (© Flight of the Conchords. Love those guys too.)

There's no way I'm getting back to sleep so I take the two lists
Thomas gave me out of their plastic sleeve and put them side by side
on the bed. *SOTD* locations, or Existential Quest? My head says
SOTD; my stupid heart says otherwise.

I flip a coin. Existential Quest it is.

You win.

Doris and Her Puppies

Doris Henry, aka Mrs C, isn't first on the list, but there are good reasons to go visit her first. One, she knew my dad before anyone else did so it kind of makes sense chronologically, what with past and background being important to build the picture and all. Two, she's old and it would be just my kind of luck for her to pass, like, the day before I get to meet her. Also, three, the train to Devon, where she lives, leaves from Paddington station, which as you already know is close to my hotel. It's a four-hour train ride to Torquay, the town where she lives, and I'm jet-lagged as hell, so I plan to sleep the whole way. It doesn't quite work out that way because apparently it's compulsory to eat potato chips on Brit trains – I have to switch coaches twice because the sound of people crunching makes me want to smash my fist through the window.

The county of Devon is in the southwest of England, in the peninsula of Devon and Cornwall. On the map it looks like an elephant's trunk. Torquay – pronounced Tor-key – is a small beach town on the south coast and Mrs C lives there, on a street called Daddyhole Road. I almost piss my pants when I read the address, but once you get over the name of the street it's really kind of picturesque. Considering my reason for visiting it'll be kind of ironic to walk up Daddyhole Street, Road, whatever.

The GPS on my phone tells me it's a thirty-eight-minute walk from Torquay railroad station to her house. There is no mass transit option known to Google and I don't believe in riding in taxis, which is maybe why I don't see them coming when I'm crossing the street.

I walk much slower than usual – dragging my heels, Thomas calls it. The sky is totally 3-D and the clouds have all been drawn with a straight edge at the bottom. There's no real reason to be nervous about meeting an old lady, I met a bunch of them when working my high school community service hours at the Sunrise Home for Senior Citizens in RB (cruel optimism, right? Should be Sun*set*, surely). If they acknowledge your existence at all they're generally nice to you in case you're a relative they forgot about. Sometimes they smell bad, and sometimes they're cranky, but who can blame them – it can't be fun going back into diapers after you've experienced the trajectory of a whole life without them, right? Maybe I'm nervous because I expect old English ladies to be different. Or maybe I'm psychic. Like my dad believed he was.

Mrs C's cottage is pink and faces the sea, or at least it overlooks a small park that runs from the front of her house to the edge of the cliff you'd need to throw yourself off to get to the sea. It's kind of a relief to see a bike chained to the fence in front of her house. I'm thinking it means she already has a visitor, another human presence to absorb the impact of my arrival. (Mrs C has no phone number so she doesn't know I'm coming, and I'm anticipating excitement on her side. I learned at the Sunrise that excitement in old people can be fatal.) Her neighbour's house is blue and I kill a few more minutes admiring the straightness of the line dividing the two colours. There is no actual line, just two colours bumping against each other. There's a large basket in front of the bike, wound through with yellow and blue plastic flowers, all faded by sunshine and greyed by road dirt, and I use up another few seconds speculating about who the bike belongs to. Daughter? Niece? Kindly neighbour? Grocery delivery girl? Turns out none of those is correct. At eighty-three years old, Mrs C considers herself too old to drive a car, but not to ride a bicycle down the hill every morning to the market and back up it again with a full basket of shopping.

I'm still stood there, pretending to admire the bike and my general surroundings, when I realise I'm being barked at. If barking is the right word to describe the noise that's coming out of the mouth of the small, long-haired creature with a bow on its head and a plaid quilted comforter fixed over its shoulders. Its hot, excitable doggy breath is steaming up the glass in Mrs C's front window. It has good reason to be angry, dressed up in that lame outfit, but once you zone in on the noise it's making, it's horrible, like a chainsaw stuck in a tree. The GD would not approve.

Behind the dog, hidden in the dark space between the white lacy drapes, is Mrs C. Or at least there's an old woman, with a pale, pinched face, who I assume is Mrs C, seeing as she's in Mrs C's house and she doesn't fit the description of any person I had imagined riding the bike. Gawping at me slack-jawed like I'm the ghost of Hamlet's father's son (Hamlet).

We're held in a kind of staring contest; I'm waiting for her to disappear and reappear seconds later at the door; she's waiting for me to disintegrate into pieces of silvery nothingness. Meanwhile the dog is getting super-hysterical so I break the deadlock and let her know that I'm not a ghost or a passing member of the Vintage Bicycle Admiration Society by knocking at the door. At which point the dog goes apeshit, literally starts throwing itself at the glass, and finally Mrs C quits staring and moves away.

Somewhere near my right hip there's a harsh squeak and a voice says, 'Who is it?' She's talking to me through the mailbox. I never knew Brits have their mail delivered through a hole in their door, and I guess there's no reason I would know that, except that it's the kind of trivial comparison favoured by a certain Mr T Hardiker – and it's not the voice of a frail old lady, all wobbly and polite and only too aware of her vulnerability, but the breathless squawk of a fairytale witch.

'Mrs Henry?' I say, bending at the waist. 'My name is Sonny Agelaste-Bim.' I'm aiming for speedy recognition by using my dad's last name.

'Wait a minute,' she says.

She calls out to her dog – did she say *Binky?* – and finally the stupid mutt quits jumping at the window. The barking gets more distant but doesn't stop. It must be delightful living next door to Mrs C; hopefully her neighbour is hearing-impaired. By this time, I've decided the bike belongs to someone else entirely and figure this is

probably a rare event and that not too many people come to the door
to set Binky off, and I feel bad for Mrs C until she opens the door and
stands there in a fog of what appears to be cigarette smoke.

'I shut the dog in the kitchen,' she says. 'Don't like strangers.'

Mrs C's hair is not white and softly curled like the customers
of Noreen, the visiting hair stylist at the Sunrise, but wiry and grey
(except for where it's stained yellow in the front) and hacked into a
longer version of the buzzcut that is the speciality of Jim, the barber
who also visits weekly to tend to the Sunrise men. (Noreen and Jim
dispense uniform 'styles-'n'-cutz' at 'special discount' prices for those
no longer able to venture out of doors and so have no idea how much
a haircut costs any more. Noreen drives a Hummer, Jim a vintage
Mercedes in tiptop condition.)

Mrs C's wearing a kind of plaid coverall in shades of once blue
and green with a heavy-knit grey vest over. Her front teeth are stained
brown. My mind makes the unnecessary calculation: cigarette smoke
plus brown teeth equals heavy indoor smoker. Yuck. No wonder the
dog has such an annoying bark; it probably has throat cancer from
breathing in all the second-hand smoke. But who am I to judge, right?

A single black hair coils from under her chin, so I guess her near
sight isn't so good and there's no Noreen to pluck it out for her. I try to
estimate how far it would stretch if you pulled on it – two, maybe three
inches? The shiny black leather shoes on her feet don't fit the picture.

She doesn't invite me in and I actually would prefer not to get any
closer, it looks kind of rank in there, but I've come here to brighten
her day and so I persist. I introduce myself again and she cuts me off,
says she heard me the first time.

'I think you knew my father when he was a child,' I say to the
shiny shoes. 'Robin Agelaste-Bim? I was hoping you might be able
to help me with some information about him. About his childhood.'

Above the shoes her legs are bare, her skin grey and mottled. I
force myself to look up at her face again and smile. And I immediately
know how Willy Loman must have felt in the face of extreme
commercial disinterest.

'I suppose you're trying to find him, but if you think I can help
you, you're mistaken. I haven't seen him for more than fifteen years.
I've no idea where he is.'

I didn't plan on being the one to break the news of my father's passing to anyone. I assumed they'd all know. I don't want to be responsible for causing Mrs C to have a heart attack right here at her door, she doesn't exactly seem to be in the best of health, so I decide to not tell her yet.

'No, I'm not looking for him. I'm collecting information about my family history, for a kind of summer project. It shouldn't take too long. I could meet you somewhere else tomorrow if you prefer?' (Did you pick up on what I was doing there? Passive-aggressive manipulation, a skill I learned from a master, my aforementioned father.)

She raises two nicotine-stained fingers to her lips and then drops them again immediately when she remembers there's no cigarette between them. 'Come back tomorrow morning,' she says. 'I'm usually home from church by nine. I'm not sure what use it'll be, though, if you're not trying to track him down.'

I'm trying to work out if she just contradicted herself when she starts closing the door. I lean sideways so she can still see me through the closing gap and thank her for her help. While we're speaking, Binky the dog's voice finally gives out and its bark reduces to a rhythmic squeak like a dying car alarm. On the subject of cars, I also have a least favourite word: *lube*. Makes me want to vomit.

On the park behind me, a couple kids aged eleven or twelve or so are playing football. A regular pair of homies, riding their pants low to show the top of their chonies. As I walk towards them their ball swerves my way so I chip it back and drop a gnarly pass on to the right foot of the other little guy, the one who didn't kick it to me. Just flexin', bro. Actually I'm not a bad player as it goes. Me and the other kids in Brazil played hours of barefoot every day, and when I was twelve and we'd moved to RB I was picked for the Galaxy Youth to play midfield. I killed it for a while, but I guess I'm not really a team player. And I think it's safe to say that twelve going into thirteen was kind of a difficult phase for me. And that's the definition of understatement, right there.

I feel like goofing around for a while with these guys to get some blood into my muscles, so I say, 'Hey,' and stop to take off my backpack. My shoulders need a break from the weight and it feels good to get some air under my shirt. They're cool. I show them a few

tricks, a couple Touzanis, which they can already do well enough so
I show them how to do the Rivelino Elastic and tell them about the
Galaxy and how I could've trained with Beckham if I hadn't bailed
a couple years before he got there. They're super-impressed by that
even though it's something I didn't do, and if I'm entirely honest the
Galaxy are crap, which reminds me of Thomas, ranting on about how
the Brits worship mediocrity. Also on my unwritten list of things to
do here: go to a real game, with real crowd noise made by real live
supporters, instead of a recording played while the audience chats
and crunches its ten-dollar popcorn.

Maybe it's because Mrs C was so underwhelmed to see me,
maybe I'm knocked out of whack by the jet-lag, but for some reason
I'm coming on to these guys like I'm The Dude. I hear myself and it's
pathetic. I try to cool it a little, make it more about them.

I ask them how many balls get booted over the cliff in an average
year, and they say thousands, so I tell them they are probably the
sole (get it?) reason all the fish in the ocean are dying from plastic
poisoning, which makes them laugh. Their names are Josh and David
and they are both twelve and have been best buddies their whole
lives. Their accent is like the villagers in *Hot Fuzz* (second movie in
the Cornetto Trilogy) – the female villagers, that is; their voices didn't
break properly yet.

They tell me that once a boy was chasing a ball so hard he ran
right off the edge of the cliff. His body was smashed to a pulpy mess
on the rocks below. The council put up a fence to stop it happening
again and people tied plastic flowers to it, but then it all got blown
apart in a storm.

Somehow I twist the conversation round to *SOTD* and I'm stoked
when they say it's their favourite movie so I pull the list of movie
locations out of my bag and tell them about my plan to visit them all,
which gets them real excited.

We take turns to count keepie-uppies.

I haven't yakked off like this in years; it's like I never fell into the
meth-hole. It's the football: it bypasses all that shit and takes me back
to being a kid.

When it's time for them to go home for dinner (they call it tea)
they tell me I can get to my hotel quicker by walking along the cliff

path and show me how to get on it. We walk over there together, kicking the ball in tight triangles, discussing the merits of certain pizza toppings and Lionel Messi, all the way to the other side of the park. We stop at a section of low wooden fence with two steps on each side to help the less limber climb over. They call it a *stile*.

We high-five each other and they pick up the ball and run back towards the cottages. I'm kind of sorry to see them go. It's like watching my old self running away from me all over again. Only my old self didn't run so much as strap himself to a rocket.

I send Thomas a panorama shot of the view so he knows I've touched down in Torquay. Thomas is partial to views. He texts back: *Nice*.

It's five a.m. and I'm awake. The sky outside my window is SoCal blue. By six I'm out of bed, in my shorts, vest and sneakers and ready to run the Agatha Christie Mile, which I learned about from a leaflet in my room. I never read anything she wrote but according to the leaflet, Agatha Christie is like the queen of murder mystery. Apparently she was born in Torquay and the Mile is a trail that links all the places she used to hang out and get inspiration for her stories.

I don't know if the Mile is an actual mile or a fictional mile, but I jog there and back along it four times (Torquay has palm trees!), which I guess is like eight fictional miles. It's actually pretty sick if you stop to read the signs. There's a beach right by my hotel where she almost drowned once, and a special garden where they grow all the poisonous plants used to murder the victims in her novels. I guess the best part of being a writer is getting to plan and commit murders without having to clean up the mess or do time for them, which is awesome, right?

I'm showered, shaved and eating a Full English Breakfast long before it's time to go to Mrs C's. I'm dressed in my raggiest clothes. Not that all my clothes aren't raggy, but these are the ones I'm gonna least mind getting stunk up by cigarette smoke on Daddyhole Road.

There's the occasional fluffy white cloud and the temp is like a warm spring day back home with no marine layer to put a chill in the air. A kite trapped in a tree makes me think of Thomas. When he was a kid, his father used to call him a daft kite, because he was always floating off and getting tangled up in things. I guess they gave up on untangling him.

Real, not fake, church bells pealing in the distance (that's what church bells do, right – they peal?) remind me I'm in England, on my way back to Mrs C's house, and this time I'm nervous not because I'm scared of disturbing her, but the total opposite.

I take the cliff trail again. There's a heavy scent in the air, which I guess is coming off the yellow flowers on the huge spiky bushes growing either side of the path. A red and black butterfly flitting around above the flowers brings back the memory of the bow on top of that frickin' Binky dog's head.

I get a bad scratch on my right leg when I step aside to make room for a dog-walking couple, but like a true English gent I swallow my pain. I suck in my breath and bid them good morning. Thomas would be proud.

There's some kind of kiddie football game happening on the park. I say 'some kind of' not because I'm SoCal inarticulate but because all the kids are wearing different jerseys and it's impossible to tell who's playing against who; they don't even seem to know themselves. The players are all ages but I don't see my Josh and David anywhere among them. I guess they're off doing whatever twelve-year-old kids here do on a Sunday morning. Hopefully not the same as I was doing at that age.

It's a different Mrs C that opens the door today. For one thing she's smiling, and inside that smile her teeth seem less brown, more a regular Brit yellow. Her fingers are more pink than yellow. As if she's been up all night scrubbing all the brown stains off her body. The stupid Binky dog is even quiet, but probably because it's being carried by its owner. Rule one of dog ownership: keep the dog at ground level at all times or it'll think it's the boss. I don't say that out loud; we aren't quite on those terms. She (Mrs C, not Binky) is wearing a floral dress with stockings and a white knitted vest. (Did I tell you Thomas likes to knit? He learned in prison, knits pillow covers and hats and all kinds of shit to sell at NA fundraisers.) The black shiny shoes look right today too. In context. Maybe an injection of God has rejuvenated her spirit. Maybe when I saw her yesterday she was in withdrawal and in need of her Godly fix. Or maybe my own anxiety altered my perception; it happens. I wish her a good morning and she welcomes me into her smoke-free home.

The space around her is lit up by sunshine and it all looks somewhat inviting as she leads the way in to her old-lady lounge. The walls are decorated with framed pictures of all shapes and sizes with the floral wallpaper showing in between them – brown, old pictures of boats and people and people on boats or next to boats. And random close-ups of fish. And people with fish. It's cosy, but a person could get seasick in here.

With the stink of *los cigarillos* gone I feel bad for not wearing smarter clothes. Disrespectful.

'I like your house,' I tell her. It's the truth: her house is awesome. Never lie to old ladies, they always can tell. Hopeful-looking china puppies perch all over the lounge: on shelves, on the table, on top of the TV – it's like a kind of rescue centre for ornamental doggies.

Mrs C puts her real dog down and it immediately jumps on to my lap. Yes, its name really is Binky and now it's licking my hand. Nobody tell the Great Dudini. The GD is no lapdog and his tolerance of those who are is off-the-scale low. Mrs C – 'call me Doris, dear' – doesn't even ask me if I would like to join her in a beverage, she just goes off into the kitchen to make it. Binky responds to a bit of a shove from me and follows her to the kitchen and I wipe the dogspit from my hand on the lacy cloth that's draped over the arm of the chair.

They're only gone two minutes before Binky's tongue reconnects with my hand.

While she pours tea into floral cups Mrs C asks me if I'm staying at the youth hostel. When I tell her the name of my hotel I see her face morph momentarily into yesterday's Mrs C, which triggers a memory that has nothing to do with her: me and another person – who I don't recall – pissing our pants laughing because whoever it was said to me, 'When you smile, the sun disappears behind a cloud.' Okay, so we were probably high.

Ha. How much use can memory really be if it's so fungible?

I sense a prejudgment forming so I go into a spiel about how I chose that particular hotel for its proximity to her house without realising it would be quite so luxurious and that anyway it was actually really cheap from one of those last-minute booking sites, and

I redeem myself enough for her to pay me a compliment. Or what I think she intends to be a compliment. 'You really are the spit of him,' she says. 'It's quite uncanny.'

What's uncanny is that even her voice is different today, like she never so much as looked at a pack of cigarettes.

I ask if she's okay with me recording on my phone whatever she's going to tell me. She says, 'Of course, dear, if you think it will help,' and sits down in the armchair next to the window, saying, 'I had a good think about it all last night. Whatever will help you to find him.'

Now seems like the right time to break the news about him being dead. Dishonesty makes me uncomfortable.

I wouldn't say she shrugs it off exactly. I know how it is with old people: the death of old friends, relatives, whatever, *who*ever, becomes a part of your daily routine, like reading the newspaper or watching *Judge Judy* or taking a pill to make the poop move through your pipes.

'Tell me what you need to know,' she says.

'I don't know anything at all, so just whatever you remember.'

'Well, just stop me if I wander off track, then,' she says, and pats her knees for Binky to come be petted by her as she talks. I guess the stroking sets her into the rhythm of her story.

'I first met your grandparents, Mr and Mrs Agelaste-Bim, in September 1970 when they took me on as their daily help. Old Peggy Jackson was retiring and suggested me as her replacement. I happened to be pregnant with my Sharon at the time, but it was early days and I wasn't showing yet, so I decided not to mention it in case they changed their minds about giving me the job. We needed the extra money, you see, with a baby on the way.

'I'd only been working there a few weeks when I heard that Mrs Agelaste-Bim was expecting too. I didn't hear it from her, of course; some old busybody in the village told me. Idle gossip was nothing short of an Olympic sport in Applesham. I'd promised myself I wouldn't get dragged into gossip about the goings on at the house, but it was impossible to avoid it. Menopause mishap, they called it. I wasn't exactly young myself at thirty-seven, old enough in those days to have given up on ever being a mother really. Mrs A-B must have been a good ten years older than me and I felt sorry to hear her being talked about so disrespectfully. I'm sorry to tell you, dear, your grandparents weren't well liked in Applesham, but that didn't stop people being interested in their business; if anything it made them nosier. Human nature, I suppose. Don't let your tea go cold, dear. Is it sweet enough?'

I take a sip and nod enthusiastically. I want her to stay on track. And I don't want to be hearing my own voice when I listen to the recordings. They say never eat or drink anything with sugar in the top three ingredients. Now I understand why her teeth are so bad.

'The problem with your grandparents was that they hadn't always lived in the village, not that they cared about that, but people didn't like outsiders in those days. A double-barrelled name and being filthy rich didn't help much either. I was still a teenager when they arrived – it must have been a couple of years after the war ended. To me it was as if they'd descended from a planet made of gold. Everything about them was shiny: their cars, their clothes, their skin, their hair. They bought the Grange, which was the second-biggest house in the village after the Rectory, and made it into the first-biggest by building a huge modern extension on the back and side. All wood and glass, it was. You'd have thought people would be pleased the house was coming back to life seeing as how it had been sitting empty all those years, but no, you'd hear them rattling on in the post office about how much better it was before, even though they'd been just as nasty about the previous owners when they were around. Those poor devils were killed during the war when a bomb flattened their London house. People said they must have been too drunk to hear the air-raid sirens and slept through them. That's how nasty they could be.

'Anyway, the Agelaste-Bims moved in and spent an absolute fortune doing the house up. It was a devil to clean, but I loved it, all that light and space. It seems ridiculous now, but it felt like a privilege to look after it. People don't have the same pride in their work these days. I think what really upset everyone most about them was that they never made any effort to get to know anyone outside their circle, never invited anyone from the village to their house unless it was to do them a paid service of some kind, never even so much as set foot inside the pub or the local shops. I suppose the common feeling was that if they weren't going to spend their money in the village, they were of no use to anyone. A bit like the French must feel about

Monaco, my Frank used to say. Frank's my husband. Was. He's dead
now. That's him over there.'

Mrs C points to a framed photograph of a man holding a fish.
He's wearing a huge fisherman's hat that covers his eyes and his face
is hidden in its shadow.

'They were never short of visitors, whizzing back and forth in this
or that sports car. Theatrical types, writers – the poor posh, Frank
called them. Lots of parties. Some of their guests were famous by all
accounts, but I didn't recognise them; the Swinging Sixties hadn't
really made it down to Applesham. We didn't watch much television
in those days and the nearest theatre was miles away in Bristol. Do
you know –' she quits stroking Binky a second and leans towards me
'– even the debris left behind after one of their parties was other-
worldly: a golden feather here, a fallen star of a broken earring there.
I swept up quite a little collection of fancy litter in the aftermath of
those dos. Nothing valuable of course; I wouldn't want you to think
me a thief. I never took anything that wouldn't have otherwise been
headed straight for the bin. I brought it home in the pocket of my
apron and put it by in a jar for my little Sharon to play with when she
was old enough. Not that she'd been born yet. I was like a jackdaw,
collecting shiny things for my nest.'

She stops for a sip of tea and then stares at me as if she's really
looking at me for the first time, as if the tea has somehow opened her
eyes. 'The absolute spit,' she says.

'Well, when word got round that Mrs A-B – I took to calling her
that privately after I'd been there a couple of months – was expecting,
Frank and I reckoned the most upsetting part of it for the old fuddy-
duddies was that a middle-aged couple could still be having sexual
relations, but nobody ever came right out and said that; it was all
folded arms and sucked-in breath, you know how people are. Instead
they said things like "How on earth will they cope?" As if they were
concerned for their wellbeing, when what they really meant was,
"Well, that'll put the mockers on their footloose and fancy-free lives."
It was almost as if they wanted it all to go wrong for them. No, I'm
afraid nobody liked them, dear. Jealousy can be very ugly.

'Having said that, the Agelaste-Bims weren't the most domestic
of people. Having seen them at relatively close quarters, I have to

say I secretly agreed it was hard to imagine them doing anything so practical as raising a child. Not that they were unpleasant or bad people; they were always charming to me and never criticised my work. As long as they had food to eat and wine to drink and clean clothes to wear and a radiogram to listen to and dance around to and books and newspapers to read and talk about, and friends to entertain them, I don't think they noticed much else. I suppose he worked, but I never did find out what at. In the end I think the real reason people didn't like them was the same old chestnut you still read about day in, day out in the newspapers now, dear: they were different.'

Mrs C stops for a sip of tea. 'Is this the kind of thing you had in mind? You must stop me if I'm rambling.'

I nod and give her the double thumbs-up.

'All right, well, going back to your father. To her credit, Mrs A-B took pregnancy in her stride. There were none of the histrionics that you might expect from a woman of her class. She never troubled the midwife outside of her routine visits. She carried on as usual right up to the day young Robin arrived. I'd go so far as to say that she behaved as if she was the one person in the village who hadn't been told she was pregnant!'

She slaps the arm of her chair, wakes Binky up.

'The upside of that from my point of view was that they seemed to not even notice my own pregnancy, even though my belly grew as round and bulbous as hers was sophisticated and discreet. That suited me fine – it meant I could relax and stop worrying about losing my job and concentrate instead on dreaming about all the lovely family holidays down in Cornwall my wages would pay for in the future.

'Looking back, I must have been naïve but it honestly never once occurred to me that a pregnancy that failed to register in the mother's consciousness would likely produce an unwanted baby. I must have been the only person in Applesham not to work that one out. To me a baby was such a precious gift; it just didn't make sense to reject him. It wasn't that he didn't look like them: he was the most beautiful little cherub with his smooth olive skin and large, dark, unblinking eyes. Anyone could see he would grow into the handsome child, and then man, that he did. But it wasn't his fault. It was about them not wanting anything to inconvenience their social life, and for them that

was a perfectly acceptable reason to hand over the responsibility for
their child to an employee they scarcely knew. In the end the villagers
were right. It's what people of their class did. When you have money,
no problem is insurmountable, and an unwanted child is a problem,
no more, no less.'

Her eyes move around the room as she talks, like she's talking
to each of the pictures and china doggies in turn, like they're her
audience and she talks to them all the time. Maybe she does.
Occasionally, like now, her eyes turn to me in the front row and seem
surprised to find me sitting there.

'Have you been to Applesham, dear? It's only about twenty miles
from here. You might find it interesting to see the house and the
school. The last I heard, the school had been converted into one of
those health farms. I haven't been to see what they've done to it, I
couldn't bear it if they've destroyed Frank's garden. I'm sorry, dear, I
keep going off on a tangent. Just tell me if I'm doing it wrong.'

I wave at her to keep going. It's hard not to speak. I'll need to
explain so she doesn't think I'm rude. I'm no psychologist, but I guess
I've already discovered the reason my dad was such a fuck-up. Quite
the cliché, right?

'Anyway, your father was born in one of the guest rooms at the
Grange because it didn't occur to anyone to prepare a nursery until
after he'd been born. Well, it did occur to me, but it wasn't my place
to say. Your grandmother gave birth with very little fuss, named the
baby after the first thing she saw when she opened her eyes later that
day, a robin on the windowsill, then got up and on with her life.

'My own pregnancy ended a couple of days later with the stillbirth
of my little Sharon. Black as coal she was when she came out, and
cold as the sea. These days, people take pictures of their dead babies
and give them proper funerals. Nothing like that happened then.
Little Sharon was whisked away to I don't know where without me
getting a proper look at her, let alone a kiss goodbye.'

Another sip of tea. I wonder if all the pictures on the wall are to
compensate for that one missing photo.

'So there I was, childless and distraught and with enormous
bosoms overflowing with milk sufficient to nurse a whole field of
calves, never mind the baby Robin Agelaste-Bim. My sorry state of

affairs couldn't have suited the A-Bs better if they'd planned it. Do you understand what I mean by "nursing", dear? They call it breastfeeding now. They offered me a lot of money and I was shell-shocked enough to take it. I would have gladly fed him for nothing, but I accepted the payment because a relationship with the likes of me only made sense to them if there was a financial transaction involved. So they paid a high price for the milk that should have nursed my Sharon. I'm not ashamed to say that the first eighteen months of your father's life provided for the complete redecoration of Applesham Lodge. That was the gatehouse at Applesham Manor School, where Frank and I lived. I had it in mind to dress the place up in a style similar to the Grange, which made Frank cross, and looking back I suppose the result was a real poor man's version. Frank was the groundsman at the school and the Lodge wasn't ours, it came with the job, but I didn't mind spending the money on it because it was ours until Frank retired and we weren't planning on moving anywhere else. People thought differently in those days: where you lived was your home, no matter who owned it. These days it seems like everyone's a landlord, and no one can afford the rent.'

I want to tell her about our landlord in RB, to offer another perspective and sweeten the bitterness of her words, but she's talking to the pictures again.

'Naturally when my breastmilk dried up I expected my wages to return to normal, but they never did. I tried to bring it up and Mrs A-B just shooed me away. I was convinced she would realise her mistake one day and ask for the money back, so I never told Frank and never spent a penny of it. I hid the extra away just in case. Mrs A-B was conscientious all right, but she was more like an overseer than a mother and I can't have been quite right in the head because I came to think of the boy as my own. She'd pop into the nursery once or twice at first, to check we had everything we needed. Once the weather was warm enough and Robin was big enough for us to go out and about she more or less left us to our own devices.

'It made me proud to see him growing into such a strong, healthy little chap and I would wheel him into the village in his big pram to show him off – like a Rolls-Royce it was – or the mile or so up the lane to the school to coincide with Frank taking his lunch break. I was daft enough to try to encourage a bond between Frank and young Robin to match the one we had –' she's talking to the picture of Frank and the fish and I imagine she's seeing a baby in place of the fish '– but, whenever I offered him the baby to hold, he would stand up shaking his head and say, "It'll never be a two-way street with that one." I never understood what he meant by that and the only sense I could make of it was the obvious fact that Frank could never love a child that wasn't his own, but I never gave up hope even when I knew people were talking about me behind my back.'

Back to me. 'All this yakking's making me thirsty; let's have another cuppa. I bought some posh biscuits on the way home from church – would you mind going to fetch them in? I'm always leaving my shopping out on the bike, I hope the gulls haven't got to them.'

Which is how I discover that she rides that heavy old bike down the hill to town and back up again every day.

Before we start again, I explain why I'm not speaking on the recording. She seems okay with it, says, 'As long as you're alright with me rambling on, dear.

'We'd only just celebrated Robin's first birthday when Mrs A-B told me about their plans for his future. From the age of five the poor little mite would be sent to board at Applesham Manor, the school where Frank and I lived and Frank worked. Not that there was anything wrong with the school, it just seemed so young to send him away from home, even if it was to a school in the same village and I lived in the grounds. I suppose they thought he would be close enough to me that I could keep an eye on him, and to them that he wouldn't forget who his real parents were. Well, it turned out I'd misunderstood their intention entirely. When the time came he took the upheaval in his stride and I tried to too, but as soon as he'd gone his parents disappeared from the Grange as mysteriously as they'd arrived. I turned up at work one morning to find it all locked up. Even though the house wasn't sold for years, they never came back. I believe they moved to the Middle East. Jordan, or one of those places. Do you know where they went, dear?'

I shake my head. I never even knew they existed until now, besides the obvious fact that my dad must have come from somewhere other than outer space.

'We arranged with the school for Robin to come to our house every Sunday morning after chapel and stay until after teatime, just so he wasn't completely abandoned. It broke my heart to see him all trussed up like a choirboy in that uniform. When I say *we*, I mean me really. Frank never quite cottoned on to my plan for him to be a surrogate father to the boy. Even out of pity. On the contrary, he took to getting up earlier on Sundays than he did on a work day, to go fishing. He'd pack himself a flask of tea and a pile of sandwiches and be gone before I left to pick the boy up.

'During the school holidays Robin was allowed to stay the whole day, and no matter how many times I asked Frank to take the boy fishing with him the answer was always, "Maybe next time," but it never happened. Not that I had anything better to do with my Sundays, I was no churchgoer in my younger days; I only started going when I moved here, as a way of meeting people. And before you say anything I'm not the only one, they're a right godless bunch round here. I'm not even sure the vicar believes.'

We both laugh at that and I forget about not speaking and tell Mrs C about the church in RB that writes a new pun on its signboard every week – SOULER ENERGY USED HERE – that kind of thing.

'Ooh, I like that,' she says. 'I must suggest it to our vicar. So, where was I? Oh, yes. Occasionally in the holidays Frank would get home before Robin left of a Sunday evening, if the weather was bad, or maybe just to please me. He never said anything but would hand over his catch, usually a large trout or a perch wrapped in soggy newspaper, and wait in the hall while I got Robin into his outdoor things. Then he'd take him by the hand and walk him up the driveway to the school. They'd both let go of hands as soon as they thought I was too far away to see. He did that just often enough to stop me nagging. The fish would always be gutted, filleted and in the pan by the time he came back. Nothing tastes like trout fresh from the river.

'Robin wasn't the only child who stopped at the school over the holidays, there were a few others, but he was the only local boy. Every week I told him to ask his housemaster if he could invite a friend to come the following Sunday, but he always turned up alone. I didn't read too much into it. I was all he had, so it was only natural he would want to keep me to himself.

'He was definitely more of a thinker than a talker. Every now and again, though, he'd come out with something that made me chuckle. One Sunday – he must only have been about seven – we were sitting at the tea table, listening to the hit parade on the radio while we ate our scones, when he announced that he was an "abecedarian". At first I thought it was something to do with school, like being milk monitor or cloakroom monitor, neither of which I could picture him sticking at, if I was honest, but I congratulated him anyway. He said I didn't understand what he meant and explained. His mother was Mrs A-B, so I was Mrs C, and when he got married his wife would be Mrs D. I told him he was clever to have come up with it. He always had an unusual imagination and I used to tell Frank I thought he would become a writer or a painter when he grew up. Maybe even a poet, he was such a quiet boy. I never told him about the alphabet thing, though; I thought he would be insulted that the boy didn't want to call me Mrs H for Henry and I didn't want to give him any more reason not to like the poor child.'

See? He was even weird as a kid.

'One year, Robin was about seven or eight, it happened that my birthday fell on a Sunday. All my presents – I make it sound as if there were hundreds but there were probably only five or six and none of them large – were piled up on the table when he arrived. From the look on his face you'd think a spaceship had landed slap bang in the middle of our dining room. I'm forty-three years old today, I told him, or whatever age I was. He just stood there, gawping, and it dawned on me then that he'd thought they were for him and that if he'd ever had any memorable birthday experiences of his own, he would have known to wish me a happy birthday, or make me a card. I suppose I'd always assumed his parents would at least have come up with the goods on his birthday and arranged for him to have a little party at the school. He'd never mentioned it, but then he never talked about anything that happened over there. I felt so guilty. Naturally when his birthday fell on a Sunday I would bake him a special cake, but we were too poor again after he started school to stretch to presents, and I was mindful that Frank already thought we did too much for the poor boy. As he stood there, his dark little eyes darting from the presents to me and back to the presents, obviously willing me to let him open one, I decided to let him in on a secret that not even Frank knew about. I told him to go and wash his hands in the kitchen because I had something to show him that was to be our special secret, just his and mine.'

I guess my own dark little eyes must have been darting back and forth between Mrs C's face and the cookies because she says, without missing a beat, 'If you want another biscuit, dear, just help yourself.' And goes right on with her story.

'I gave Robin the two smallest presents to carry and I took the rest and we went through the back hallway to go upstairs. That side of the house faced north and was always dark and chilly, even on a summer's day, not like this place – always light here except when it's stormy. We'd tried to cheer it up by putting Frank's tropical fish tank out there and I'd expected Robin to be fascinated by the angel fish and their long feathery tails and the neons with their luminous colours, but he had no interest in fish, living or dead, thank you very much. No interest in nature. I'd tried to teach him the names of the flowers in our garden because I thought it might please Frank, but he refused to take in the information, as if he knew what I was up to, and insisted on calling them all *daisy* whether they were roses or wallflowers. "*Daisy* rhymes with *lazy*," I used to say, and tap him on the nose with my finger. I'm getting off the point again.'

'No, this is all good,' I say. And by good, I mean revealing.

'Robin had never been, or even seen, inside the spare bedroom before. The door was always kept shut. Of course he'd been upstairs to use the toilet and to wash his hands before and after meals, although sometimes I let him wash at the kitchen sink if he promised not to tell the master, who could suspend his Sunday visits if he found out; they had some strange rules at that school. It was only a boxroom really but it was special to me because it would have been Sharon's room if she'd lived. Some of the breastfeeding money went into doing it up so we wouldn't be thrown into chaos by the arrival of an unexpected overnight visitor, not that that ever happened. I furnished it with a lovely walnut-framed bed with a matching wardrobe and bedside table and lamp. All very modern. We'd made a special trip to Exeter one Saturday to choose it all: lampshades, curtains and a quilted bedspread. Orange, to give the room a warm glow even in winter. I picked it out while Frank trailed round the shop behind me, God bless him.'

Mrs C pauses and smiles to herself. I wait.

'In the room, under the window where you'd put a radiator now but we had no central heating then, was the wooden trunk my father made me as a wedding present. I still have it up in the attic, one of the few things I kept when I moved here. The style of it didn't really fit with the new furniture but it was a beautiful piece of work so rather than get rid of it I found a special use for it. It has a high curved lid like a treasure chest and a lock, which even then I'd long since lost the key to. I suppose it's all covered in cobwebs now. Frank assumed it was full of baby clothes so he never ventured to look inside it.

'Anyway, I knelt down on the floor and set the presents down beside me and gestured to Robin to come and do the same. I said he reminded me of one of the Three Wise Men visiting the newborn Baby Jesus. His little face was a picture. "Solemn as a salmon," I said. He liked tongue-twisters even if he didn't like fish. As I lifted the lid his eyes grew big as saucers. The chest was full of even more presents, some wrapped in Christmas paper printed with baubles or robins or Santas, others in bright birthday paper. A few were still in their brown paper with my name and address written in big black letters, as if the postman had only brought them that morning. Not that the postman delivered on a Sunday, but you know what I mean – untouched. Robin watched me put the new presents one by one into the trunk. "Go on, then," I said to him, "pop them in." And reluctantly, he put his two in. Then I shut the lid and told him the story.

'After I lost Sharon... come to think of it I probably didn't mention Sharon. I don't think I ever told him about her; I didn't want him to think of himself as second-best. Anyway – after that I noticed that people stopped giving me useful presents, just more boxes of hankies and bubble bath and talcum powder sets, things I already had too many of, things to help me feel better I suppose, but it was as if people didn't know who I was any more. Even so, I appreciated that they had thought about me for long enough to choose something they thought I might like, and wrap it up and bring it over or go to the trouble of taking it to the post office to send it, and that was enough. Every gift

I received from that day on went straight in the trunk without being opened and if I ever felt lonely or unhappy I would go upstairs and remind myself of all the people who thought about me from time to time and cared enough to send me a present on my birthday. Eventually I didn't even need to go upstairs; I could just think about the trunk, no matter where I was and it would have the same effect.

'Robin sat very still and listened. Then he said, "How do you know who sent you what?"

'"That's not what's important," I told him. "Over the years some of the people who've sent me presents have died and their boxed-up best wishes are particularly special to me, but if you were to ask me which ones are theirs I'd never be able to single them out."

'I offered to wrap a little something up from my house for him to take back to school and keep in his locker to look at when he felt lonely, and he said, "I'm never lonely, because of God." Well, I admit I was a bit taken aback by that because he'd never mentioned God before, and I'm not sure he ever did again. I shrugged it off as another of his funny little ideas.

'Every Sunday after that, he insisted on abiding by school rules and refused to wash his hands anywhere but upstairs in the bathroom. The water would stop gurgling in the pipes and I'd hear him tiptoeing – at that age you believe you can make yourself invisible and inaudible – across the upstairs landing and into the spare bedroom to sneak a look inside the trunk.

'Then he developed a habit of feeling unwell of a Sunday evening as the time drew close for him to leave. The first time he did it, I begged Frank to run over to the school with a message for the housemaster that Robin Agelaste-Bim was going down with something and would stay with us until morning so I could keep an eye on him. I promised to send for the school doctor if he took a turn for the worse, but of course that was never necessary. He didn't try it every week, but those special Sundays when he could wangle a night in the spare room definitely became more frequent. And his symptoms would come on earlier each time so that he would be already in bed before the time he would normally leave. On those nights, he would be too unwell to say his prayers, but could always be relied upon to raise the energy to creep over for one last peep into the trunk before settling into bed.'

Mrs C giggles. I think she's even forgotten I'm here now.

'Your father was generally an even-tempered boy, but he could resort to tyranny as well as the next child and he was as unattractive and ungrateful as any other when he did. I loved him all the more then; his tantrums made him more human somehow. He seemed so disconnected a lot of the time.

'I don't know if he was an especially bright child, but he had charm enough to persuade anyone, except perhaps Frank, around to his way of thinking, which helped him get on at school. As a rule only the much older boys were entitled to a study bedroom of their own, but he managed to wangle one for himself at eleven.

'Just after his eighteenth birthday, so not long before he left school, a funny thing happened. Not funny ha-ha, funny strange. A letter came, addressed to me, from his parents' solicitor in London, informing me that Robin Agelaste-Bim's allowance would increase on his eighteenth birthday to three thousand pounds per month!' She shrieks and bangs the arm of her chair, waking the frickin' dog up again. 'Per MONTH, mind you! That's still a small fortune even these days! It said the increase was made on the understanding that the boy would be living independently. Reading between the lines, I took this to mean they didn't want him to think he could go and live with his parents, wherever they were. Why they were writing to me, I had no idea. I didn't even know he had an allowance, never mind an increase. And I don't know what he did with it all because he certainly never needed to buy anything except maybe sweets from the school tuck shop. I was sure he'd never set foot inside any other kind of shop in his life. I supposed it was all just piling up in a bank account somewhere.

'There was a catch to it, though. If he didn't manage to spend the full amount one month, the following month's allowance would be reduced to whatever he had spent the month before and could only be increased again after due application to the solicitor. I was supposed to keep that last bit of information to myself, but I told Robin because I thought he'd been badly treated and it wasn't fair for him not to know what he was up against.

'When I told Frank he said, "That's the last you'll see of him." He was wrong about that. But it was the last Frank saw of him. I still have the letter somewhere if you want it.'

I shake my head.

'Well, give me your address and I'll send it to you.'

'No, really, it's okay,' I am forced to say. 'I have envelophobia.'

She looks at me like I'm mentally defective and starts talking again, but I miss the first couple minutes because someone walks past the house and sets Binky barking. At first I think Mrs C hasn't noticed, but then she turns and says, 'It won't be anyone for me, dear, but maybe we should stop there because I'm running out of steam. Can you come back tomorrow, or are you leaving today?'

'It's fine,' I say. 'I can wait until tomorrow. I'm still tired from jet-lag and could do with a nap.'

'I suppose that's a modern thing, a man taking a nap during the day,' she says.

Binky gets all excited when we get up and move around. I fantasise about grabbing the stupid creature out of Mrs C's arms, running out with it to the middle of the park, setting it down like a ball on the penalty spot, and kicking it way up into the air and over the edge of the cliff. Fish food.

I don't take a nap. I check out the coastal trail on my phone and hike the few miles to a spot on the map called Hope's Nose. There's nothing there, but what optimist wouldn't want to check it out? And if I'm giving you the impression that I'm an outdoorsy kind of guy, it's not that so much as I like to keep moving.

Disclosure. I get these weird pre-sleep movies that run in my head. They're not dreams, I'm still awake when they happen, but it's like I'm watching them on a screen. The Germans have a name for it: *Kopfkino* (head cinema). I can turn them off by just opening my eyes, but I don't get to control when they start. They're not in colour or monochrome, they're always in red and black and always of people having accidents and dying. They are completely random and have nothing to do with my life and they don't happen every night or even every week. I've had them since I was a kid so they are not a result of my adventures in methland. They aren't fantasies, I'm not even in them, I'm just a passive observer. The people in them are tiny like I'm passive-observing from thousands of miles away in outer space. One time it might be a guy falling off a horse and getting trampled, another it might be a kid falling out of a tree. Occasionally I get a close-up on a face that zooms in and out like a psycho, leering at me. Its mouth might be moving like it's trying to tell me something, but there's no audio so the effort is wasted. Tonight's is nothing special, far away and kind of dull, a guy lying on his couch watching TV. He slips from being alive to dead without anything in the scene actually changing, but somehow I know that he's just passed. Weird, right?

Awake at five. Run. Shower. Breakfast. Back to Mrs C's. We chitchat a little while she makes tea. Nothing interesting. We sit down, I line her up with where she finished yesterday and she sets right in.

'Robin came over as usual the last Sunday before he left for university. I could tell he was hoping I would give him the trunk to take with him, but I told him it would be his when I die. As he died before me, perhaps I can persuade you to take it away with you? It really is a lovely piece of craftsmanship.'

I shake my head and point at my phone, meaning let's discuss it when we're not recording. Hopefully she'll forget.

'I was surprised he had signed up to study religion, but I found out later from Mr Todd, the Head at Applesham, that the reason he'd been given the study room when he was eleven was because he'd put in a special request for a quiet place to practise meditation and prayer.

'He went to Sussex University, in Brighton. I saw less of him then but he still visited the first Sunday of each month. He'd come down on the train in time for lunch and leave after tea. And every month he brought a parcel, two thousand five hundred pounds in twenty-pound notes, brightly wrapped like a present, money drawn from his parental allowance to dodge the rule I told you about. Of course, he never told me what was in the parcels, he pretended they were gifts for me, and I never let on that I knew, but I'm not as green as I look. Instead I said, "Thank you, dear, just take it up and pop it in the trunk, would you?" Exactly as he expected me to.

'He took lodgings in his second year with a divorcee by the name of Marsha Ray, whom he took to calling Mrs F. A nurse. I assumed that D and E had been girlfriends in his first year. I mean I hoped they were, because Frank used to say Robin would turn out to be one of *those* – you know, batting for the other team. Said it was very common among men from his background.'

Mrs C picks up her tea and blows into the cup. She takes a few long slurpy sips and kind of chews on each one while she sits petting Binky and staring at the photograph of her husband on the wall. I turn to look too so I don't have to watch her. It would be rude to put my fingers in my ears so I can't do anything about the noises except promise myself I can edit them out of the recording later.

'Frank passed away on the 14th of June 1991. He was only fifty-eight. His heart gave out while he was pruning the roses around Mr Todd's window and he was gone. It was so sudden. The doctor said he wouldn't have known anything about it. I hope I go that quickly. Sometimes I think I'm going to be here forever, pushing that bloody bike around. Mr Todd saw to all the arrangements, booked the funeral for a Wednesday and all the children and staff came from the school, even the governors. The school choir sang the hymns so beautifully. Frank wouldn't have appreciated it, though, he could be a right miserable so and so, but funerals aren't really for the dead, are they? "Just plant me in one of the flower beds when I go," he used to say, "reckon I'll make a decent compost thanks to all the good food you've put inside me over the years." Obviously they wouldn't let me do that, so I had him cremated and put his ashes on the roses. That would have cheered him up.

'Robin was in the middle of his exams, so naturally he couldn't come, but he sent me a beautiful card. I still have it, upstairs in the trunk. Are you sure you don't want to go up and bring it down?'

Yep, still sure.

'He said he had two recollections of Frank. One of his silhouette in the distance, hunched over a wheelbarrow or a lawnmower, and the other a close-up of the hairs that protruded from his nostrils in thick wet strands, like the untrimmed tobacco that poked from the end of his roll-up cigarettes. That's exactly how he described it; he had a way with words when he could be bothered.

'The governors were very good to me. I suspect Mr Todd had a hand in persuading them to let me stay on at the Lodge. He brought gardeners in from the village to do Frank's job. Three men to do the work Frank used to do on his own – no wonder he had a heart attack! I knew one of the new chaps from my days up at the Grange and he told me they were under strict instructions not to change anything Frank had done, not to do anything that might upset me, just to maintain things as they were. The only time they came close to the Lodge was on their way in and out, and except for that one man – I forget his name now – who used to give me a cheery wave if he saw me, they all kept their heads down. It wasn't as if Frank was Capability Brown or anything, but I appreciated their respect. "Stay in the Lodge for as long as you need to," the governors said, but after six months I couldn't stand it any more and moved away.

'He was a lovely man, Mr Todd. Lifelong bachelor, we used to call them in those days. The absolute opposite of Frank, who always had dirt under his nails no matter how hard he scrubbed them and smelled of damp earth and rotting leaves in the autumn. "Call me Alistair," he said, and then made a habit of popping in to check I was all right. When I got a job in the local greengrocer's shop to tide me over until Frank's money came through, he came every Wednesday afternoon, when I'd be home because the shop was shut for half-day closing. I'd say regular as clockwork, but I've never had much luck with clocks; Frank used to say my animal magnetism upset their workings. All we'd do was sit drinking tea and eating cake and talking about Frank. He'd always ask after Robin too, but when I passed on his regards Robin always claimed not to know who I was talking about.

'When Frank's insurance money came through I moved here for a fresh start. I found a job as a dinner lady at the primary school down the road and joined the church and life became very busy, what with working and all the new friends I made. It wasn't like at Applesham where I never saw a child other than Robin from one week to the next, despite living in the school grounds. Here children would knock at my door when they came to play in the park and I'd give them a sweet or a biscuit and in the summer I'd leave a jug of iced squash and some paper cups out for them. Some of them bring their own children now, so I always keep a biscuit in the house. I always made sure to be home on my own for Robin's monthly visits, though.

'Before I left the Lodge I cleared all my old presents out of the trunk to make more space for his packages. That was the most fun I've ever had in one evening. I poured myself a glass of wine – I don't make a habit of drinking alone, but it seemed like a special occasion, all my birthdays and Christmases come at once you could say – sat on the floor and opened them all one at a time. Most of it was junk. Have you ever sniffed twenty-year-old talcum powder?'

A few years back I would have sniffed anything vaguely powderish. I keep that thought to myself and shake my head.

'Well don't bother, it smells of nothing. And don't bother trying to peel the wrapper off a twenty-year old bar of soap either. There were a few boxes of stale chocolates, which I didn't dare open, put them all straight in the bin. Some of the linens were pretty, hankies and whatnot, so I took those down to the charity shop.

'I wasn't short of money in those days, what with my wages and Frank's pension. I could afford to buy shop jam instead of making my own, and a ticket to the cinema in town once a week, and sometimes if I felt wasteful I'd go to the bingo. All those little changes joined up to make my life unrecognisable from the way it used to be. I never gave a moment's thought to Robin's parcels of money in the trunk, and even if I had been dirt poor I wouldn't have touched them.'

I stifle a yawn, and smile apologetically when I realise she saw me.

'If Frank had come back from the dead, I dare say he wouldn't have known me after I moved here. You wouldn't think so to look at me now, but I was still an attractive woman in my fifties and sixties. I never felt the need for another gentleman friend after Frank though, I enjoyed my freedom too much.

'Then Robin stopped coming. The first time, I was beside myself with worry thinking he was ill or had been in an accident. When he'd missed two visits I went over to the phone box on the green to call his landlady in Brighton supposing she would know if anything had happened to him. When I eventually tracked her down, boy did I get a shock. Not only was Robin about to become a father, but he was in prison! She either didn't know what he'd done or she didn't want to tell me, she just said where he was and gave me the address: HM Prison, Isle of Sheppey, in Kent. I wrote three or four times, but he never replied to any of my letters. I supposed he was too ashamed of himself to write back. I never did find out what he'd done. Do you know, dear?'

I say I don't, and that I'll let her know when I find out. But that was before I knew, right?

'I only saw him once more after that, in 2000. I suppose he'd not long been released. He'd grown a big bushy beard and was dressed all in white as if he was stopping by on his way to a judo class or a pyjama party. He drove up in one of those big camper vans – not the small, hippy kind, more like the ones people my age clog the roads up with after retirement. Not that he was driving. I don't think he ever bothered learning to drive. He had another young man with him, very well spoken, very polite. Tom, I think his name was, or Thomas. He gave me the creeps.'

'Thomas is my guardian,' I say to pre-empt any further insults.

She chews on her cheeks a bit more.

'Well, anyway, Robin comes in carrying a big green holdall, breezy as you like. Of course I knew why he'd come: his allowance would have dropped off while he was in prison. So, I come in here, thinking they're both behind me, but when I turn around only the Thomas chap is there. Your father's gone upstairs. Thomas keeps me talking, asking me questions about the house, about my job, small talk really, and all the time I'm listening to Robin's footsteps upstairs. Thomas acts pleasant enough, I suppose, but it feels a bit uncomfortable, as if he's been told to corner me in my own sitting room. Then, it can't be more than a few minutes later, I hear a thud on the path outside and Thomas's eyes flick to the window and he interrupts himself to say, "Well, Mrs C, it's been very nice meeting you, but I need to go back to the van now to make sure we don't get a ticket." And off he goes. "No need to see me out," he says. And I'm thinking, a ticket, here?

'While I'm waiting for Robin to come down, I watch the other one pick up the holdall – Robin's thrown it out of the bathroom window – and carry it over to the camper, casual as you like. Next thing, Robin comes charging down the stairs and into the sitting room. I'd never seen him exert so much energy; he'd always been such a languid chap. Too much being carried and wheeled in early life, if you ask me. "Sorry I can't stop," he says and gives me a big hug, something he's never done before, it brings tears to my eyes. I watch him walk over to the van and all I can think of is how thin he is, that I should have offered him something to eat or made sandwiches for his journey. I didn't even get a chance to ask him if the baby was all right. And that was the last time I saw him. I got the dog after that. Not this one, his mother.'

She pauses a few seconds to pet Binky.

Wait, Binky's a boy dog?

'He'd emptied the trunk, of course. I didn't dare think about how many thousands of pounds he'd driven off with or what he was planning to do with it; it was none of my business.

'I tried calling his landlady again a couple of months later to see if she had any news or an address for him, but the man who answered the phone said he was looking after the house while she'd gone to live up north and had never heard of Robin. I wrote a couple of letters to her address in Hove in case her post was being forwarded, but when nothing came back I had to give up. For a short while I had things all muddled in my head, got all worked up thinking Robin had passed on a bad gene and you'd been stillborn like my Sharon, and then I remembered he wasn't my son. Old age does that to you.'

Mrs C insists on making us lunch before I leave. We have cold ham, beets, tomatoes and cold potatoes with a suspicious blob of yellow cream on the side of my plate that she tells me is salad cream not mayo and forces me to try it. I have to say it actually is quite delicious, not bland like mayo, and I take a picture of the bottle to send Thomas so he can pick some up on his next trip to Burbank. Mrs C kind of sucks her food and I have a hard time staying at the table, but at least the sucky technique requires her to keep her mouth shut once the food's inside it. Binky sits on a chair at the table and watches us eat.

'He likes you,' says Mrs C. 'Do you have a dog?'

I tell her about the GD, about how we rescued him, and somehow we skip from that to the tomato tomato conversation. Yeah, it doesn't really work written down. I've often wondered why the rule doesn't also apply to potatoes, but Mrs C doesn't know and neither does Thomas, we've had the same discussion at home a million times. It's just one of those mysteries of the English language. We get, by way of tomatoes, potatoes and the whole deadly nightshade genus, to talking about Agatha Christie's poison plants garden. Apparently her friend helped build it. 'Frank would have loved it,' says Mrs C, and sighs and says, 'There are so many different ways to die,' which reminds me of my weird night scenes. I generally don't think about them during the day. As soon as I go to sleep I forget they ever happen, until the next time.

Dessert is another cup of tea with a chunk of ginger cake – which she emphasises is bought from the market, not home-made; I get the impression she's done with cooking – and more chewing and sucking.

She gives me a second chunk of cake wrapped in foil to eat on the train and makes me promise to come visit again when I've finished my investigations. She says she'll wangle us a special pass to go see the poison plants when the garden is closed to the public. I actually would like to do that. And apologies to *fungible*, but *wangle* is my new favourite word.

Before I check out of the hotel – late but I wangle off the extra charge by lying about having gotten lost – I'm emptying out my backpack to separate my clean clothes from the not so clean, and that's when I find Thomas's envelopes. Before I turned twenty-one, I don't think I ever got a letter and now every motherflipper is writing to me. Letters must be a feature of adult life. He must have shoved them into my bag when I wasn't looking and I guess he doesn't want me to read them all at once because they're in separate envelopes, numbered one through five. He knows I can only take in so much information at one time. I open number one.

Dear Sonny. There are things I still haven't told you.

Uh oh.

That's not how the letter actually starts but it's what my eye puts together out of all the words on the first page. Too much already. I toss the envelope and fold the letter into my pocket to read on the train. If I feel up to it.

Things We Can't Undo #1

I go all-out and travel first class. I need to be relaxed to think about everything Mrs C's told me, not tense and distracted the whole journey because of other people's sticky mouth noises and one-sided upspoken phone conversations. I look out the window a while at the pink rocks on one side and the ocean on the other. It's not that I forgot about Thomas's letter, more like I'm consciously choosing not to remember it, but then the train turns inland and we're into open country and all there is to look at is sheep and cows, so I get it out of my bag. It's short, just one page.

Sonny,

Wherever you are when you read this letter, I hope things are beginning to piece themselves together for you. The past is a giant jigsaw puzzle and I'd hate for you to reach the end of your trip with whole sections still unaccounted for. Sorry, that's a terrible start. What I'm trying to say, by way of rather clumsy metaphor, is that there are things you don't know about me, that nobody knows because I've never told anyone. Suffice it to say, I still have major amends to make with many people, above all with you.

Where to start. Do you remember that time I completed the programme and you asked me why I needed to start over again?

Thomas messed with drugs when he was younger too, so, when I
started going to NA, he did as well, to show solidarity, he said.

> *I gave some glib reply about the cathartic value of forever*
> *digging deeper when in truth I was doing the exact opposite.*
> *I'm not saying it's all been a charade, but I've tripped over*
> *step nine without reaching resolution too many times now to*
> *maintain any delusions.*

In case you don't know the programme – and why would you, right,
your life is perfect? – step nine is about making amends to those you
have harmed.

> *When I saw you get to step twelve and go straight back to step*
> *one without really being able to articulate why, alarm bells*
> *rang and I knew it would be impossible for you to get clear*
> *without knowing the whole truth. I've waited until you were*
> *mature enough to handle it, and I have to admit to being more*
> *than a little scared even now that what I have to tell you will*
> *throw you off kilter again.*
>
> *So, before I go any further, I want to tell you that it's been*
> *an absolute honour and a privilege to be your guardian these*
> *last ten years or so. You are a remarkable young man, Sonny,*
> *and have faced challenges head-on that a person of twice*
> *your years and life experience would run from. The upside has*
> *been a varied and interesting life, but, as we both well know,*
> *varied and interesting is often only a minor crisis away from*
> *chaotic and precarious. But I am convinced of your strength*
> *and that everything you have faced up to and dealt with so far*
> *will stand you in good stead for what comes now, and for the*
> *future, however varied, dull, chaotic or peaceful you decide to*
> *make it. I have to believe that, and so must you.*
>
> *When you've read these letters, I will completely under-*
> *stand if you choose to cut me off. Andrew and Ruth have both*
> *promised to be there for you if you need someone to talk to.*
> *They are both good people. The best.*

What the hell?!

> *As for what I have to tell you, I'll try not to bore you by*
> *repeating things you already know, this isn't about me, but*
> *inevitably there will be moments. All I ask is that you please*
> *just take your time and hear me out, read each letter in turn,*
> *and please, keep reading to the end, however long it takes.*

Okay, that's enough for now. My envelophobia, letterphobia, whatever, has kicked in again. I'm not ready for what comes next, whatever it is and whatever Thomas believes. I get out my tablet and book a hotel close to Ruth Williams's address in London and then, to stop my mind asking questions about Thomas's letter, I watch some *SOTD*. I write Thomas a message to tell him I found his letter, then delete it without sending.

Tonight's death scenes: an old man falls out of a hammock; a young guy skis into a tree. I don't know if these are real deaths that I'm tuning into telepathically, which are happening to real people in real life/death at the exact moment I tune into them, or if they are happening in some other space-time continuum. Or maybe they're hallucinations brought on by self-inflicted brain damage. I never asked anyone else if they ever had the same experience and I never told anyone about mine, not even Thomas. If one starts up and I don't like the way it's going, I have a simple strategy. Open my eyes and watch *SOTD* instead.

Ruth of the Living #1

Ruth Williams still lives in the same house she lived in when you met her, back in the late 1980s, way before you had me. I check out the satellite view of her address and locate the roof of her house at the top of Parliament Hill, by Hampstead Heath, one point four miles and twenty-seven minutes by the most direct walking route from my hotel.

Ruth functions better in the morning so we've arranged for me to be at her house by nine. I walk over there real slow, enjoying that everyone else is either dragging kids to school or rushing to get to their job, all fresh out of the shower, stinking of perfume and aftershave and all the other chemical crap people wash down the pipes to pollute the water supply. I know it's wrong but I can't help thinking that now I'm a multimillionaire I could live my whole life without ever having to do any of that shit.

The streets are still wet from overnight rain and the air is damp and chill and grey clouds block the sunshine every few minutes. I picture you, the young woman who became my mother but never my mom, making the same journey thirty-some years before, your long hippy dress trailing in the dirt, beads jangling on your wrist. You stop to hug one of the big old trees that are evenly spaced along both sides of Ruth's street. But all that turns out to be a false imagining. You only started to dress like a hippy after you moved to Scotland, as a kind of disguise. In my experience, disguises only make people stand out more; you only have to watch the Z-list TV stars shuffling self-consciously along Hermosa boardwalk in their big-hat-and-shades disguises while every normal person is hatless and relaxed to know what I mean. I guess they want people to look at them really or else they wouldn't be on TV in the first place. Even I could have told you that dressing like a Deadhead was never going to stop my dad finding you.

If I was nervous to meet Mrs C, then the words don't exist to describe how I feel on my way to Ruth Williams's house, and that's because Ruth is the first person I ever met, not counting my dad and Marsha Ray, who knew you really well.

Ruth doesn't shout at me through the door like Mrs C did. In fairness to Mrs C, she didn't know I was coming whereas Ruth does. She opens her door with a wide smile and holds a hand out for me to shake. When our hands connect, one of us is trembling and I can't be sure it isn't me. I'm grateful she doesn't attempt any awkward observations about which parent I resemble most, just lets me be myself and only compares me to the version of me she met when I was very small. My anxiety eases off a little.

Her living room has a huge fireplace and the furnishings are minimal compared to Mrs C's clutter. I wonder if it's a gas fire that can be lit easily like the one we have in RB. It's supposed to be summer, but I am really feeling the cold. But I guess I can't just walk into a stranger's home and insist they light the fire. All I can do is stare at it hopefully.

'It's Edwardian,' says Ruth, misreading my thoughts. 'This style of house was built during the reign of Edward the Seventh. Make yourself comfortable. Would you prefer tea or coffee?'

'I'm a tea man, thank you,' I say. 'My parents were both Brits, remember?'

I have no idea why I say that – nerves, I guess. My tea habit comes from Thomas, not from you, or my dad, who only drank herbals, and I feel bad for Ruth when she slaps her hands on her skirt as if to say she should have known that. She's gone again before I get the chance to apologise.

The room is in the back of the house and has a clear view over the red and brown rooftops of the houses on the street behind. Beyond them is a large grey pond and beyond that an area of green, which I guess is the Heath. We don't have large public parks in RB, and if we did Donald Trump would probably have bought them and

remodelled them into golf courses for rich old men to drive around
on in their buggies.

The thin layer of dust on the window frames and shelves in Ruth
Williams's house is the same dust that settles on everything in the
rooms of the old people at the Sunrise: tiny particles of dead skin,
shed by the old and dying, whose eyesight is too weak to see it and
even if their vision is okay their muscles and bones are too tired to
care about sweeping it away. Sometimes their brain has forgotten
what dust is and what you're supposed to do about it. But don't get me
wrong; there is nothing weak or forgetful about Ruth Williams.

Two chairs are arranged at an angle to the window, positioned to
look out over the view. It's obvious which chair is Ruth's favourite:
the one with the reading lamp set right behind it and the slanting
seat cushion with the ends of a newspaper poking out from under it.
I guess this is where she likes to sit and talk, and when there's nobody
to talk to it's where she likes to sit and read, or sit and watch the
seasons change. A low, round wooden table is set between the two
chairs and I knock my knees against it as I sit down because I'm not
about to start rearranging the furniture.

While Ruth sings to herself in the kitchen, I mess with my phone,
send myself the recording of Mrs C because I forgot to back it up,
check the weather in RB (sixty-eight degrees), and write another
message to Thomas, which I send this time, so he knows I found his
letters. *One thing. Those challenges I faced head-on were of my own
making, not anybody else's.* Shaun has to stop defending Ed's actions
before he can grow some, and I had to stop defending meth-head
Sonny's actions. Right?

Ruth has arranged cookies in the shape of a flower. A low tower of
round, pale wheat cookies in the centre form the flower's eye, and
six or seven chocolate oblongs with BOURBON etched into their
tops are the petals. Later, before I kill the last petal, I take a photo to
remind me to buy a pack on the way back to my hotel. This is one
kind of bourbon I'm allowed.

I double check that Ruth's okay with me recording her story and
she warns me that her speech can get a little slurred when she's tired
and makes me promise that if it gets so I can't understand what she's

saying, I'll stop her and continue tomorrow. Like Mrs C said about there being so many different ways to die, there are so many different ways of being old. As many different ways as there are people, I guess. Not that Ruth's so old, just a little stooped from her condition. There's an old guy at Sunrise, Mr Somethingowitz, who is bent over at the waist. He used to set the type for a newspaper. He calls it his *occupational posture.* 'I've been looking at the floor since 1968,' he says. I tried it one day, doing everything bent over at ninety degrees, and man, it kills. Once you've tied your shoelaces, everything else is hard. Thomas refused to participate because he said you couldn't have two people in a house like that; nothing would get done. So I guess the moral of that tale is that, when life bends you over, you need an unbent helper, right?

As Ruth settles into her chair, I feel myself getting antsy again. I have so few memories of the time I was with you. But, as Ruth rests her hands on her knees and closes her eyes, prepares to speak, I remember the anticipation of being told a story and naïvely associate it with you.

'Is it recording?' she says.

Her voice is soft and clear, like I imagine a dolphin's would be if it could speak.

'I'll start at the very beginning, as they say in *The Sound of Music.* The first time I met your mother. It wasn't long after they diagnosed my Parkinson's disease. I have only ever had mild symptoms, but we didn't know then how it would progress and someone at work suggested meditation might help. I wasn't into any of those New Age therapies, but I thought it couldn't hurt to learn to relax properly, particularly with a job as stressful as running a school.

'Nor do I believe in signs, but when I spotted an advertisement in the *Ham & High,* our local paper, for an alternative health fair up at the library, I thought I should go and take a look. This was in 1988, I'm not sure of the month. Most of the stalls were selling useless paraphernalia, crystals and incense holders and suchlike, and your mother was the only stallholder not selling anything. There she was, sitting behind a bare wooden decorator's trestle covered by a white sheet with *LifeForce Meditation* printed on it in big blue letters.

She had her nose in a book, was deep in concentration, obviously hadn't had too many interruptions. When she sensed me hovering, she looked up and smiled.

'Your mother was a remarkably pretty girl.' Ruth Williams opens her eyes and squints at me. 'It's no surprise you're so handsome. Although you have your father's eyes; hers were the clearest blue. Her hair was coal black, like yours, tied up in a long glossy ponytail. Her skin was clear but for the sprinkling of freckles on the bridge of her nose and she was the smartest-dressed person in the whole room. A badge pinned to her blouse said her name was Suki, which hinted, I assumed wrongly, at an oriental heritage.

'I explained why I wanted to learn to meditate and she offered to teach me, right there and then. A couple of cushions were set out on the floor behind her and she invited me around to her side of the stall. I wasn't the type to worry about who might see me, so I sat down and shut my eyes as instructed – my movements were still brisk in those days – and she sat opposite me. She talked me through a simple deep-breathing exercise and in those few minutes I experienced such peace as I've never achieved since. It was as if every muscle in my body had been put into neutral and every worry transformed to insignificant litter floating around on the breeze. Five minutes and I was hooked, regardless of whether it could help my condition. Suki gave me her business card and invited me to join one of her meditation groups. She seemed so mature and pragmatic that it didn't occur to me she might be involved with a cult; she didn't seem the type.

'Of course I found it much more difficult to meditate alone. So the following week I went to a meeting. The address was a private house in Camden, so not far from here.

'The meeting started with a short meditation, followed by an inspirational talk, or "discourse", as it was called. I don't remember the subject; it would have been trust, openness, our inner child, something like that. After that, more meditation, followed by tea and biscuits and a general chat.

'Over the weeks I learned a little bit about the group, a real mix of people: professionals, artists, students, unemployed people looking for a meaningful pastime or some supernatural luck. Fifteen or twenty of us in all, of which around half of us were beginners like

me, or "uninitiated", to give us our correct label. The others were a
mix of first and second initiates, people who'd climbed to a higher
rung on the spiritual ladder, although hadn't yet reached the top.
Suki was a second initiate and told me that first initiates meditated
on a personalised mantra and second initiates meditated on light and
sound. I said she did seem to have a certain glow about her, which
made her laugh. I learned that by practising meditation I was aspiring
to the highest possible spiritual state: enlightenment. There were
apparently some within the LifeForce organisation who had reached
that hallowed state. They were known as "adepts", and they didn't mix
with anyone less evolved than a second initiate.'

And there I was, hoping you'd turn out to be the normal parent.

'There was a lot of talk about us being on a spiritual path and
the importance of staying on it. Initiation was the big mystery for us
beginners, the carrot that kept us going back every week. I admit I
found it all a bit competitive and tedious. I was too old to care about
enlightenment. My only ambition at that point was to perfect my
meditation practice and stay in good health as long as possible.

'A faint alarm bell rang when Suki told me I needed to be
seen to be making progress. You need to progress from breath
meditation to truly benefit, she said, and insisted on giving me a basic
mantra to repeat over and over during meditation, a string of seven
sounds that would have a healing effect on my aura and help prepare
me for initiation. It was gobbledygook really but I didn't want to get
her into trouble by not conforming, so I promised to try.

'When she announced she was moving to Brighton – she'd been
accepted by Sussex University for a research post in philosophy – it
came as a surprise to think of her having a life outside LifeForce,
though it was no surprise that she was clever.'

I guess I get my brains from you, then, right?

'Brighton was famous for its hedonism, and for all her maturity
and pragmatism I found myself worrying about how she would fare
amongst other less ethereal beings. When I expressed this to her
she emphasised that she wasn't leaving LifeForce, that she'd chosen
Brighton because there was a fledgling group of initiates there who
needed her guidance. When I told her she'd be missed, she said I
should channel my emotional energy into my meditation, that I

should get initiated, so I could also go to meetings in Brighton and even spend time with her outside meetings. I didn't want to be left behind, so I increased my meditation from twenty minutes to an hour each morning and evening.'

Suddenly Ruth opens her eyes. 'I hope I'm not being too long-winded.' I wave at her to keep talking; this is the first time anyone has told me anything about you EVER and I want to know every detail. She nods and closes her eyes again.

'Apparently my reluctance to socialise with other non-initiates was also a hindrance, and the more gregarious members of the group overtook me on the path time and again, but like the proverbial tortoise I persevered and, a few months after Suki moved away, I was invited to attend a "special meeting".'

She makes those cute little finger-waggling movements for the speech marks.

'Four of us were taken into a darkened room and instructed not to leave under any circumstances. The ceremony consisted of us being tapped on the forehead by an unseen adept. It could have been anyone and was over in seconds. I barely noticed it, but one of the others experienced a hallucination of gold and silver flying doughnuts while the other two declared internal firework displays of municipal proportions. I kept quiet, but I wrote and told Suki my news and within days she wrote back, inviting me to Brighton.

'Things changed after initiation. The adepts came into the picture more, as did the big boss, Ishvana, our guru, whose "grace" –' waggling fingers '– had to be switched on for initiations and enlightenment to take place. He was the great puppet-master behind the organisation, and the recipient, no doubt, of all the donations. As initiates we were expected to donate ten per cent of our income to the organisation. Perhaps to justify the expense, initiates made ridiculous claims about their meditation: enhanced insight into the thoughts and behaviour of uninitiated people, heightened aura-detection, taste and smell, superhuman powers of concentration. It was Thatcher's Britain, after all; people expected value for money. I fluctuated between feeling inadequate and irritated by their nonsense, but kept quiet in case Ishvana decided to uninitiate me, if such a thing were possible.

RUTH OF THE LIVING #1 61

'Suki completed her research and that summer I went down to Brighton for a week to have a little holiday and take her out for a celebratory dinner. I was allowed to stay with her and Andrew, another second initiate, in their little rented house in Kemp Town. I loved waking every morning to the sound of gulls calling to each other across the rooftops. You don't get that in London.

'One evening, I was helping Suki prepare the room for a meeting when she told me she had invited someone new along, a student from the university, and wanted my opinion of him. The way she tried to stop herself smiling as she talked about him gave me the impression she thought he had some special spiritual quality, and I couldn't help but feel a little sad. LifeForcers had a tendency, because of the celibacy rule, to dress up any sexual attraction as mutual recognition on a deep spiritual level. I felt sorry for Suki that she had learned to sublimate her natural feelings in order to justify them and I was sad because I had hoped that she would fall in love with Andrew, who was such a kind, gentle person and clearly smitten with her. She had achieved so much intellectually at such a young age that I often worried whether her emotional development wasn't a little retarded, if that doesn't come across as too much of an insult.'

Ha ha. So maybe I got the emotional retard gene from you as well as from my dad.

'I was quite friendly with some of the regular Brighton gang. They were a funny bunch. Alison, who was the unhealthiest-looking nurse I'd ever met, had spent her adult life trying to give things up – smoking, food, drink, poor hygiene – and was delighted to have found an arena in which to flagellate herself legitimately; Alan, a lovely silver-haired man in his fifties, hyperactive, obviously gay and terrified of it and using LifeForce as a kind of reinforced closet – Ishvana condemned homosexuality as unnatural – and Amber, a dance student, who I think was there hoping to meet a boyfriend who wouldn't hurt her. I don't know if she ever found one.'

Ruth looked up and caught my eye. 'But I'm drifting off the point; you want to know about your parents.

'By then I knew a little about Suki's upbringing. Her parents, your grandparents, were strict Anglican Christians, very High Church, who had sent her to a single-sex Anglican school and expected her to marry within the church community. Her dedication to Ishvana and his teachings earned her the strong disapproval of her parents and their religious friends, who all but ostracised her. For all its restraints and control, LifeForce was Suki's spiritual rebellion. But I couldn't help wishing she'd do something truly rebellious, truly worthy of rejection, like being arrested for drunk-driving or lashing out at someone who annoyed her instead of smiling with compassion. But religion was part of her make-up and she couldn't be someone she wasn't. In the end it didn't seem to matter too much, because she always seemed so happy with her lot.

'I'll cut to the chase. The person she'd invited along that evening was your father, and I'll be frank with you, I didn't like him from the start. Of course in LifeForce you weren't allowed to say anything about anyone that might be construed to be a negative criticism.'

'It's like that in SoCal too,' I tell her. Personally I find all that positivity exhausting, and so does Thomas, which is why we're allowed to be as negative as we want at home. As long as it causes nobody harm. 'Why didn't you like him?'

'He was faking it to get in with Suki. I understood the attraction, though; those narcissistic types are always charming. He was as striking to look at as she was and charismatic with it. They even looked alike. Not so much a physical resemblance, but they shared an ethereal quality that might lead you to assume they were brother and sister, even though he was fair to her dark. Please excuse the LifeForce cliché but I had this overwhelming sense of him being her shadow.'

She opens her eyes. 'Have you seen that Austin Powers film where Dr Evil says "you complete me" to his Mini-Me? Yes? Well that's how it was with them: he completed her, but in a negative sense, if you don't mind my saying that.'

I tell her she has great taste in movies and that I appreciate her honesty. I don't want her to hold anything back no matter how anxious it makes me feel.

'You could generally spot a newcomer at their first meeting by their posture. Usually they cowered and slumped, intimidated by the presence of us so-called spiritually advanced beings. Not so Agelaste Bim; he sat there erect as a flagpole from day one. He had no interest in me so I was free to observe him at my leisure, and I watched him

closely in the hope of finding some positive encouragement to give
Suki when she asked for my opinion.

'Do you mind if we stop for a while? I could do with a break.'

Ruth suggests I take a walk over the Heath while she rests, so I show
her my list of *SOTD* locations and ask how close they are. On the
map they seem really close, but I have no sense of scale here. In
Redondo, if a place looks really near on a map, it probably takes three
hours to walk to it.

'Oh, yes, most of these are in this area. This one's in Highgate,
over the other side of the Heath. Probably a bit too far for you to go
now.' She's tapping her fingernail on the address for the apartment
building where Shaun's girlfriend, Liz, lives. I can't stand the sound
of it and pull the paper away. She doesn't seem to notice. 'What's the
title of that film again?'

I set off over the Heath to Hampstead, following Ruth's directions,
sucking up the post-rainshower smells, which are so rare in RB. My
sponsor told me once that drug addiction can be caused by a sense of
loss at the deepest cellular level and I wonder, since I was born over
here but grew up in warm dry places, if my deep sense of loss is rain-
related. Could be, right?

Hampstead's kind of a swanky neighbourhood. Swanky and shabby
all at the same time, like you'd expect the heart of Trustafaria to look,
and I wonder if that's why Ruth sent me to check it out, to be among
my own people. There's no bling here, people hide their wealth
by dressing shabby, but they live behind high walls and cameras
and it's clear they have plenty of the most valuable commodity of
all, according to Thomas: time. Time to shuffle along the street at
the pace dictated by their expensive little doggies. The main street
runs uphill and I walk up looking for a deli, in search of a sandwich
without mayo; I settle for the market and an Indian pastry.

I sit on a bench across the street from the library and eat, staring
and thinking about the first time you and Ruth Williams met inside
that actual building, and, while I'm sitting there, watching the world
of privilege run its errands, that woman with the crazy hair who's in
all the Tim Burton movies walks by. No hat, no glasses, and nobody,

except me, gives her a second glance. Look and learn, Hollywood, look and learn.

Ruth opens the door and, before I can step inside, says, 'What a wonderful film.'

I look behind me, confused. It's not the word *film* that confuses me, Thomas says that all the time, just I forgot we talked about it. Then I remember. '*Shaun of the Dead*? You already watched it?'

'Yes, I often watch films while I'm resting. Thank you so much for recommending it; I would never have come across it otherwise. I enjoyed it very much. In fact, I've had an idea. Rather than sit in this gloomy old house tomorrow, why don't we visit a couple of the locations together? I can talk as we go. Unless you'd rather go alone, of course.' She's all excited and I'm still standing on the doorstep.

'Definitely, sounds good to me. You didn't mind all the cursing?'

She stands aside at last, waves me in. 'Oh, no, I've heard much worse than that in my time, believe me, most of it from the mouths of six-year-olds. It may not look like it to you, but I have lived a bit, you know.'

We chat some more about the movie while Ruth makes tea. Her kitchen's all black and white and green. She has a huge crush on Bill Nighy, the guy who plays Philip, Shaun's stepdad in the movie, says what a great actor he is, and how in her younger days she would have also thought Ed in *SOTD* very handsome. When I point out that they aren't exactly of a similar type, she says it's something in their voices; that my dad had the same thing going on, with the opposite effect. I don't know her well enough yet to tell her how weird that is.

'Please would you carry the tray?' she says, kind of apologetically. 'As you're here. They tell me not to carry and walk because of my condition, but it's just a Health and Safety thing and I'd like to know how anything would get from A to B in this house if I didn't.'

In these first couple days with Ruth I sense a kind of challenge in the small tasks she sets me, as if she needs to see me demonstrate the possession of certain qualities, to assure herself I've turned out to be the kind of person she hoped I would. Or, more specifically, that I'm not the person she's scared I might be – my father.

We sit down and Ruth closes her eyes – I guess she's entering the meditation zone where the old memories are easier to find – and picks up where I tell her she left off.

'That first day I met your father he was wearing a bright turquoise suit with a pale blue shirt and red tie. Most young people would have been embarrassed to be seen in the street dressed like that, even in the '80s, but you could tell he was the type to relish the attention. My first impression of him was not of someone needy, desperate or vulnerable, as so many were, but determined and single-minded, and it was obvious to me that the object of his determination was Suki.

'We all sat cross-legged on the floor in a semi-circle, as usual, and waited for Suki to start the discourse. The room was lit by a single lamp and several candles, and the curtains were drawn to keep out the last of the sunshine.

'Suki smiled at each of us in turn then fixed Agelaste Bim with those blue eyes that I had presumed to be so clear-sighted, and said, "Welcome to LifeForce, on behalf of us all. Tonight's discourse is on the subject of trust, but first let's meditate together for a few minutes." I half-closed my eyes so I could carry on watching him. As a newcomer, he was expected to sit and absorb the beneficial vibrations given off by the group, but he didn't even bother to pretend to be affected by them. While everyone else straightened their backs and assumed a look of serenity, he kept his eyes wide open, looking at the little hammock Suki's skirt made of the loose fabric between her thighs, where her hands were resting. He stared at her, challenging her to open her eyes and engage with him. But in those days nothing could break her concentration.

'At the end, there were the usual questions from the group about how to trust in the face of adversity, that sort of thing, and Bim pretended to listen intently, but I could tell he was waiting to jump in with his own question, not that he gave any outward sign of impatience. I hope you don't mind me calling him Bim, I don't mean to be disrespectful but the name is a bit of a mouthful. Anyway, his question was, "How long does it take to get enlightened?", which at a LifeForce discourse was a bit of a showstopper. Suki put her hands together and said, "Let's talk about it over tea," and so he scored himself a double success, nipping all the other nonsense questions in the bud and guaranteeing a private chat with Suki in the break.

'Suki knelt down beside him and gestured to me to join them.
"How did you find that?" she said, and he smiled at her, nodding
slowly like the proverbial cream-filled cat, and said, "Fantastic." To
be fair to Suki, she treated him like any other newcomer, asked if he
had ever done yoga and he replied that he'd tried it. Did he want to
learn how to meditate? Of course he did. And then she trumped him,
clever girl. "Okay, then," she said. "Why don't you arrange to meet
Ruth here in the next couple of days and she can start you off with a
basic breath meditation."'

Ruth laughs. A long and wicked laugh.

'He was miffed, to say the least. A date with me had not been on
his agenda. As for me, I was flabbergasted! Suki of course chatted on,
asked him about the origins of his name, and he lashed back at her
with, "When you were born, were your parents expecting a parrot?"'

I tell Ruth I don't get it and she sings a little song about someone
telling Polly to put the kettle on. I still don't get it.

'I knew Suki wasn't her real name, it was the one Ishvana gave
her, but she didn't tell Bim that, just smiled at us both and went off to
speak to one of the others, leaving us to make our arrangements. I was
less concerned for her welfare after that and I've often wondered since
if that was the point of the whole performance.

'I met him for his lesson at Suki and Andrew's house a couple
of days later. Suki was upstairs, a few hours into an eight-hour
meditation. His shoes were like nothing I'd ever seen, sky blue leather
with the big toe separated off from the others, like a thumb in a
mitten. When I commented on them he said he'd had them made to
his own design by a cobbler in London. They made his feet look like
cloven hooves, but I refrained from pointing that out.

'Anyway, to get back to the story – he asked whose house it was
and I told him, deliberately implying Suki and Andrew were a couple.
But he knew I was trying to put him off and gave me that smile of his,
to let me know he knew better.

'To tell the truth, I was a little scared to be alone with him. I was
glad Suki was upstairs even if she was as good as on another planet.
I was still hoping the LifeForce rules would put him off before we
even got round to the meditation, so I reeled them off, right there
in the hallway: "We all follow a strict vegan diet: no meat, no dairy,

no animal products or processed foods. This is essential to keep the system free of toxins and stress and aid the movement of energy through the chakras during meditation. For the same reason the use of alcohol, drugs or stimulants of any kind, including cigarettes, is prohibited, and we limit our intake of tea and coffee. Natural remedies and homoeopathy are preferable to prescribed medicine." We didn't usually release all this information at once in case it put people off, but not him, he just stood there, unfazed, with that arrogant smirk on his face. I had a feeling the restrictions on clothing wouldn't bother him either, but told him anyway. "Certain colours help to channel different energies," I said. "Blue is protective and healing. Black blocks our energy and has a negative effect on our aura. White is too powerful for anyone other than second initiates and the enlightened to wear." He interrupted to say he always instinctively wore his favourite blue shirt when he was feeling unwell. I ignored him; I was building up to my *pièce de résistance*. "You may have noticed fewer men than women at the meeting. Our meditation and healthy lifestyle makes the young women in LifeForce extraordinarily attractive, which often entices men along to one or two meetings, but, once they discover what is truly involved here, that we uphold a strict rule of celibacy outside marriage, they soon lose interest." I paused for him to say something, but he just stared at me, showing not the slightest sign of discouragement. My ace was on the table and I was running out of options. I had one last go at putting him off.

"'Everyone involved in LifeForce is on a spiritual journey towards enlightenment, both together and alone, and the foundation of that journey, the path itself, is the meditation. So, before I teach you the first stage of meditation, I will need a commitment from you that you will sit down to meditate twice a day, first thing in the morning and last thing at night, and that you will endeavour to live by LifeForce rules. It's a lot to take on, so if you need to go away and think it over that's fine, or if you have any questions now, please ask."

"'So," he said, "are Suki and Andrew married?" He put his face closer to mine and whispered, "Or was that intended to put me off?" He had the upper hand and he knew it, and like all assured champions he didn't linger on it. "I don't think any of that will be a problem for me," he said. "Though I may find it difficult to give up cheese." I could have smacked him.

'After he'd gone, I picked up a framed picture of Ishvana from the little shrine in the living room and remembered how I'd felt the first time I saw it. With his white suit and long hair and sideburns, he reminded me of a TV detective from the '70s. One thing LifeForce had taught me was to look beyond the physical, to view the body as nothing more than a vessel for spirit, for grace. I knew it would be difficult to apply that lesson where Agelaste Bim was concerned, but I had to try, for Suki. Anyway, all I could do was come back to London and try to forget about him.

'If you don't mind, maybe we could stop there for today. It looks as if we're in for a storm.'

I've been staring at Ruth's face for so long that it's shape-shifting, morphing like the faces in one of my night scenes from old lady to fairytale princess to young girl and back to old lady. I look away. The sky over the rooftops has turned a deep shade of purple and the street lamps on the next street are lit orange. Ruth switches on the lamp behind her chair, and I quit recording. I take a slug of cold tea and ask if it would be okay to have another beverage before I leave; I'm feeling quite chill.

'Of course,' she says. 'You should stay until the storm's blown over in any case. You're welcome to use my spare room, you know, if you need somewhere to stay.'

I thank her and tell her I already have a hotel room.

We sit in silence, sipping our tea, deliberately not talking about you and my dad, watching the storm develop into a spectacularly heavy rain shower. We talk about the rain and the song about it never raining in SoCal and by the time we've finished our tea the dark clouds have been replaced by blue.

We say goodbye until tomorrow and she waves me off from the door.

I detour to a joint selling burgers made of organic meats I never even heard of at Trustafarian-only prices, order myself a wild organic elkburger – all that vegan talk, right? – which I eat standing at the counter. When I get back to my hotel I'm too mentally exhausted, and physically weighed down by delicious elk meat, to do anything more energetic than lie on the bed messing with my tablet. I wonder what Thomas is doing. He didn't reply to my last message, I guess it didn't need a reply or else he's waiting until I've opened all his envelopes. I post a photo of the pack of cookies I bought on the way home and tag him in with the message: *Hitting the Bourbon*.

I fall asleep watching TV and wake up again at four a.m. with the TV and all the lights still on. I switch it all off, but then I'm lying there in the dark, eyes wide open, thinking about you and how finding out more about you only makes you seem like more of a stranger. I calculate that it's only eight-twenty p.m. at home and while my body is still stuck in that schedule I may as well indulge it, so I turn on the light, call room service to order a pizza, then man right up and read Thomas's second letter.

Things We Can't Undo #2

Brazil. As good a place to start as any. Getting off the plane in Recife was like walking into a furnace. I'd slept on the flight but was still exhausted. No sooner had I shut myself in my room than your father came and told me to get up, that he had a job for me. I begged a few minutes' grace to get my bearings and go and sit and smoke a little skagerette out on the balcony – that's how I spoke in those days, I was a complete tosser. 'Balcony?' he said. He was so pissed off that I had a balcony and he didn't that he didn't even register that I'd smuggled a few days' supply of heroin across the Atlantic. Anyway, he handed me some notes he'd scribbled on a sheet of paper, stapled to a photograph of the entrance to Quilombo Novo and wrapped around a thick wad of reals, then sent me on my way without even giving me time to shower. He was paranoid that someone else would get there before me and foil his plan.

He had read about Quilombo Novo, when we were in prison, in his favourite book, Great Spiritual Masters of the Twentieth Century. *It was established in the sixties by a chap called Guru Mehdi.*

Yeah, so Thomas was in prison with my dad; it's where they met.

Your father claimed to have received a message from the Universe that Guru Mehdi had died and that he was to be

Mehdi's successor, charged with the task of restoring the
commune to its full spiritual capacity. My job was to travel
ahead as a kind of envoy and set things up for your father's
arrival. I didn't know any of this until we were on our way to
Manchester airport. Not that I would have argued; I was more
than happy to leave England and it all sounded like a great
laugh. I said something like, "So the Universe didn't tell them
you're coming, then," and he answered, completely straight,
"No, it may not have. You need to make sure that Mehdi
didn't appoint a successor before he died." Your father wasn't
famous for his sense of humour and I'm ashamed to say that
his failure in that department never stopped being a source of
entertainment.

From the hotel in Recife, he sent me to Olinda to find you
all a place to stay, which turned out to be surprisingly easy. A
woman in the tourist office made a phone call to a family who
she thought would gladly vacate their house for a few months,
in exchange for more money than they would normally earn in
a year. They even agreed to leave their eldest daughter behind
to work as a maid as part of the deal – your Maria.

Maria! The only truly happy memories I have of my childhood
feature Maria. It was love at first sight and I guess partly I loved her so
much because she loved me. She taught me how to do so many cool
things: how to sweep the floor and how to stab a straw into the top of
a coconut and drink its sweet juice. Taught me the names of flowers
and how to mimic the calls of the noisy colourful birds. How to mash
manioc in the kitchen. How to greet the storekeepers at the bottom of
the hill – *bom dia!* – and the stallholders in the market at the top of
the hill – *bom dia!* Day after heavenly day, I watched her firm round
buttocks switch from side to side in front of my face as we trudged up
the hill in the heat, from the store to our house, or further up the hill
from our house to the market, her yakking away to me in a language
I didn't understand, but who cared, right? And in return I must have
told her stories about you and Andrew and my friends at school
because that would have been all I knew then. And we both made
listening noises and neither of us cared that we understood none of

it; words didn't matter, we had so many ways to communicate, Maria
and me. She showed me how to tickle the pink and purple medusas
washed up on the shore with a straw of broken reed. Taught me to
tread carefully to avoid the spines of puffer fish half-buried in the sand
and showed me the spot where the turtles buried their eggs. Told me
stories of sharks and surfers. Sat me down on the terrace at the public
library and showed me pictures of her beloved goddess Yemanja.

I could go on forever, but this is Thomas's story.

*First mission accomplished, I returned to Recife for one
night, strictly against orders, to replenish my dwindling drug
supply, in the scariest bar I've ever spent time in and come
out of unharmed. I bunked up at a decrepit hotel near the bus
station and didn't sleep a wink, expecting to be murdered or at
least robbed at any moment, but presuming I was marginally
safer there than out on the streets. Next morning I caught the
earliest possible bus to Cabrobó, twelve-hours into the Sertão,
Pernambuco's desert hinterland. Quilombo Novo was a few
miles on from Cabrobó. I'd been instructed to settle in first
then write to your father via the tourist office in Olinda as soon
as I'd cleared the way for him to make his appearance.*

*You may be wondering why I was so keen to do your father's
bidding. The truth is I was financially dependent on him,
needed him to fund my habit. Contrary to what I've told you
before, it was never my decision to stop drawing on my trust
fund – it was blocked by my family when I went to prison,
never to be reinstated under any circumstances, either to me or
any future progeny.*

Thomas is, or was, heir to his family's arms-manufacturing company,
and until he got caught running a neat little business on the side
exchanging guns for drugs, most of which he consumed himself, he
was also their employee. Thomas says that arms companies in the UK
like to keep a low profile, so when he got caught and caused a massive
media scandal they disowned him immediately. You can imagine
the hoo-ha, maybe you even saw it in the news. Anyway, once he
was incarcerated he went back to conducting business as usual. Or

not *as* usual, *better* than usual because there was a) a ready-made clientele, right there on his doorstep, and b) less chance of being caught. Ironic, right? Thomas made new contacts on the inside, his colleagues on the outside supplied weapons to their colleagues on the outside, and in return his new contacts on the inside supplied him with drugs and protection. And that's what kept him and my dad from getting beat up, which they definitely would have otherwise, for being posh (Thomas), and posh and weird (my dad). Soon as Thomas got out of prison, he folded his business, which is why I guess he needed my dad.

My release date was a few weeks before your father's so he had me run a couple of errands before he got out, said he was thinking of setting up a spiritual retreat in the Lake District and it was my job to find a house to rent, etc. But mainly he wanted me to find out where you were. He'd never seen so much as a photograph of you, what with him being behind bars when you were born and your mother taking the opportunity to disappear. Well, not disappear exactly – she was easy enough to find. I've gone off the subject. I was in Brazil.

You must remember how lethal the roads were. Dogs, bikes, carts, buses, people pushing wheelbarrows, all swerving around on the same narrow stretch. It was a long way to Cabrobó and I needed to be out of it. I nodded off in the warm breeze that blew dust in through the open windows and that was it until the driver woke me at the refreshment stop. Some enterprising person had set up a stall in the middle of nowhere selling coconuts and water and home-made pastries. I took a piss behind a tree, bought a coconut and sat under a different tree to drink the juice and smoke a skaggie to see me through the rest of the journey. The other passengers stood around chatting. I was drenched with sweat just in my shirtsleeves; they were wearing jackets. I hadn't washed for three days. Brazilian people are the friendliest you'll ever meet, but even they knew to give me a wide berth. Except one scruffy little kid, who appeared out of nowhere to sit next to me. I entertained him by blowing a few smoke rings and gave him a fifty-real note and he legged it at top speed. It's incredible how fast those kids can run in flip-flops – he probably could have gone at the same speed with a football at his feet too. It felt good giving him money, especially as it wasn't mine. Come to think of it now, though, it was probably yours! I hope you don't mind. Five minutes later the boy returned with his mother, or big sister, trying to give it back. I put my hands in my pockets and got back on the bus to get away from them and the driver took that as a signal to scuff his cigarette end into the dust, say goodbye to his mate the coconut seller and get back behind the wheel.

We arrived in Cabrobó late afternoon. The bus dropped me by a scrubby tree and drove off in a cloud of dust and diesel fumes. I sat on a wall for a smoke, watching the sun go down behind the low flat-roofed buildings and waiting for the cooler darkness to swallow up the shadows of the palm trees at the side of the road. A cart drawn by a pair of black, sharp-horned cattle came up the street towards me, its flatbed loaded with rubble. The driver walked alongside, flicking a switch and shouting. Hard to tell if he was encouraging the cattle to keep going or if he was buying or selling – rubble? – or if he was simply announcing to the whole town that he was on his way home from work. Once they'd passed I set off in search of a bar and a bed for the night. I didn't want to arrive at the commune in the dark. I sauntered down the road with this image of myself as an enigmatic, smartly dressed stranger arriving in town, more tax inspector than spiritual emissary, a far cry from the emaciated, fluorescent-faced rat of a junkie that I actually was, with my filthy, sweat-streaked shirt hanging down over my baggy-kneed trousers.

Halfway down the street, a thin, grey-haired man with lines set deep in his face sat dozing under a light pestered by insects, the back of his chair propped against the wall. A brighter light spilled through the open door beside him, and through it a man with a frizzy afro was hacking at the end of a green coconut on a heavy wooden counter. I went and stood in front of him and he put down his cleaver, cracked a wide white smile, wished me bom dia *and reeled off a list of possibilities.*

Cachaça? Caipirinha? Whisky?

As if on cue, my room service order arrives: hot chocolate, cold beverage, soggy margherita pizza and potato chips. The guy calls me sir, comes right into the room uninvited and replaces the packs of cookies I ate earlier. I'm glad of an excuse to put Thomas's letter to one side; he's walked into a bar so I can kind of tell where it's going. If you didn't already guess, Thomas is a recovering alcoholic as well as a drug addict.

But the food doesn't have the soporific effect I was hoping for, and I'm kind of intrigued, so I pick the letter up again.

I woke up in a windowless room behind the bar with a plastic strip curtain for a door. My bag, and the money and drugs inside it, were on the floor beside me, untouched. Needless to say I had no memory of the night before. A small, dark-skinned lad, maybe ten years old, woke me. His green eyes and ball of reddish frizzy hair suggested a genetic link to the proprietor, who was nowhere to be seen. The boy waved at me to follow him into the bar, sat me down, brought me coffee and a plate of couscous in the shape of a disembodied breast and cheesy butter to spread over it. I knocked the coffee back in one gulp and tuned into the sound of voices and general kitchen noises off somewhere in a back room. As it's common practice for a Brazilian family to welcome a stranger to their table, I assumed I'd overstayed my welcome, probably done something shameful the night before, which was nothing out of the ordinary. I picked at the couscous, slipped a large apologetic tip under the plate and headed off down the street to find a taxi.

The taxi office was shut. It was early, not even six-thirty, so I sat under the tree for a smoke while I waited for it to open. A few minutes later, the boy from the bar turned up, leading a cart and two oxen. 'Taxi?' he said. I showed him my list of instructions and pointed at the name of the place I wanted to go, hoping he could read. 'Trinta,' he said. I gave him a fifty and gestured at him to keep the change. He climbed up on

to the cart and beckoned to me to follow. In one corner was a
rolled-up hammock, which the boy pulled out and patted, then
pointed at me and put his two hands together at one side of his
face to suggest sleep. He jumped down, the cart jerked forward
and yet again I saw nothing of the journey.

When I came to, the cart had stopped. At first I thought
the glimmers of light against dark above me were stars in a
black sky, then my eyes adjusted and the stars morphed into
specks of sunlight through a mass of foliage. The cart was
parked on a narrow track under a canopy of trees, its wheels
stopped by large rocks. The boy and his oxen were nowhere to
be seen.

I followed the track to the edge of a river. I knew the
commune was close to the São Francisco so I deduced we were
at or near our destination. I saw the oxen first, stood cooling
their ankles in the shallows. The boy was sitting watching
them, his back resting against the trunk of a palm tree, a
newspaper spread on the ground beside him as a makeshift
blanket, over which were scattered the remains of a picnic. The
boy looked up and waved me over and I propped myself against
the tree next to his. He held out a spoon and a plastic box and
babbled something at me in Portuguese.

The box contained a mix of rice and black beans and a few
chunks of sausage. Feijoada. As the first spoonful approached
my mouth, one of the oxen lifted its tail and dumped a string
of turds as big as footballs into the water. I screwed up my
nose and the boy fell sideways laughing, clutching his belly
and rocking. Although the food was delicious, my appetite
was knackered and when he wasn't looking I tossed a couple of
spoonfuls into the trees behind me.

When he calmed down, the boy looked at me, weighing
me up, then patted the tree-trunk behind him and said: árvore.
So I did the same and said tree and we went on like that for
a while: leaf, stone, water, oxen, sky, shit, shoe, shorts, and
trousers, until the boy got tired or bored and lay down on his
newspaper sheet and fell asleep. I sat and had a smoke and
read through my instructions properly for the first time. Your

dad had written one of his inspirational quotes at the end of his notes. You know the kind of thing: A Master can show you the path that leads to the doorway of understanding, but only a True Master will hand you the key to pass through it. *I was always impressed by his ability to come up with such twaddle without the aid of chemical stimulants. This is my all-time favourite:* History imprisons the mind. Science imprisons the soul. Sensual pleasures imprison the aura. Only fools allow themselves to become trapped. Unlearn it all to become Free.

Something tells me he thought that one up in prison.

When the boy woke up he jumped to his feet, ran into the river and splashed around shrieking. I called over and pointed to the shit to remind him but he just laughed and mimicked my accent. After a few minutes he shook his hair like a dog and set about urging the oxen to their feet. We processed at ox-speed back to the cart. Water droplets glistened in the frizz of the boy's hair like dew on a cobweb. I shudder now to think of the litter we left behind, newspaper, plastic containers, water bottles, but that was normal there, remember?

I had to walk the rest of the way. The boy – we'd exchanged names but I'd already forgotten his – pointed me in the right direction and I burdened him with a further fifty reals and for some reason my gold watch, probably a pathetic attempt on my part to make memorable for him a day that I would most likely forget myself. Although, even more strangely, I haven't, mainly because of the watch, which had belonged to my grandfather and was worth a fortune.

The sun was burning the top of my head, and after just a few minutes' walking my feet were hot and heavy and my shoes were tight as if they'd shrunk. I had sobered up enough to consider that I might have paid a hundred reals and one priceless gold watch for the privilege of being taken into the wilderness and dumped, but not really enough to care. I was without food or water, had nothing to sustain me but a bottle

of cachaça I'd found in my bag without having any idea how
it got there. The river was still visible through the trees, but the
road was definitely moving away from it. I took a swig from
the bottle and had decided to look for a place to sit and finish
it off – if I was facing a slow death by sunburn, I might as
well be cooked in something nice – when I spotted something
glinting at the side of the road up ahead. It turned out to be a
large wooden M (for Mehdi, I discovered later), mounted on
a wooden plinth and decorated with random scraps of silver
foil and thin streamers of faded fabric, bleached pale by the
sun. It marked the beginning of a track through the trees, the
branches of which were decorated in similar fashion, with
streamers and wooden windchimes that clunked together in
the breeze of my passing. Ah, good, I thought, hippies. Where
there were hippies, there were drugs. I crossed the log bridge
and was at the wall and listening to life on the other side – a
child shouting, a dog barking, someone whistling, I don't know,
you probably remember better than me how it sounded. I sat
down on the track with my back against the wall and polished
off the cachaça while rehearsing my 'bringer of good tidings'
act to be performed on the other side. I chucked the empty
bottle into the undergrowth, and followed the wall to the next
bridge and the open gates of the commune, where I was greeted
by the sign WELCOME TO QUILOMBO NOVO written in
English, Portuguese, Dutch and German.

Most of what happens next I already know, because it's part of
Thomas's first rehab story that I've heard sooooooo many times, so
I'll abbreviate. T shows up at the commune and they think he's a
bum, he's such a stinking, drunken, drug-stung mess. The doctor
there, Ken, takes him in and cleans him up, which isn't a simple case
of showering him off and washing his clothes, it takes three whole
months. Ken gets him off the junk and booze and on to methadone
and vegetable-farming. What I don't already know is that, when
the resurrected Thomas finally emerges from that first house of
reformation and gets round to remembering why he's gone there in
the first place, he hits a major stumbling block. The part of the story

I've never heard before is that it turned out the Universe lied to my dad about the leader of the commune being dead. Good old Guru Mehdi was in extremely good health.

> *The law of inevitability says that if you write down one word after another you will eventually find yourself forming the sentences you've been trying to avoid. I've reached the point of no return, and I must keep going because you have a right to know who I was, who I still am. We can never leave ourselves behind; we can only know ourselves better. I'm beginning to sound like your father. Sonny, I'm not like you, the drugs didn't turn me into an arse; I got into drugs because I was an arse. Saw myself as the big man upending the system, when all I did ultimately was land my family in jeopardy. In those first few months at Quilombo Novo I might have come off the junk – thanks to Ken – but I was still the same person in terms of motivation. Under the skin, I wasn't so terribly different from those zombies you're so fond of.*
>
> *On the subject of the undead, Mehdi still being alive was a huge problem. While he was still there your father couldn't take over and if I didn't contact your father soon I'd be stuck out there in the Sertão, miles from civilisation, stranded, sober and broke. I had no interest in staying clean; I needed your father to come and rescue me so I could get off the methadone and back on to the real stuff. So I exerted my recently unaddled brain to come up with the best possible solution to my dilemma.*
>
> *Quilombo Novo under Guru Mehdi was a happy and healthy place. The commune seemed to run itself, with Mehdi as its benign leader. Children and adults from the surrounding villages came and went as they pleased to make use of the school and Ken's clinic, and Ken treated villagers out in their homes if they were too sick to visit the commune. The word 'leader' doesn't best describe his relationship with the rest of the community; Mehdi had the best house because he had bought the land and settled there first, but the vision was a shared one and he helped build every other house there. He wasn't old,*

in his fifties or early sixties, nor was he even sick. He was fit
and well and everybody loved him. He swam in the river every
morning at dawn and this was his private time. Otherwise he
was never alone.

This is what happened. Start again: this is what I did. One
morning I waited for him down at the river with a cloth and
a bottle of chloroform stolen from Ken's clinic. I hid behind
a tree and watched him take off his pyjamas, fold them and
place them on a small boulder – he always swam naked. As
soon as he had both feet in the water I pounced on him from
behind. He was tall and wiry but there were hidden depths
to my strength that only a junkie in need of a fix can muster
and I managed to keep walking him out into the river as we
struggled. The chloroform didn't work quickly like in films,
he didn't fall into an instant swoon, but, once he was out, I
pushed him face-first into the water as if I were baptising him
and held him under until the bubbles stopped rising to the
surface. Then I dragged him further out and let him go.

WHAT
????????????????????????
THE
?????????????????????
FUCK
??????????????????
??????????
????

Ruth of the Living #2

I haven't slept. Ruth says we can postpone if I want to go back to my hotel or else I can rest at her house. For once I don't want to be alone so I say I'll be okay, that I need to beat the jet-lag and that it was probably the elkburger that kept me awake.

Then we're outside, trudging up to the top of the Heath and I try to relax my shoulders and breathe. It's warmer today, or else I'm acclimatising. I should be genetically programmed for this climate, right?

I guess you're wondering how good of a writer I can be if I don't describe what's going on around me. What can I say? I'm in shock. There are dogs, trees, people. Leave me alone.

I drift ahead of Ruth without meaning to. I guess I'm not ready for her to pick up her story. I stop and wait for her to catch up then find myself ahead again. I wait at the top of the hill and when she joins me she needs to rest so we sit on a bench overlooking a view of downtown and I tell Ruth I haven't seen any of it close up yet. She says it's prettier from up here anyway and tells me the weird names of some of the weird-shaped buildings: the Gherkin, the Walkie-Talkie, the Cheesegrater, the Shard. I say they should call them all the Penis and be done with it: Penis 1, Penis 2, Penis 3, Penis 4. Seriously. Which makes her laugh, and me kind of proud for making her laugh.

Ruth breathes easier on the downhill so she's keen to start recording again. I shuffle along beside her, thinking of Thomas up to his middle in the São Francisco.

'I came home late from work one evening to find a message from Suki on my answering machine. I hadn't been back to Brighton since the episode with Bim. She wanted me to call her urgently. She sounded so excited that I immediately assumed Ishvana had enlightened her at last. Naturally I called her right back, but whatever it was couldn't be told over the phone and she begged me to visit as soon as possible.

'Now I say I'd pushed Agelaste Bim to the back of my mind, but not so successfully that his name didn't ring warning bells as soon as it came up. Not that she mentioned him on the phone, but when I arrived in Brighton a couple of days later it was Agelaste Bim this and Agelaste Bim that, which was troublesome enough, but on top of that she seemed to be thinking about leaving LifeForce, and that's when I started to worry.

'Suki confided that they had become quite close, albeit according to the strict restrictions imposed by LifeForce. As for the cause of her excitement, he hadn't even been initiated yet, but that hadn't stopped him taking her aside one evening and claiming to have achieved enlightenment. And she fell for it.

'Apparently, a few weeks before, he'd tried to persuade her to set up a new group with him or to come and give a talk, something along those lines, but she'd refused because LifeForce initiates weren't allowed to give discourse anywhere outside the LifeForce centres. So evidently he'd gone away and raised his game, but unfortunately that wasn't how she saw it. It was impossible that Ishvana had extended his grace to a non-initiate – or indeed anyone, of course – but, Suki being Suki, she couldn't help but be intrigued. She made a deal with him that if he kept his "enlightenment" secret from other LifeForcers she would break the rules and meet him at the house in Hove where he lodged with that Marsha Ray woman, so he could show her whatever proof he had to offer.'

I must be paying attention because, when Ruth asks me if I've been to see Marsha Ray, I answer.

'Not yet,' I say, 'but I remember her from Brazil.'

'Oh, she was there too? Well, my overriding memory of Marsha – correct me if I'm being unfair – is of one of those women who dressed like a twenty-five-year-old despite being well into her forties. I didn't know if this tendency had been a contributing factor to her husband's defection or was a reaction to it and I wasn't interested enough to find out. Either way, my first impression was that despite the considerable difference in their ages her fascination with Bim was more than simply custodial.'

Eew.

'The reason I mention her is that Suki told me Bim had shown her something at Marsha's house that had convinced her that, even if he wasn't enlightened in the LifeForce sense of the word, he had accessed, if that's the right word, a higher spiritual force that was ripe for exploration. That was her choice of word; exploitation would have been mine. It was his intention to set up a group and he wanted Suki to help him. She still hadn't made any commitment, but it was clear she was close to waving goodbye to the Good Ship LifeForce.'

Ruth hesitates and looks at me. 'Forgive me, I don't mean to speak ill of your father, I'm sure he had many good qualities. I certainly came to witness many people enthralled and convinced by his performances and insights. His followers talked about him in the same way LifeForcers talked about Ishvana, said they only had to look at a picture of him to feel his love, all that. But at the same time it's important to understand how unworldly your mother was, how beautiful and unspoiled, and how vulnerable to manipulation.'

'I need to know the truth,' I say. 'What you thought of them.' It strikes me that, since Thomas fessed up to being a killer, Ruth Williams has become the most trustworthy person in my life at this point and I've only known her two days. Not even.

'Well, in the end, I decided it was better to support her in whatever she wanted to do than to try to persuade her against it, or more specifically him, and better to be around to pick up the pieces when it all went wrong than to alienate myself, to stand on the shore and watch her drift off on the tide.

'Needless to say, she left LifeForce. She was given permission to stay in the house with Andrew, perhaps in the hope that he would persuade her back into the fold. But I had to find somewhere else to stay when I visited. Marsha offered me a room in her house, and withdrew the offer when Bim found out, but I wouldn't have taken it anyway and had found a nice bed and breakfast in Kemp Town, the

Avalon, close to Suki and Andrew. I decided to stay in LifeForce until I was certain Suki's departure was permanent. Even after she and Bim set up their group, which they called Trembling Leaves –'

Ruth raises an eyebrow at me and I manage to raise a smile.

'– I continued to keep a foot in each camp. It was quite exhausting.

'There were a few other defections from LifeForce to Trembling Leaves. Amber, the dancer I told you about, and Alison, whose face had never quite fitted – quite literally because she suffered from some form of hirsutism and had a perennial five o'clock shadow – and one other woman, whose name I forget. Oh, and Alan. Plus me, of course. Alison in particular was frustrated by her lack of progress within LifeForce, but in the main they just loved Suki too much to not follow her.

'The first Trembling Leaves meeting was held in the summerhouse at the end of Marsha's garden, an old 1920s tennis pavilion, built for ladies to take their afternoon tea in the shade and sip iced drinks laced with sprigs of mint plucked fresh from the herb garden – all very Nancy Mitford – while their menfolk expended excess summer energy on the tennis courts. Apparently the courts had been sold off after the war and houses built on the land, but the pavilion had stayed on Marsha's side of the wall.

'I walked all the way there from my B&B, which was further than I thought, so I was last to arrive. I took off my shoes and lined them up with the others on the verandah. Bim's strange cloven-hooved affairs were there, slightly off to one side with Suki's sandals.'

We reach the road. I'm just thinking it's too noisy on the street to keep recording when Ruth says, 'Should we stop for a bit, dear? We're almost there. Why don't we pop over to that shop and buy ourselves a Cornetto each, like in the film? I think we've earned it, don't you?'

Ruth Williams, I love you.

I'm still too shaken up to be hungry, but a Cornetto isn't food, it's sugar, and, as any recovering addict will tell you, sugar can be a welcome false teat.

The crosswalk is one of those with black and white poles on each side of the street with a flashing orange light on top – *zebra crossing, belisha beacons*. I stand at the kerb waiting for the cars to stop but Ruth just steps right on out into the road.

'Come on,' she says, 'they won't want to run over an old lady.'

After taking a strawberry Cornetto out of the freezer and holding it until it's at melting point, Ruth changes her mind and goes for mint instead. I choose the straight vanilla. Outside the store, we chink them together like champagne glasses, peel off the wrappers, and start up the hill.

A writerly observation for you. This city has so many trees and shit.

'This estate was built as council housing,' Ruth says when we get up there, 'but it's all privately owned now. These flats sell for a small fortune.'

My multi-millionaire brain wakes up. I have a small fortune. I have a *large* fortune. I could buy one. I could live here and be friends with Liz from the movie and walk over once a week to visit Ruth. We could sit on a bench together at the top of the Heath and monitor the erection of new phalluses downtown. I could eat Cornettos every day for breakfast. I need never return to RB and my murderous guardian.

I feel a little better.

Ruth walks to a bench under a tree and sits down so I follow, nervous. 'Are we allowed to walk on the grass?'

Ruth points at the ground. 'You didn't notice the desire line?' She laughs at my dumb expression and explains that *desire line* is the official name for an unofficial pathway. Sure enough, the grass between the bench and the road is scuffed as bare as the Great Dudini's coat before he got his thyroid pills.

'Cool.'

She passes me what's left of her ice-cream while she searches in her bag for a tissue to wipe her mouth.

'Which one is Cunningham?' I say, looking around at the identical apartment blocks.

'Cunningum,' corrects Ruth, just like Thomas, 'one word. A name, not a manipulative pig.' (That eyebrow again. We both know who she means, right?) 'There'll be a map of the estate somewhere; why don't you go and look for it?'

I guess she wants some alone time, and I'm glad to go because I am at risk of busting through my shame barrier and telling Ruth what I know about Thomas.

She takes a photo of me on my phone outside the main door of Cunningham House, pointing at the sign with what's left of my ice-cream, which is mostly wrapper, before we go sit in the shade of a tree, this time on the actual grass where Shaun perfects his zombie-slaying swing. Ruth yells at me for tossing the pointy end of my Cornetto wrapper into the trash. 'That's the best bit!' she says, 'Now we'll have to buy you another one.'

For a while we speculate about how Shaun could have climbed up on to Liz's balcony. We argue about which floor she lives on, I say second and Ruth says first, until we realise we mean the same thing. After that we just sit a while. Ruth closes her eyes and I wonder if she's meditating. Maybe meditation would help me. Maybe I should join LifeForce. Yeah it still exists. Ruth says it's a huge international concern now, everywhere apparently. Maybe you went back to it in the end. What do you think – could you teach me to meditate?

There aren't too many people around, a couple moms pushing strollers, a guy in a uniform who Ruth says is reading gas and electricity meters, all moving in slow-motion, all pretty zombie-like. Ruth says it's quiet because people are at work and the kids haven't broken up from school yet. I like that it sounds as though the kids and school were lovers.

Ruth suggests that as I'm so tired we should have a change of plan and go back to her house for some lunch, and visit Crouch End tomorrow instead. I agree.

I'm wondering if Ruth needs me to help her up on to her feet, and how to offer without offending her, when she goes right ahead and, well, not springs exactly, but you get the picture. She's not so old really and sometimes her movement is completely normal. I guess the sugar perked her up too.

'Let's be on our way,' she says, 'before I forget what I was talking about.'

'The first Trembling Leaves meeting,' I tell her, pressing the record button.

'Ah, yes. Well, in the summerhouse, all the ex-LifeForcers were massaging each other's shoulders. Massage was the LifeForce-approved and prescribed method of dislodging and expelling toxins from our auric layers. A lot of massaging went on in those celibate initiate households, all those young people starved of physical contact.

'I got the impression they had been waiting for me because as soon as I arrived Suki jumped up and pulled me across the room to introduce me to the great Marsha Ray herself. There was no sign of Bim. One corner of the room was partitioned off by a wooden screen and I presumed he was lurking behind it. I made small talk with Marsha, told her how fortunate she was to own such a beautiful place, until at last Suki went and sat cross-legged in the centre of the circle and closed her eyes, indicating the start of the session.

'Once the room was quiet, Suki opened her eyes and told us to close ours. "Listen to your heart," she said. "We say this because our heart is where the Master places the answers to all our questions." I could tell by her voice she was smiling. "Welcome to the inaugural meeting of Trembling Leaves," she said. "Before we go any further, Guru Bim will show each of you in turn the reason you have been invited to join him this evening."

'She told us to open our eyes, then stood up with her arms stretched out to the side and started spinning, ever so slowly. "We are like a wheel," she said, "whose connections to the main axle have become rusty and loose. We are in danger of becoming completely disconnected from it and from the energy that drives us. But there is a way to repair the damage and that's why we are all here at the gateway to this new path. In a few moments you will close your eyes and we will begin our restorative journey towards repair by meditating together. When you feel a light touch on the top of your head –" she folded one arm to tap herself on the crown of her head and then unfolded it again, like an air stewardess getting her routine muddled "– you may open your eyes. When you feel a second tap, you must close them again. There will be no discussion about what you are shown."'

Ruth nudges my arm with her elbow. Quite hard, actually.

'Well, there was no way I was closing my eyes, I can tell you. I wanted the whole performance.

'The sun was setting and the room was already quite dark when Bim finally emerged from his hiding place. His white outfit seemed to glisten, but that was probably because my eyes were watering with the strain of being held half-closed. He tiptoed into the centre of the circle, not speaking, his attention fixed on Suki, who moved out of the circle, went to stand behind Marsha. Then he closed his eyes, raised a hand to his chest and took a few long slow breaths, sliding his hand about as if trying to locate his heartbeat.'

Yeah, that probably took a while, right?

'Then his whole body began to shake. At first the tremors were light and only apparent through the movement of his clothes, but as he went on they became more and more violent. By the time Suki tapped Marsha on the head, he was convulsing. When Marsha saw the spectacle before her she lifted her hands as if to burst into a loud, spontaneous applause, but Suki intervened. I heard Amber, the dance student, stifle an embarrassed giggle, so she must have been peeping too. I was last to be tapped on the head and midway through my turn he stumbled, as if about to fall on top of me. I felt certain he did it deliberately to give me a fright, but anyway Suki stepped in to steady him and lead him safely out of the circle. When she returned, she urged us one by one to open our eyes and get on to our feet, whispering, "Listen to your heart, listen to your heart." We were to imitate what we had seen Bim do. "Unleash your joy," she called out, "unroot your sadness. Banish your anger. Reach out with new and willing tendrils. Listen to your heart."

'I went at it more gently than the others but even so my heart was going like the clappers and I managed to whack somebody on the chin. I braced myself for their retaliation, but whoever it was I hit – I don't remember now – smiled at me as if I'd just promised to do their ironing every day for a year.

'I was the first to retreat to my cushion, and one by one the others fell down exhausted as Bim had done. Alan stayed on his feet the longest, trying to shake the homosexuality out of himself. Alison sat muttering under her breath, reciting her LifeForce mantra. Amber was giggling. We sat on our cushions, listening to Alan grunting and careering about, until at last he fell over. He lay still while we all sat in awkward silence, then, just as Suki tiptoed towards him, he sat up, all wild-eyed and expectant.

'Suki nodded to Marsha, who got to her feet, with a rather self-

important expression on her face, I thought, and went to fetch a pile
of leaflets from the corner of the room. She divided them up and gave
us each a small bundle.

'"Next week will be our first open meeting," said Suki. "Please
do your best to bring people along. In the meantime it's not
recommended that you practise alone, or with anyone outside this
group. If you have any questions about your shaking practice, you can
make an appointment to talk to Guru Bim at the end of next week's
meeting, or you can ask me." She looked around for Marsha, who
was hovering by the door, waiting for Suki to give her the nod to go
across to the house and fetch the tea and biscuits. Bim stayed behind
the screen.'

Ruth looks up and stares through me, caught up for a second in
a sad memory, a regret, maybe just a fleeting shiver of unhappiness,
hard to say.

'Suki had changed, seemed happier than I'd ever seen her. When
I got back to my room at the Avalon that night I tried to be happy too,
but I must be honest, it didn't come easily. I had presumed she would
ask me to wait for her after the meeting, would want my opinion
before making any lasting commitments, but instead she thanked me
for coming and wished me safe home along with all the others and I
realised that she had no further use for my opinion. She had invited
me to show me her mind was made up, that she had moved on. She
hadn't even asked where I was staying.

'I understood that this was her rebellion, and there was no
disputing he had a certain charm, but it wasn't the rebellion I had
hoped for, especially as it seemed to involve pushing me away. The
desire to protect her became stronger than ever. So, while I made
no effort to distribute leaflets or attract other members to Trembling
Leaves, I committed to going down once a week to attend the
meetings. I don't suppose it ever crossed her mind that I was anything
but happy for her, that's how naïve she was.'

Ruth stops for a few seconds with her hands on her hips, gasping
like a marathon runner at the finishing line. She looks so sad that if
I were the kind of person to indulge in public displays of affection,
comfort, whatever, I would give her a hug. She smiles at me as if to
say she knows that, and the thought were enough, and resumes her

walking and talking.

'Trembling Leaves took off remarkably quickly. Every meeting brought new members – the usual vulnerable, needy types – and they kept coming back. I gave up going to LifeForce meetings because it took too much energy to keep up with both groups, but I stayed in contact with Andrew, because that was the only way I could find out how Suki was. And I've never stopped meditating. I really do believe it has helped me.'

I ask if she thinks it could help someone like me and she says it wouldn't do me any harm if I wanted to try it.

'In a couple of months, the group had grown so big that the few of us original members were given blue outfits to wear, which I believe Marsha "acquired" from the hospital, to separate us off from the rest. Suki and Bim had worn matching white outfits from the start.

'Bim had already stopped coming out from behind his screen. The newest members never saw him; they learned to shake from Suki and the rest of us. As for us in the core group, or Blueys as we became known, we were allowed to see him by appointment only. The others were always scrambling to put their name on a list to get behind that screen and ask their inane questions about how to shake their way to enlightenment. They were desperate for his attention, whereas my principal inclination was to avoid him.

'Eventually the summerhouse was so full on a Tuesday night that the group was split in two. Suki ran Tuesday meetings for newcomers and non-Blueys, assisted by Marsha, and our meetings with her were moved to Thursdays. I don't know if Bim ever attended those Tuesday meetings but he continued to hide behind his screen at ours and I supposed the reason for his presence was to check Suki was doing things the way he wanted them done and to ensure his supremacy remained intact.'

Ruth's cheeks are red with the exertion of walking uphill. As we're near the top, I suggest we take time out to sit and look over the view of downtown again. To be honest I stopped listening to her some time ago. I've been thinking about Thomas again. About all the different Thomases. Thomas the junkie. Thomas the alcoholic. Thomas the gun-seller. Thomas the prisoner. Thomas the murderer. This new Thomas seems so far removed from even those other wayward

Thomases, never mind from the one I've seen every day for most of my life, who raised me for the last ten years, who was father *and* mother to me and who saved his money to bring me here to London to find out about you and my dad. I'm not sure the state of being twenty-one is transformative enough in itself to help me deal with all that.

Back at Ruth's house, I sit like a zombie while Ruth makes us sandwiches, tuna no mayo for me, cheese with cucumber for her. Afterwards we wash the dishes together. She has a dishwasher but the activity is good for her hand muscles. Ruth washes. I dry.

As we say goodbye at her door, Ruth pulls an envelope out of her bag that she forgot to give me earlier. It's the card you sent her to congratulate her on her initiation. My envelophobia is so bad now I can't even tell her. I shove it into my pocket. We already arranged to meet the next morning at the railroad station at the bottom of her street so I just walk away. Despite my earlier fears about my state of mind I am actually pleased to be alone at last. It's been a really weird day and my feet are kind of aching but I keep on walking until I'm sure I'll be too tired to think, just in case.

Dinner is a basic margherita from room service and while I wait for it to arrive I keep myself busy, backing up the day's recordings. Normally I would send Thomas the photo of me outside Cunningham House with my Cornetto wrapper but there is no normal any more.

I open the envelope Ruth gave me and immediately start to freak. I'm only just coming to terms with the idea of you as a real person who really existed, exists even, so to hold a card in my hand that you've held in your hand, that you went into a store and paid for and then sat down to write in, is a bit of a mindfuck. But then I read it and right from the start it's all such blissed-out nonsense that I have to stop. *Sister Ruth? Welcome to the inner space of light and sound?* If I'm not ready to accept that Thomas could murder someone in cold blood, I'm even less ready to believe that someone related to me could write the kind of shit you wrote in that card.

I think about listening to a couple of my dad's tapes because how bad could they be after that, right? And besides, they are taking up too much space in my bag. I even pull them and their special little player thing from the bottom of my backpack, but I don't have the nerve to take the idea any further.

The Grace of Guru Bim #1 & #2

I'm awake at five-twenty a.m. Too early in any language. But later than yesterday so I am optimistic for tomorrow. It's important to believe in progress, right? It's too early for breakfast and the pool is closed until seven a.m. The tapes are still there at the side of my bed and I'm still dozy enough to think I can take it.

It's kind of fiddly getting the tape into the machine and I only think at the last second to check if it needs batteries, but Thomas the fixer was there before me, and everything works. Surprising really because these tapes must be, like, twenty years old. So here we go, Part One of the recorded autobiography of Robin Agelaste-Bim, aka Guru Bim. It's short. My anxiety hardly has time to wake up and it's already over.

> *One two one two. I knew a girl at university who said she always listened carefully to what a man said about himself in the first ten minutes because that was the only time he would tell you the truth about himself. She was Mrs D. She never heard my first ten minutes. This is my first ten minutes. I am an abecedarian. I was a menopausal aberration. Sent by the Universe to upset the Apple(sham) cart. I was born… under a wandering star. No. I was born… between parties. To Mrs A-B, a son, a Robin. The little red-breasted thing on the window sill cocked a snook at my mama and she said that'll do… Oof…*

It sounds like he's shifting positions. One thing I remember about him now: one or other of his body parts was always hurting.

> *… That'll do. To Mrs C a dead baby daughter and two milky bags full. Their contents sold to the highest bidder. All worked out very nicely, thank you. For a mistake. For an aberration. Mrs A-B a beauty, Mrs C not. Mrs D, I remember only her words… her shiny hair… Mrs E not at all…*

A wheeze, possibly forced.

> *… 1968, the when of it, England, the where. This is my first confession.*

The tape clunks off. I check to see if it broke but nope, that's all there is. It's weird to hear him speaking almost like a normal person and not in his preachy voice. To be honest, it could be anyone, except he knows the stuff Mrs C told me that nobody outside his family could know (playing kind of fast and loose with the word *family*, right?), that only Mrs C could've told him.

I fumble around for the next tape, number two. Probably Thomas numbered them; that doesn't seem like something my dad would have done himself. There weren't many things my dad would do himself. Take a piss, maybe. And anyway, he would have lettered them, what with being an abecedarian and all.

Here we go, then, Part Two of the recorded autobiography of Guru Bim. He's singing, real slow and croony:

> *Suki take it off again, Suki take it off again, Suki take it off…*

Yeah, I switch it off immediately. That's the song Ruth sang. I have enough of a clue to know where it's going and I sure as fuck don't want to hear it. Damn straight.

May as well be the first man down for breakfast, hit the bacon before it shrivels. I unpause *SOTD* and find the scenes at Cunningham House to play while I pull on a T-shirt and jeans, to bring me back to the present. To remind me I was just there. Site-specific viewing, man, that is the shit!

Ruth of the Living #3

I get to the station early, and Ruth's already there. She's checked out the trains, bought the tickets, everything, and I feel bad because she probably thinks I have no money. Even I still think I have no money most of the time. I try to imagine a more regular experience that's as hard to get a grip on as being suddenly super-rich, that you forget about until, right bang out of the blue, you're reminded of it and it knocks you sideways. All I can think of is death, my mind's favourite topic. Or discovering that the person you relied on most in your life is a murderer. Those lottery-winner guys get special counselling, right? Strategies? That's what I need.

When I try to give her the money for my ticket she says, 'It's your turn to buy the ice-creams, and this time you have to eat all of it.'

She has more crap for me. 'I brought you this,' she says, and gives me a flyer with a picture of purple flowers in one corner and the branch of a tree in the other. I recognise it by its genre; there are a million of these things in cafés and stores all over California. Thomas loves them. When we go hiking up at Topanga, he stands outside the General Store laughing at the notices for angel readings and aura predictions and all that crap, while I go buy us snacks and water. I kind of know what this one's going to say, but as Ruth's made the effort to find it, and as she's standing right there in front of me with an expectant look on her face, I force myself to read.

In these challenging times it takes courage to live in the light

and avoid the shadows. Release your individual luminosity
through shaking to the rhythm of your own beating heart.

Agelaste Bim is our spiritual Master, who tells us: 'In these
troubling times we are all as fragile as leaves, trembling to the
rhythm of an external power. By relinquishing control of our
own trembling we rediscover our individual power and reclaim
it from those who have wrenched it from us.'

Shaking with Trembling Leaves is meditation in movement
and is the only effective catalyst for healing, creativity and true
change in our lives.

Classes cost £5 and begin Tuesday 30 July at 6.30 p.m.
Bring loose clothing, a beating heart and a desire for
magical change, to the Summerhouse, 19 Westbourne
Avenue, Hove.

'I can't believe people actually go along with this kind of crap,' I say
as I try to give it back. Ruth doesn't want it either and looks at me
all Great-Dudini-wants-a-treat. I guess she's kept it for me when she
really would have liked to burn it, so I fold it up and toss in the trash
as we get on the train.

'I think your parents wrote it together,' she says, as if that makes
any difference.

And yes, it does. It makes it way worse.

Our first train ride takes no more than two minutes. We've hardly sat
down before we get up again to switch. As soon as we're on the second
train I remind Ruth where she got up to with her story and we start
recording again.

'One Thursday, I sensed something was up. Suki was pale and
red-eyed and seemed upset, and at first I thought something had
happened to her parents because she started the meeting with a
short discourse on families. "When we shake together," she said, "we
share an intimacy greater than any family bond. In our dysfunctional
genetic families there is often little care or respect –"'

No shit, right?

'"– but among chosen family members, such as we are, there can exist true intimacy, true empathy and understanding and true support. Listen to your heart." *Listen to your heart* had become the Trembling Leaves catchphrase – every discourse started and ended with it, and it replaced *hello* and *goodbye* in our dealings with one another. I think it makes people feel special to use language that so-called unspiritual beings don't.'

I agree. All those a-holes who say *reach out* instead of *talk to* and *share* instead of, well, *talk to*. What are they? They are a-holes.

Sorry, Ruth is sharing, I mean talking.

'Anyway, that Thursday, as we sat waiting for Suki to lead the shaking I supposed Bim was behind his screen as usual, but then the summerhouse door opened and in he floated, like a spectre in his white linens. It was the first time I'd seen him in weeks. He was thinner than ever, his hair was down to his shoulders and his beard was an unkempt bush. He crept towards us, placing each foot carefully on the floor as if we were playing What's the Time, Mr Wolf? and it was his turn to be wolf. Except he made sure all eyes were on him. All eyes except Suki's, I noticed, although it was clear to me she knew exactly where he was.

'He took her hand and pulled her to her feet and they stood side by side at the edge of the circle. He placed a hand on Suki's belly and whispered, "We have been blessed. In two hundred and fourteen days from now, Suki will give birth to my first child."

'I did my best to disguise my horror. The rest of the group were all whooping and clapping and clasping their hands to their hearts. Alison had tears in her eyes. Suki was smiling – but not beaming, I noticed – at her feet.'

Not beaming? That was me in there, right?

'When Bim crept away again to do whatever he did behind his screen, Suki asked us to keep the news secret until she'd had her scan, and I sensed a tone of annoyance in her voice that we had been told at all.'

We have to get off the train again here and find the bus to Crouch End, where Shaun and Ed's house is, but Ruth is on a roll now, keeps going. I don't get all of it; I fill in the gaps the best I can.

'Suki didn't shake with the group any more after that, and that evening as she watched us, her strange non-genetic dysfunctional family, I wondered what was going through her mind. When Marsha got to her feet even before the last man – it was always Alan – had dropped to the floor, declaring it was time for celebratory tea and cake, I knew. Prior to that evening Marsha would have waited for Suki to give her the nod, and in that small aberration I recognised a subtle shift of power, a loss of status, as if conception had forced Suki into a process of reverse metamorphosis so that she had become the tiny speck of life in her belly, a being to be cherished and protected, but without autonomy. She had become the burglar-proof casing around a precious jewel in a museum, transparent almost to the point of invisibility. She smiled across at me, and, when her smile went unreturned, came and sat close to me, so that our arms touched, her way of extending her own vast perceived good fortune and privilege to a poor, sick, courageous woman. I found her pity repulsive. I couldn't speak to her; all I could think about was Bim sitting there behind his screen, gloating over his victory.

'At the end of that meeting there was a universal clamour for appointments with him the following week. I was the only member of the group not interested in speaking to him, not desperate to offer my congratulations. So, when I got home, it didn't come as too much of a surprise to find a message from Marsha on my answering machine, summoning me to a private "audience" with Bim the following Thursday. I assumed he was going to kick me out of the group and considered saving him the trouble by just leaving. But I wasn't ready to abandon Suki, my attachment to her was too strong, and instinct told me she was going to need my help.'

She takes a deep breath. 'I think we should stop for now,' she says. 'We're almost there.'

Yay! We're on Weston Park, the street where Shaun, Ed and Pete live in the movie. The IMDb trivia page says Simon Pegg lives here in real life but I doubt that. Just because a movie star owns a house, it doesn't mean he lives in it. Cool if he did, though, right?

The bus stops right outside Nelson's store, and not one of the zombies on the bus even turns their head to look. The driver couldn't give a shit either. Everyone makes such a big deal of anything movie-related in LA, but I suppose that's all we got, right? When you have

Big Ben and Buckingham Palace and rain and a river with water in
it and buildings in the shape of giant dicks all over downtown, who
gives a flying banana about some dumbass movie? Me. I do. And
Ruth does, and the damn bus driver should realise that when there
are new faces on the bus they are probably on a *SOTD* sightseeing
trip and make an announcement just for them. Us. A simple *That
store right there appears in* Shaun of the Dead, *one of the greatest Brit
movies ever made* would suffice. How would that hurt?

We cross the street to 83 Nelson Road. It's just a normal house
and they didn't even shoot the interior scenes there, but even so I am
just about pissing my pants with excitement and Ruth is grinning like
a letterbox (new Brit simile). I expected to see crowds of other kids
there, zombie-walking in the street, paying homage, slouching back
and forth between house and store with a Cornetto and a can of soda,
tripping over the sidewalk. But it's just Ruth and me. Seriously, what
is up with these people?

I say, 'I know it's only ten a.m. but I've been up since five and I am
really ready to eat ice-cream.'

Ruth says, 'Me too. Let's go for it.'

I fake-trip up the sidewalk to make her laugh and I can't believe
she remembers that detail when she's only seen the movie once. She's
not the kind of woman who would normally laugh at someone falling
in the street. Not a *schadenfreude* kinda gal.

We take photos of each other outside the store with the
storekeeper, Cornettos raised, then cross to number 83 for more
photos without the storekeeper, then we head off down the street in
search of a quiet spot to record some more.

As we walk, Ruth tells me that she always suspected my dad's
name was made up, so one day she checked out the etymology. After
that she was convinced it was, because it's unbelievable how perfectly
his name fit his personality. In Ancient Greece an *agelast* was a man
with no sense of humour. If you told my dad a joke he would just stare
at you. *Bim* is from 13th-century English and means *balm*, which is
more how my dad *thought* of himself than how he actually was. I tell
her my grandparents had the same name, but who's to say they didn't
fabricate it to add to their own enigma?

We go into a café for a cup of tea. I guess Ruth must still be tired from yesterday's hills but she doesn't complain. It's pretty dark inside and we're the only customers but Ruth wants to sit way in the back of the room so I get the feeling she wants whatever she's going to tell me next to be as private as possible. I go order our beverages at the counter and when I come back to the table Ruth has written a quote on her napkin that she found in a book and never forgot: *Lors de son passage dans l'espace cosmique, l'âme du veritable agélaste ne saura pénétrer en paradis.*

She translates: '*The soul of a true agelast, travelling through space, would not know how to pass into heaven.* Rabelais,' she says.

Kind of cool. And kind of ironic, right?

A sip of tea and Ruth's ready to go again. For an old lady with Parkinson's, she is unstoppable.

'I went behind the screen and there he was, sitting cross-legged with a blue sheet draped over himself, like a statue under a dust cover. "Who is this?" he said. Either he had forgotten or was pretending to have forgotten that he'd called me in. I reminded him. It was pretty noisy back there with all the chatter and shuffling around on the other side of the screen and I had to listen quite hard to hear him. I don't remember word for word what he said, but you'll get the gist.'

She shuts her eyes, goes into the zone. '"I have been observing you in my meditation," he said. "By taking control of your inner trembling and releasing it through daily practice, you are challenging the power of those negative internal forces that have made you sick, but your spirit is too weak for you to make significant progress. You are becoming more and more depressed." Which admittedly I was, but not because of my illness. "The path ahead of you is narrowing and your symptoms will worsen considerably in the coming months. Spiritual progress is no longer possible for you. The time is fast approaching for you to escape the pain of your deficient physicality and move beyond the constraints of your mental and physical disease. If you wait much longer you will find yourself without the power to help yourself. When you are ready, come to me and I will help you. That is all. Meditate on what I have said and come back to me next week if you have any questions. Listen to your heart."

'It wasn't until I got home and really thought about what he'd said that I let myself acknowledge the subtext. Of course he'd been canny enough to leave his meaning open to interpretation, to imply just enough threat to be disconcerting. What was doubly upsetting was that I couldn't discuss it with Suki; I knew she would deny any negative interpretation. He had succeeded in ruling by division, the preferred *modus operandi* of the narcissist. I didn't sleep for a week worrying about it, swinging between conviction that I was hearing a threat where none was intended, and fearing for my life. I decided to go back and ask him some direct questions.

'I had a dictaphone, a little tape machine that I sometimes used at home to record dictated letters or notes for my secretary at work, the same as we're doing here with your phone. It wasn't my intention to trap him; I just wanted to record what he said in order to be clear that he was really saying what I thought he was saying. Nonetheless, I didn't want anyone to know what I was doing and was terrified someone might see the little red recording light shining through my pocket. In any case there was a strong chance it wouldn't pick up his voice over all the background noise. But somehow it did.'

She's talking so quietly now I can hardly hear what she's saying, so I move my phone closer to make sure it picks up every word.

'I asked him to explain in more practical terms how he could help me and he came right out with it. He had a prescription for me, which he slid out from under the sheet. A plastic bag containing one syringe and a vial. He said the vial contained a fatal dose of insulin that would send me into a painless coma. It would look like suicide. As soon as I was ready, if I needed their help, he or Marsha would come to my house and administer it for me. He emphasised that this service would be free of charge. He'd drawn up an astrological chart to identify a selection of auspicious dates, all within the following month, which he'd thoughtfully written down on a sheet of paper for me, to help me decide when to do it.'

Ruth stops and sighs and looks at me to see how I'm taking it. I nod to let her know I'm fine. She's sitting right there in front of me, so I know he didn't go through with it.

'I felt that if I didn't get out into the fresh air immediately I would die right there and then. People were saying their goodbyes so it was easy for me to slip out unnoticed – at least no one tried to stop me. I supposed that if Marsha was in on it, it probably meant Suki was too. I walked as quickly as I could away from the house to go and sit on the beach to try to organise my thoughts. There was no way I could cope with the train journey home to London, and anyway the thought of going back to that big, empty house was suddenly terrifying. I took a taxi to the Avalon and luckily they had a room available.

'I don't remember all of what happened that night, but no matter how hard I tried I could not get off to sleep. I didn't need to listen to the recording; his voice was there in my head repeating over and over how my depression was getting worse and my condition was deteriorating. I had so often imagined a far worse future for myself than has transpired in reality that his predictions chimed only too easily with my own fears.

'Muddled in with all this was the increasing belief that Suki wanted me gone too. One thing led to another and the next thing I knew I had unwrapped the vial and thrown its contents into my throat, like a Turkish man with his morning coffee. The doctor explained later that it wouldn't have killed me because my digestive juices would have taken the sting out of it, but it did make me ill enough for Paul at the Avalon to insist on calling an ambulance.

'The police came to the hospital. They wanted to know all about Bim, where he lived, how long I had known him, if that was his real name, and so on. And about me, my occupation, my illness, how I came to meet him etcetera. They took my dictaphone. I didn't understand how they knew about your father's involvement but it turned out the insulin had been prescribed in his name; the evidence was right there on the vial.

'I supposed they would issue Bim with a warning and was worried he might retaliate. They advised me to go home to London and said an officer would pop in every day to check I was okay.

'A couple of days after I got home, Suki called me. I was screening my calls so I just listened while she left a message. Bim had disappeared. At first I assumed he had told her to call, to pull me back in, but she seemed so genuinely upset that I called her back. Either she didn't know what had happened or was pretending, but she apologised for having been so distant and explained that, the very day Bim had so proudly announced her pregnancy, she had caught him having sex in the summerhouse with one of the Tuesday group women. She said she knew I disapproved of him so had been too ashamed to tell me, but now she was convinced he'd run away because he was terrified of his impending fatherhood. She'd got herself into such a muddle, made it all her own fault, wanted *me* to find him and tell him it would be okay. She was heartbroken.

'In the end I believed her of course but I refused to go to Brighton, told her I was unwell, which wasn't a complete lie. If the police had interviewed Bim about the insulin and that had caused him to run away, Suki would soon find out and I didn't want to be around when she did. So I said that a man like him would see a child as an extension of himself and was unlikely to just give it up, I was sure he'd be back soon, and I said that Andrew and Marsha would look after her. It broke my heart to push her away like that, but I didn't know who I could trust any more.

'I thought I should let the police know she had called so I phoned them, and that's when I found out Bim was in custody, charged under the 1961 Suicide Act. Apparently, when they questioned him he didn't even try to deny what he'd done, and when they charged him he told them that if he ever saw me again he would finish me off, which I don't suppose garnered him too much favour. I didn't leave London again until the trial.

'I was surprised to see Suki at the court. She was heavily pregnant by then. Marsha was there too, sobbing in the witness box and denying all knowledge of Bim's threat, which was probably the truth, but given that she had fiddled the prescription for him she wasn't completely blameless and the prosecutor scared her enough to stop the tears.

'Bim put on something of a performance in his turquoise suit with his hands together in *namaste*, describing me to the court as a negative forcefield who had a detrimental influence on everyone I came into contact with. He said my life was miserable and that he had been doing me, and everyone who knew me, a favour by offering to help me remove myself from it.

'Poor Suki was called as a character witness and he clearly expected her to support his argument. Instead, she held her nerve and called him a manipulative charlatan. She said there was no room for him in God's kingdom, which made him laugh out loud. The judge sentenced him to eight years. When it was all over Suki came and gave me a big hug. She told me she was moving to Scotland with Andrew to have the baby and invited me to visit once you'd been born.

'I knew Bim was too much of a coward to do anything himself, but I'd be lying if I said I wasn't worried he might send someone to come after me while he was in prison. All those criminals to exercise his powers of manipulation on… well, it would have been entirely feasible for me to meet with a nasty accident. And while nothing actually happened it took years to push the possibility to the back of my mind. With hindsight he probably really did believe I was about to die a horrible death or that Karma would deal me a suitable punishment for what he imagined I'd done to him. It's safe to say his grasp on reality was somewhat warped.

'Suki and I were never as close again as we had been, but I was happy to think of her settled with Andrew. I went up to Scotland once, when you were a year or so old and just walking. You lived in the middle of nowhere, about half a mile or so outside a tiny village called Drongnock, quite isolated. Andrew had taken you on as if you were his own and you seemed to adore him in return. You were a confident little chap. I'd intended to stay a whole week, but it was clear Suki wasn't comfortable with me around – too many reminders of the past, I suppose – and after a couple of days Andrew asked me, on her behalf, to leave. By then I'd been without her long enough to construe her rejection of me as a positive sign, that she'd moved into a happier phase of her life.

'After that, communication dwindled to almost nothing: the occasional card, usually written by Andrew, with a photograph or two tucked inside.'

She searches through the crap in her bag to hide the fact that she has tears in her eyes. Pulls out another envelope.

Seriously?

'I've brought you a few photographs – I don't know if you've seen them before – you are welcome to keep them. One of them is the official photo we were given of your parents together after the announcement of Suki's pregnancy.'

Okay, so how did I go from living in a village in Scotland with you and Andrew to a weird commune in Brazil with my dad? And where are you now?

Ruth looks at me and shakes her head as if I've spoken out loud. 'That's all I can tell you, Sonny. I'm sure Andrew will be able to fill in more of the detail. I'm sorry,' she says.

We're riding the bus back to Ruth's house, both lost in our separate daydreams, when she says, 'Oh, by the way, I searched on my tablet last night for information about the Winchester pub. It's not there any more. It's been converted into flats, so it's probably not worth your while to go all that way across London to see it.'

'I guess not.'

'Will you go and see Andrew?'

'Sure.'

'Please send him my love. And you will stay with me when you come back to London, won't you? I want to know more about your life in California.'

'Okay.' And I smile to let her know I mean it.

I guess you've deduced by now that I'm not big on talking. That is, I don't like to talk about myself, and I find people who report every inane detail about every mundane minute of their life tedious as hell. Consider Ruth and me. We just spent three days together. If you gave each of us a questionnaire and told us to mark as true or false ten statements about how the other lives their life, what they do day to day, we would have no clue, we'd have to guess because we haven't discussed that shit. But we know what kind of people we are. Spend a little time with someone and the human brain can work it out, that's all I'm saying.

Listen to Your Heart, Right? #1

I weigh it up, who to visit next. Marsha Ray or Andrew Harrison? Get the worst out of the way now, or delay it a while longer? I toss a fifty-pence coin and the coin says Marsha Ray, aka Mrs F, aka The Worst. So, I take the tube across London to Victoria station.

There's a couple kissing noisily at the other end of the car; this is my first bad omen. I switch cars at Oxford Circus but they get off there anyway. And no kidding, EVERY person on the Brighton train is crunching potato chips, and there's no first-class car to escape to. I'm on my way to hell.

Mrs F – Marsha Ray – is still a pain in the ass. Even hearing her voice on the phone makes my skin creep. She wants to come meet me at the station. I don't want her to come meet me at the station. She wants me to stay at her house, I don't want to. With Mrs C it was easy: she didn't offer and I sure as hell didn't want me to. Ruth is awesome; I'd stay with her any time. No way would I ever stay with Marsha Ray, not for all the fish in the ocean, or whatever the saying is, but she won't take no for an answer, like she thinks she has some kind of ownership over me, and the more she insists, the more I don't want to. Even telling her I already booked a place to stay isn't enough to throw her off; I could cancel it and sleep in the room my dad used to sleep in, she says. Like *that's* going to swing the argument her way.

In the end I lie, make up a bunch of crap about staying with a girlfriend from school. I tell her my imaginary girlfriend is meeting me at Brighton station. Well, that gets her real excited and she wants to know all about the girl, asks for names in case she knows her family. I tell her I have to go find my train and that I'll call her tomorrow soon as I'm settled. She says she'll come pick me up from wherever I'm staying. I say I'll call her. Some women will do anything to be somebody's slave.

The Avalon, the B&B where Ruth nearly died, is still owned by Roger and Paul, a sweet gay couple. I call and tell them Ruth sent me, and it kind of pays off. They say I can book myself in for a week and cancel if I want to leave sooner and when I get there they make a big fuss of me and give me their best room, the one they save for honeymooning gay couples. It has a four-poster bed and flouncy pink drapes. I'm no homophobe, but I don't want to think about what's happened in the bed I'm about to sleep in.

I last saw Marsha Ray, Mrs F, whoever, like twelve years ago, in Brazil. She stayed behind after Thomas and I left. I don't remember her physically so much as how I felt about her, which, if you didn't already pick up on it, is not positive. But I want to know what happened there after we left, and she's the only one who knows. Plus, there's a small chance that maybe you're still in touch with her.

I want to meet in Starbucks. She says Brighton people don't go there, which I soon discover is a lie, when I pass by on my way to meet her and it's as busy as all the other coffee shops. Obviously she means *she* doesn't go there, out of some kind of high-minded, self-righteous principle to do with American Imperialism or Oligarchic Capitalism. I heard it all in school, but you know what? In a free society, if people want to drink shit coffee, you have to let them. Still, as my overall aim is to avoid going to her house and suffering the guided tour of where my father slept and where he did a crap every day etc etc, it's a small sacrifice on my part to meet any place she wants that isn't there.

First observation. Brighton has shopping zombies and bike path zombies like you've never seen. I always thought they were the special preserve of Redondo and the Beach Cities – great name for a band, right? – but not so. It also has street drinkers, and homeless people begging for money, which you don't see so much of in RB. There's a noticeable lack of people of colour.

Little kid Sonny found Mrs F huge and overbearing, and let's just say some things don't change. If you were to pin me down about the detail, to list exactly what it is I don't like about her, I could say it's the horrible simpering voice emanating from the oversized body, but it's more than that, it's beyond physical. There's this gut feeling that stirs even at the mention of her name(s), and that feeling has a name of its own: suspicion. In real life – putting physical size and emotional expectations (hers) to one side – I'm sure she's a decent enough human being. I just don't like, respect or trust her. End of.

The café she's chosen is actually pretty cool and I guess the idea is for me to think that she's pretty cool too for knowing it even exists. The couple cool places in RB? This beats them both. It has a store mannequin's hand for a door handle, nail polish and all. It's a little grubby, though. All I can think about is how many people walk right out of the restroom without washing up and reach for the door hand.

Marsha Ray is waiting for me right inside. I step back to avoid the inevitable hug-lunge and the door hand jabs me in the kidneys.

Immediately the bombardment begins. Did I eat breakfast? Did I eat lunch? Would I like a slice of chocolate cake? And it hits me right away, the reason I never liked Marsha Ray, Mrs F, call her what you will. She behaved like she thought she was my mother. She still behaves like she thinks she's my mother. And not a nice mother – a controlling, overbearing one. If I had to pick a woman who isn't my mother to be my mother, it wouldn't be her. My ideal mother does not have that voice. However, the cake looks delicious. But since it's been sitting uncovered right there on the counter until three in the afternoon, being invisibly spat on by customers making their orders – *what sssssppppecialssssssss do you have?* – I say no, thanks.

'You haven't changed one bit,' she says.

And of course I have, it's just that she needs to say that to reinforce that she knew me when I was small. And if I haven't changed it's because she still only knows me as well as she imagined she did back then. She's waiting for me to say the same back to her. I don't oblige.

The cafe's actually pretty busy but we find a couple old, mismatched, battered easy chairs, one leather, one sweaty green velveteen, in the back of the upstairs room. I take the leather chair, figuring the bacteria count will be lower, and don't give her any opportunity to start chit-chatting, tell her right off what I need her to do. Hold the phone and talk directly into it like it's a microphone.

The café is way noisier than I expected. One always expects the British to converse so much more quietly than one's American cousins.

Marsha Ray sits up straight, wiggles her shoulders, and fakes a prissy little smile, like she thinks she's being interviewed for the *London Times* or whatever it's called. Man, she's so into herself. I remind myself that, however bad it is to be in a public place with her, being alone with her at her house would be way worse.

And off she goes.

'I met my husband up at the private hospital where I was a nurse and he was a heart surgeon – there weren't too many of them around in those days; now they're ten a penny, of course. He was nineteen years older than me, had never married and had a lot of money. He said right from the start he didn't want children, which suited me fine, I was twenty-five and after my nursing training was only too aware of everything that can go wrong with the little darlings. At that age, anyway, you believe that if you change your mind later you'll be able to change theirs too. And I'd never even read a Mills & Boon! Never mind, I don't suppose you know what that is. Anyway when he decided, at the age of fifty-odd, that he did want a child after all, he also decided to have it with a twenty-two-year-old who worked behind the bar at the golf club. Muggins here knows nothing about it until he dies and the solicitor calls me in to say I have to share the estate with this other woman and her teenage son! There was plenty of money for all of us though and they were nice enough people, so it all worked out in the end. I got to keep my beautiful home. You must come and see it.'

And this has *what* to do with me?

'We shared the cost of the funeral and it ended up being quite a jolly do with all those other people I'd never met before. Well, I went back to work after that. For the companionship mostly; I didn't need the money. I hadn't worked since we'd married. I had thought about it a few times, but it's a difficult decision when you've been living the life of Riley for as long as I had, down the beach every day in the summer, up to London once a week with a friend for dinner and a bit of culture, nice clothes, dishwasher, all the trimmings. But you soon start to notice how big a house is with just one person rattling around in it.'

Someone's calling my name and for one second I entertain the irrational hope that it might be Ruth come to rescue me but it's only the waitress with our drinks. I wave her over. Marsha chunters (new word, thank you, Roger and Paul) on.

'A work colleague suggested I take in a lodger to relieve the loneliness. I was still only in my forties, too young to be a reclusive widow, so I called the university and offered comfortable lodgings at a low price to a well-behaved and deserving student and they suggested a young man by the name of Robin Agelaste-Bim. I was worried he might be a foreigner, but in those days you couldn't ask a question like that without being labelled a racist so I took reassurance from his first name being English and the likelihood of him being only half foreign.'

Jeez, she's worse than I remember.

'He arrived in a taxi the following Saturday. It's not so unusual nowadays for a young man to not drive, but then it was almost unheard of. Do you drive?'

I shake my head, wave her on.

'Oh, anyway, it was one of those warm, sunny early June days that take you by surprise after a miserable wet May. He found my penchant for leaving windows open unnerving. I always do, except in the most inclement weather. I like a through breeze. What's the point in living yards from the sea if you shut out all the ozone? I also like to keep doors unlocked, especially the front door, which obviously I keep closed to put the opportunists off, but never locked. I expect it's because I've seen in A&E what can happen to people in those few seconds it takes the Fire Brigade to break down a locked door. For ages after your father's arrival I had terrible trouble remembering to lock the bathroom door when taking a bath or using the toilet.'

Gross.

'Anyway, a few days after he moved in he asked to have a lock fitted on his door. It seemed like a fair compromise as long as I got to keep a key in case of emergency.

'He didn't have much in the way of belongings, one suitcase and a couple of heavy boxes, which I supposed were full of books. Despite the warm weather he wore a heavy woollen sweater in a deep shade of blue and a white tasselled scarf wound several times around his neck, which set off his clear, dark eyes beautifully. Such a charming, striking young man. Carried himself like a lord despite his deprived background. He'd just completed his first year of Religious Studies. He was soft-spoken and quiet as you'd expect someone with those interests to be, but he wasn't shy. By the time we sat down for our first cup of tea together, I knew he had been orphaned as a babby –' (that's no typo, she actually uses the word *babby*) '– and that he didn't have a girlfriend.

'We sat down at the kitchen table and he said, "I may as well tell you now, I'm an abecedarian." Well, I had no idea what he meant; I had to look it up in the dictionary after he'd gone up to his room.'

I also looked this up after Mrs C told me about it. He was misusing the word. An abecedarian is a novice, a beginner, not someone who alphabeticises people.

'Because I'd only just met him and I thought he might be one of those deadpan jokers, I said, "Does that mean you only eat Alphabetti Spaghetti?"'

Hilarious, right?

'He gave me that look of his and said, "No, it means that from now on I will call you Mrs F." He was so intense – the way he stared at you, always so deadly serious. Well naturally I wanted to know immediately who Mrs A, B, C, D and E were, but he wouldn't say at first. Eventually I wheedled some of it out of him. He'd lost his virginity to Mrs D, and Mrs E was another girlfriend. He'd met them both at the university, but I don't think either of them were students because he told me he preferred older women.

'He had one living relative, an elderly aunt living down in Devon. I never met her; I suppose she's dead now. The first Sunday of every month he would leave early in the morning to catch the train to visit her. Always took a gift. It looked like the same thing every time, probably a box of cheap chocolates or her favourite biscuits, and it broke my heart that he always went to such effort. His wrapping skills were appalling, but he refused to let me help. It's the thought, not the price tag that counts.'

She says this directly to me, like she was expecting me to bring her a gift. What is it with women who can't say what they mean? Scared of the answer, I guess, and in this case rightly so.

'I wouldn't say he was domesticated. All those years at boarding school and a year in halls eating pizza out of a box, I could forgive him for not knowing how to load a dishwasher. He was hopeless. For an extra five pounds a week on his rent I agreed to provide him with a cooked meal every day, either lunch or dinner depending on my shift. He got into the habit of telling me what he thought of each meal, like one of those chefs on *Bake Off* –' (I have no idea) '– so I started leaving my recipes out on the counter for him to mark out of ten and write his comments. I'll show you when you come to the house.'

Woohoo.

'He insisted on doing his own laundry, until I found out how much he was paying for service washes and for taxis back and forth to the launderette and gave him such a telling-off that he finally gave in. Wouldn't let me clean his room, though. He enjoyed his privacy, spent a lot of time studying, trying out new disciplines connected to his studies: yoga, tai chi, astrology, Buddhist chanting. The conventional religions weren't for him – too old-fashioned and conservative. "Spirituality is a voyage of discovery," he used to say, "which requires an open mind." He was so intense and so intelligent, I loved to hear him talk about the interesting things he'd read, or heard on the radio.'

She's expecting me to agree. I say nothing.

'I told him he was welcome to invite whoever he liked round to the house – the more the merrier, I always say – he never did. He lived like a monk and I began to wonder if he was agoraphobic as well as abecedarian! It was a relief when my friend Sue said she'd seen him coming out of the cinema one afternoon, although when I asked him what he'd seen he said he hadn't been out.

'One day he came down for dinner, I'd made lasagne, and he said he'd given up eating meat and dairy. "Bad for my aura," he said. "I'm eating nothing dead, as of today." Well, I pretended to be cross that he hadn't told me earlier, but secretly I enjoyed his little enigmas. So I followed his example and became a vegan too, although we both carried on wearing wool and leather and what have you. I'd always been one of those women who is continually dieting, lifetime membership of Weightshrinkers. My husband once threatened to leave me if I didn't start serving meals with fat in them, said that if it came to divorce he'd cite malnourishment as one of the grounds. There was I, compromising my diet to keep him at home and all the time he had another woman anyway. Long story short, your father and his veganism were a blessing. I started to lose weight without even trying.

'All this talk about food – I'm ready for a slice of cake, can I get you one?'

I press pause and say nothing for me thanks and she goes downstairs to choose. Man am I glad to have a break from her voice. But it only gets worse. She comes back with two cakes anyway and winds up eating them both, groaning with ecstasy every time she shoves a lump of the chocolatey dough into her mouth, eating and talking simultaneously. Seriously? Would it really be so wrong to punch her in the face and throw her plate through the closed window? Let's just get this over.

'He never said so but I could tell he liked me to look after him, especially when he was unwell. I think he had a tiny touch of hypochondria. You see that a lot as a nurse. You only have to mention what you do for a living and people start listing their ailments. When I'm feeling mischievous I pull this face and tell them they should see their GP as soon as possible.'

She shows me the face; it's kind of Blue Steel, if you know what I mean. From *Zoolander*. You've seen *Zoolander*, right? Blue Steel with chocolate.

'You should see their reaction.'

This is hilarious, apparently. I excuse myself to go shut myself in the restroom while she laughs it out with herself. When I get back she's talking to this hipster kid, all beard and tattoos, telling him I'm visiting *her* from Los Angeles. I see her through his eyes: the pink, the make-up, the dress with all the crap dangling off it, the huge blob of chocolate cake that's trapped in the corner of her mouth. She tells him I'm interviewing her and apologises for having to get back to it. The guy's devastated.

'Then he discovered meditation. Or rather I discovered that he'd discovered it. One day he didn't come down for lunch, even after I called him, so I thought he must be feeling unwell. I took his tray up to his room, and the door pushed open when I knocked so I poked my head round. The curtains were shut and he had lit one of the little tea-light candles that I used to keep for cosy winter evenings. My first thought was that the flame would catch on the curtains and burn the whole house down, but then I saw this ghostly shape hovering above his bed. Well, naturally I screamed and switched on the light. The ghostly shape was Robin, sitting under a sheet. He thrashed around a bit until his head popped up, his hair all tousled and his voice all woozy as if he'd woken from a deep sleep. "What on earth are you doing?" he said. "I'm trying to meditate."'

This is actually pretty funny, but I don't let on.

'Even then he wouldn't tell me anything about it, said it was too powerful a tool to be bandied around. If I was interested, I needed to find a meditation group, as he had done. Which made it fairly clear he didn't want me going to the same place as him, and that was the first time I had any inkling there might be a girl involved. I tried not to be offended.'

Blue Steel.

'In spring he started meditating out in the garden. He didn't mind that I could hear him muttering and chanting through the open windows because that wasn't his real meditation, just part of his yoga practice; the real thing could only be done behind closed doors, not out in the open air where the pollutants in the atmosphere would damage his aura. He had become more and more sensitive to everything: certain foods, certain drinks – just drinking a cup of decaf could keep him awake all night – car exhaust fumes, cigarette smoke. He was allergic to the pollen of non-indigenous plants, I had to dig up my beautiful Chinese lilac and replant it in Sue's garden because it upset his meditation. Sue said I should throw him out, not the lilac.

'That's when I got the idea to renovate the summerhouse. I'd been thinking about tarting it up for years; fantasised about sitting out there on the verandah of a summer evening with a glass of white wine after a long day's gardening, admiring my handiwork and listening to the birds. I thought in the warm weather he could do his proper meditation out there too instead of being always cooped up in his dark room.' An unexplainable sigh.

It's me who should be sighing, right?

'It took a couple of months to knock it into shape: the floor needed sanding and revarnishing, everything needed repainting. My aim was to have it finished in time for a little midsummer's party, but when your father saw what a beautiful job I'd done he said he wouldn't be able to meditate in it if people had been drinking and smoking there, it would damage his aura. So the party idea was ditched, as was my "wine on the verandah" fantasy. I'd planned to paint the walls seaside colours, different shades of aquamarine and olive, but he insisted on white to aid reflection. I had free rein with choosing the floor cushions though as long as there was a red one that only he would use. Sitting on red stimulates your sex chakra, which was why he wore red underpants.'

You hand-washed them, right? I don't say that.

'I put up little shelves with tea-lights on them and decorated a corner for him with flowers and crystals as a kind of shrine. He was absolutely delighted. So delighted that I couldn't get near it and had to make do with spending my evenings over on the patio as I'd always done, with the radio turned right down so it didn't disturb him over in the summerhouse. I didn't mind though.'

She needs a bathroom break and thank God because I can't stand the sound of her voice another second. I say I want her to tell me about my mom when she comes back. She says she will, but evidently she pees the promise away.

'When he finished his degree and his grant ran out, he said he'd have to move out if he couldn't find a summer job so I told him he could stay rent-free until he found one. I offered to ask about a job portering at the hospital, but it would have been bad for his aura to be around sick people. In the end he claimed housing benefit so he could afford to keep paying at least something.

'It was around that time he started slipping your mother's name into every conversation.'

Finally.

'It was Soo-Kee this and Soo-Kee that for weeks, maybe even months, before I finally got to meet her. Instinctively I knew that this Soo-Kee was something to do with his meditation group. Then one afternoon I came home early from work and bumped into them coming out of the side gate. That same evening he was singing "Polly Put the Kettle On" as he made himself a cup of herbal tea, or at least the "Suki Take It Off Again" bit.'

Again with the Blue Steel. Please, make it stop.

'Obviously there was more going on between them than just meditation.'

I sense her working up to more detail, such as *how* it was obvious, and I really do not need that much information. When Ruth talked about you and him, it was like being told a fairytale, at first anyway, but with Marsha Ray and her *face*, and her *voice*, it feels like the truth is she'd been spying on you through the window, watching you doing whatever you were doing, and, although she'd never admit to that part, she's desperate to 'share' what she saw.

So I jump right in and ask her to move it along a bit.

'Okay, well, one day I get home from a late shift and he's waiting for me in the kitchen, all excited and fidgety. I'm so exhausted I can hardly stand, but he insists I make myself a cup of Rooibos and sit down to listen. You know how he was. Well, during his meditation that morning, he'd had a message from the Universe telling him that he was a natural teacher and that to attain enlightenment he needed to follow his true calling and help others along the path. So, he'd decided to hold meditation classes in the summerhouse, and he wanted me to be a part of it. He insisted on teaching me to meditate right away; wouldn't even let me finish my tea.'

Prolonged Blue Steel moment.

'We went out to the summerhouse. It was a beautiful midsummer night, just like last night, hardly dark at all and the scent of orange blossom and jasmine all over the garden. He'd lit the tea-lights and incense was burning on the shrine. I think it was the single most wonderful experience of my life, I will never forget that night as long as I live.'

Excruciating pause for fake reverie.

'We got it all up and running very quickly. Robin wrote a paragraph explaining what the group was about and I found a photograph I'd taken of the clematis in the garden and took it all to the printers to make into leaflets. Robin complained it looked like he was offering gardening classes, but it was too late to change it and it didn't seem to stop people coming along. Suki and a couple of others came from his old meditation group, and because she was as experienced as him at the meditation Suki became his assistant. My job was to look after the room and the refreshments. When things started to go well he asked me to bring staff uniforms from the hospital – he'd noticed them once up at A&E when I'd taken him in with suspected meningitis; he had such a retentive memory – just simple tops and trousers, white for him and Suki and blue for the rest of us. I paid for them, of course; I don't want you thinking I stole them.

'The classes were amazing: he taught us all how to shake in this special way. I had my suspicions about some of the group right from the start, though, Ruth Williams in particular. She'd been close to Suki and I think her nose was put out of joint when she realised how inseparable Suki and Robin and I had become. Robin let slip one day that she was jealous.

'It was my opinion that Suki had seduced Robin. We were all supposed to be celibate, which was not especially difficult for the likes of me and Ruth Williams, but harder for the younger ones. It hadn't occurred to us that the more enlightened among us might not need to follow the same rules. But the bottom line was that we were all delighted that Guru Bim, as we called him, was going to be a father. He told us that the baby – you – would belong to us all, and encouraged us to speak to you and meditate with you in the womb. But then he disappeared and the whole thing fell apart.'

She reaches over and touches my hand. 'I hope this isn't too much for you?'

I pull my hand away and wave her on. Please. Kill me now.

'Suki turned up at the house, all red-eyed and upset, claiming he'd run away. It was only two days since she'd seen him and personally I thought she was overreacting. It was completely normal for me to not see him for a couple of days, especially if I was working lates and our mealtimes didn't overlap, and we were living in the same house! I put it down to hormones. I tried to calm her down and said he was probably up in his room meditating. There was no putting her off, though, and in the end I gave in. At least I knew he wasn't dead up there; in my line of work you come to know the signs. So I fetched the key to his room and she followed me up the stairs. She'd never been in his room before and even I felt uneasy going in there without his permission. I gave a little knock on the door before opening it, just in case.

'The curtains were closed as usual so I put on the light. The bedding was all topsy-turvy as if he'd just climbed out of it. His spiritual books lying open and face-down all over the place – in the bed, on the floor, on top of a pile on the bedside table. Odds and ends strewn across the floor, odd socks, used tissues – he was always blowing his nose because of his allergies – cups and plates, vitamin pill bottles, a pile of his *Vegan* magazines. And a holdall I'd never seen before. "Is it always this messy?" said Suki, and even I had to admit it was a bit shocking.

'I thought something must have happened to his aunt. I opened the wardrobe to check if his turquoise suit was there because he always wore it to visit her. He didn't own many clothes; he wore his whites most of the time by then. The suit was still there, but if he'd had to leave in a hurry... Suki picked up a carrier bag from the floor. It was full of money, mostly five-pound notes, the subs collected at meetings. I said he wouldn't have gone far without money.

'Suki got down on her knees to unzip the holdall. I said it was probably full of vitamin pills – he used to buy them in bulk by mail order – but going by the expression on her face when she opened it up, my guess was a bit wide of the mark. Inside there were two stacks of twenty-pound notes, new, still bound in those paper strips. It didn't look much, but when you worked it out... Suki was about to pull a bundle out and I don't know why but instinct made me yell at her not to touch it. Too many detective novels, I suppose. I grabbed a sock from the floor and put it over my hand like a glove puppet and zipped the bag up then wiped it all down. Suki started crying, blubbing that he'd told her he'd no money to support her and the babby. "Well, maybe this *is* for you and the babby," I said, rather crossly, I'm afraid. Instead of reassuring her, that made her even more convinced that something bad had happened and she started going on about calling the police, but I said we should give it another day. I knew the police wouldn't do anything anyway, he was a grown man. I took her downstairs and made her a cup of camomile tea then told her to go home and rest. I promised to call her as soon as he turned up.

'But after she'd gone I sat there at the kitchen table, puzzling over that bag of money. I couldn't sit still for thinking about it. Where had it come from, and why would someone keep so much cash in the house when they had a bank account? Robin always paid his rent in cash, but I'd seen bank statements arrive in the post so I knew he had an account. The money must have not been his. He was on benefits, for God's sake. I found myself wondering if he was some kind of terrorist or a drug-dealer and if all the spiritual stuff was a cover-up. These people have to live somewhere and there is probably always an unsuspecting landlady somewhere in the background. I knew I was jumping to extreme conclusions. But no matter how hard I racked my brains I couldn't come up with an explanation. So I went back up to his room to look for his bank statements.

'I was more comfortable up there on my own; after all, it was my house, and I had a right to go into whichever room I pleased.'

In case you're wondering, I am still awake.

'I rummaged around and didn't find anything, then I put the bedside lamp on the floor and got down on my hands and knees to check under the bed. I pulled out a couple of dusty old socks and then noticed that pushed right up against the skirting board was a shoebox. I almost didn't see it. I managed to hook a fingernail under the lid and drag it out. I should have been a detective. His bank statements were all stuffed inside it, all curled at the edges from being crammed into the narrow box. I took the whole lot up to my room in case he came back while I was going through them.

'There was a one-page statement for every month going all the way back to 1989, the year before he moved in with me. Each one was identical – one deposit of three thousand pounds on the first of the month or thereabouts, followed by one withdrawal of two thousand five hundred a few days later and then another separate one of five hundred. No variations. He gave me thirty-two pounds a fortnight in cash to cover rent, food and bills, which he paid from his unemployment and housing benefit. I'd thought about asking him for more when he started to make money from Trembling Leaves, but didn't so he could enjoy having a bit more to spend. I felt such a fool.

'I couldn't sleep that night for wondering where the rest of his money was, because it definitely wasn't all in that holdall. I did the sums. He had lived in my house for five years. Just over thirty thousand pounds a year for five years was a hundred and fifty thousand pounds. He could have bought himself a house of his own. In those days it was enough to buy several houses. There were only two possible explanations. Either the money wasn't his, which I had to admit was looking less likely, or he had given it all away and kept only a few hundred pounds for himself. Maybe the money in the holdall was waiting to be distributed among good causes. Maybe it was for the babby. Ownership of a bagful of money doesn't make a person dishonest; if the money's his he can do what he wants with it. And if a rich person chooses to reject material wealth and live simply then he should be praised for it. And if he chose to continue to live with me when he really didn't need to, then that implied there was something special about our relationship. Eventually I came round to thinking I'd been right about him all along. Yes, he had some odd ideas and ways, but in my eyes that made him special, and he at least deserved my loyalty and for me to think the best of him. If I didn't look out for him, then no one else would.

'After work the next day, I went up to his room to see if he'd come home. Well, did I get a fright! All the stuff on the floor had been swept into a big pile. The bed had been stripped and the bedding dumped in another pile on the floor. The mattress was up on its side and had been slashed open and left leaning against the wall. Drawers had been pulled open and left hanging with socks and underpants spilling out. My feet crunched on vitamin pills that had been emptied out of their bottles on to the floor. The two bags of money were gone. I ran up to my own bedroom but, apart from his room, the whole house was exactly as I had left it that morning.

'My first thought was that Suki had come back while I was at work, taken the money and wrecked the room to make it look like a burglary. She knew I never locked the front door, and she'd seen where I kept the key to Robin's room. But then I sat down and thought about it and talked myself around to calling her. That Andrew chap answered the phone and said she wasn't there. When I said I needed to speak to her urgently he told me that she was meditating and wouldn't speak to anyone. His tone of voice was so pompous that I slammed the phone down on him.

'All I could think to do then was call the police. I could prove the money was his and they would get it back from Suki if she had it. But I had another shock coming. When I called the police station, they told me that Robin had been arrested and was being held in custody. They wouldn't tell me why so I assumed it must be to do with the money after all and that Suki had reported him.'

Wow, she really hated you, right?

'I broke down then, at the thought of him shut up in a stinking cell like a criminal. It wasn't until they came to take my statement that I found out how that witch Ruth Williams had betrayed us all.

'I called an emergency meeting of the core group. Without Suki and Ruth there were only four of us. I made up a story that Robin had had to go away. Used words like *temporary* and *postponement* and *holiday*, but I had to be honest and say I had no idea when he'd be back. I think they assumed Suki was with him. None of us could face going out to the summerhouse so we all sat and stared at the teapot in the middle of the kitchen table. Naturally I said nothing about the money; there was no reason to upset or frighten anyone. Alison broke the silence. She said it was our Karma, that we had all been too lazy spiritually. "When a Master leaves his followers," she said, "they must accept that he considers his work with them to be finished. The fault is always with the followers and never with the Master." She said she was going to see if that other group would take her back and I knew it was over. I was absolutely bereft.'

Be*what*? Who says that?

'We met in town that weekend to take back leaflets from wherever we could, and then again at the house the following Tuesday to turn anyone away who came for the general meeting. As soon as they'd all gone, I locked the front door for the first time ever and went upstairs to tidy Robin's room.

'The next year or so was a nightmare. The trial was horrible. Robin called Suki as a character witness and she laid right into him, accused him of sleeping with other women while she was pregnant and of lying to her and everyone else. It was heartbreaking for me to see him up there, under attack, but even then he carried himself with dignity.

'They sent him to the Isle of Sheppey. I wrote asking when I could visit, but he replied that the time had come for me to find my own path, that the Universe had sent him on a different course and that he would always be with me in my meditation. I experienced true loneliness then for the first time in my life.

'The other prisoners adored him, you know; he must have been suffering so much but he still managed to do so much good for others, taught them all how to meditate, even the staff, and he even took that waster Thomas under his wing and transformed him.'

I can feel myself slipping, like I've woken up on a narrow ledge halfway up a sheer rockface with no discernible route up or down. It's not just her voice, it's her whole being – her fakery. She's just like him, like she's reinvented herself in his image, it's pathetic.

The hand reaches out again. 'Are you okay? It must be hard for you to think of him in that situation. Maybe we should go back to my house and I'll make us some dinner.'

I ponder on this a few seconds, weigh it up, overcome my repulsion and cave. If I can just hang on in there another hour or two, I could be free of Marsha Ray forever. 'Okay,' I say, 'let's get this over with.'

So I'm sitting at her kitchen table (no need to describe it, you've been there a million times) and she puts a book down in front of me, real gentle like it's some fragile religious relic. Her book of recipes. For me to read while she prepares dinner. Fascinating stuff, all right. I learn that my dad rated veggie lasagne eight out of ten. I can't read his comments because his handwriting looks like the footprints of a million termites in process of destroying a house and Marsha's already back on Planet Bim so I don't ask her to translate.

'Always had the most gentlemanly manners. Opening doors for me to go through first and standing aside for me to climb the stairs first –'

'Can I ask you a question?' I interrupt.

'Of course, darling, what do you need to know?'

I let that go. 'Why didn't my dad give Ruth one of his alphabetical names?'

'Oh, that's easy: because he didn't like her.'

But I know that's not it. I just worked it out. My dad only alphabeticised the women he had control over. So the question is were you Mrs G, or not?

Marsha puts whatever vegan delight she's made into the oven and suggests we go out to the summerhouse while it's cooking. So I drag myself along behind her, through the back yard. She's a gardener all right. In RB the cultivation of flowers is done out front on the street, where passers-by can see it; the back is usually just grass. Marsha Ray's huge yard is all over flowers and bees and butterflies and bird-feeders.

The summerhouse is dope, kind of a studio version of our beach bungalow. Marsha slips off her shoes and wiggles her candy-pink-painted toes while she waits for me to untie my laces, turns to take in the full view of the garden as if she's never seen it before, sighs at the high flint (that's a kind of stone) walls, sighs at the back of the house with its two sets of french windows. Sighs a little louder to get my attention and points a finger in the direction of the second floor (okay, first floor). 'That's his room there,' she says. 'The one with the curtains shut. Exactly as it was.'

In my imagination, that untouched room, that shrine to my father, is a combination of my own room in RB and my father's room in Brazil as it was the last time I saw him, with its drips and other medical paraphernalia and the stink of the Deep Heat cream he had Ken ship in bulk from the UK. I sense she's building up to an invitation to go up there. I cut her off with a 'Shall we go in?' meaning the summerhouse. Another sigh and she pushes open the door and it's just as she and Ruth described it to me, a plain white room with a polished wooden floor like a gazillion other rooms all over the world. There are five or six pillows thrown here and there, in various shades of red, and a shrine in the corner, which seems to be dedicated to my dad.

I'm busy picturing a bunch of losers all flailing and falling over each other when she says, 'I'm fairly sure you were conceived in this room, you know.'

Gross.

I say we should end it there because I need to go meet my fictional girlfriend and she gets all upset that I won't stay for dinner, tries to persuade me to bring fake girlfriend to meet her and her friends on the beach later for a barbecue, so I say we already have plans to go dance round a fire with my girlfriend's friends and she is stupid enough to believe it.

I walk through town, listening to the soundtrack of *SOTD*, but even Ed and Shaun can't erase the snaky sound of Marsha Ray's voice from my head. Just the thought of the echo of it makes me want to punch the nearest seagull. I feel myself disappearing, being sucked along a desire line towards getting high, towards meth-land, tasting the bitter drip of it rolling from my nose to the back of my throat, reliving the burning rush of it, like my whole body is being fed through one of those high-speed hand-dryers. And I miss that place so much I want to cry. FUCK YOU, MARSHA RAY.

Someone needs to remind me at this moment why drugs are a bad idea.

Seeing how Brighton is the Drug Death Capital of the UK, it's easy to find a meeting to go to. My first since leaving RB. My first since graduation. I'm kind of angry that I've ended up here again.

I don't intend to speak or anything, I just need to be in a safe place for a while. I never did speak much at meetings, even at home. Writing, reading, listening, watching, I'm down, but talking, not so much. I guess that's another reason why I don't have a girlfriend: girls like the talkers.

Seriously, the idea of having a girlfriend scares the crap out of me. I get how life can be easier with someone else to cling on to when shit gets difficult. But what if that person turns out to be the thing that's *making* shit difficult? And what if you're both doing the clinging, like with Ed and Shaun in the movie – that can't be comfortable or easy, right? The girlfriend I told you about earlier, Anna, she thought us being together meant I shouldn't need to go to meetings any more. I should be able to talk to her, right? If I couldn't do that, it proved I didn't love her (which I didn't anyway, but let's not overcomplicate here). And not eating meals together and not letting her do those little pecky kisses proved I didn't love her. Anna said my misophonia (yeah, it has a name, she looked it up) was a neurotic construct to keep her at a distance. But when I offered real proof of not loving her, like wanting to break up, she'd tell me I was broken and just needed someone to love me.

I'm thinking all this in the meeting when I should be listening. It's probably disrespectful to say I've heard it all before, but, you know what, I really have. A gazillion fucking times.

Which leads me to thinking about the purpose of meetings in general and that thing my father had going on, Trembling Leaves or whatever, and the kinds of people who sign up for shit like that, who need it to get from one end of the week to the other. I guess I'm no different from them. What I've gotten from meetings is probably not so different from what they get from following some weird guy who says he can show them the way to enlightenment. All these things just help you avoid having to deal if you can't avoid it by having a relationship with another person or getting high.

Thomas says that people like to have something to fill in life's holes because the holes are full of questions that no one knows the answer to, like what it's like to die, and what happens afterwards and most other death-related stuff. People are scared by all the Big Questions we can't answer, so when someone comes along, an inspirational writer, a preacher, a guru, who says they know all the answers, we latch on like a baby at the nipple. *Feed me, feed me.* But Thomas says there's nothing wrong with not knowing, that we can't know everything, that Fear of the Unknown causes way too much anxiety. And that's how I came to convince myself I didn't mind not knowing about you. I guess these days I prefer to be one of those people, one of the humans, who's scared and alone, over one of those zombies who makes themselves feel better, or special, or important, or clever, by following someone like my dad, who's just using them anyway to make himself feel better about himself.

Everyone's clapping. The woman who was speaking has stopped. To bring you into the picture (yes, I was listening), her son overdosed fifteen years ago and she still comes to meetings three times a week. I get that she might be there to help other people who are going through what she went through, I get that, but *three times a week? You* lost *your* son sixteen years ago and couldn't give a shit, right? Couldn't she just have someone give out her number when a grieving parent comes along? Who needs *who* here? There's a lot about all this that I still don't get.

But one thing I do get is that a person who tells you they have all the answers to life's mysteries is lying. And a drug is the equivalent of that person in pill or powder form. Like Thomas says, learn as much as you can about the things you can know about and imagine and dream the other stuff and use it to create something worthwhile. Just because Thomas killed someone, that doesn't turn everything he says to crap. And, before you say anything, Thomas is not my guru, I just happen to agree with most of the shit he says.

The meeting has wrapped and people are up off their seats and moving towards the tea kettle. There are no cute girls present to hang out and watch and like I said I'm not of the mind to speak to people for the sake of hearing my own voice. And I need to eat. I guess I'm through with NA.

As I step out the door I get this sudden rush of adrenaline, whoosh, like I'm about to cross the Grand Canyon on a tightrope.

I walk down to the water behind a couple guys about my age dressed in identical white T-shirts and jeans so super-skinny they walk like they've shit their pants. They're holding hands and swinging their arms like a couple of eight-year-old girls. You don't see that in RB, it's kind of sweet.

Life is just life, right? We all have the same amount of it when we're alive and we all have the same amount of it when we're dead, i.e. none. Just because we can write or drive cars doesn't mean we have more life than, say, a fly, who can't do those things, it just means we can do them and the fly can't. So what? That might be too deep for you.

I already know from the guys at the B&B that the best place to get pizza is right on the beach at the other end of town. It's a little too close to Marsha Ray's house for comfort, but I'm strong enough to deal now.

It's that time of day when the light turns everything pink and gold. Milly-Anna calls it the Golden Hour. If you ever want to see an Olympic-standard display of pelican-diving, or you just want to sit and watch Milly-Anna cry, all you have to do is walk the path above the beach at RB at sunset and you'll witness a fine performance of both.

By the time I get to the pizza joint the sky is blazing, deep pink and purple like one of those nasty tie-dye shirts they sell on Venice boardwalk. Can't say I've ever seen anyone buy or wear one of those. Thomas says they've been there since the sixties and once a year they just take 'em down and wash 'em, like Thanksgiving flags in reverse. I should call Ike and Milly-Anna like I promised. I guess I won't, though. Sometimes there's too much past, right? Sometimes you just have to let yourself be swallowed up by the present.

There's a line around the block for ice-cream, but for pizza I can walk right in and order my favourite artichoke, caper and anchovy and the girl taking my order doesn't look at me like a crazy person. I love this place. If Marsha Ray didn't live so close by, I would buy a condo right next to the pizza joint, overlooking the beach.

Ten minutes later I'm sitting on the stones, chewing away. Imagine if my own mouth noises made me angry – I'd starve, right? But I guess it's nature's mercy to keep us blind, or deaf, to our own faults.

It's kind of warm, like spring back home, and people are jumping around in the water, their skin all orange glow in the light of the low sun. I choose a spot close to a family – mom, dad and daughter – so maybe people will think I'm with them and won't try to talk to me. They're kind of cool, throwing stones at an empty coffee cup. Whoever knocks it off whack has to get up and straighten it. When it's the daughter's turn to get up they pretend to throw stones at her and make jokes about the Taliban. I totally get this Brit sense of humour. I sneak a photo of them on my phone and study it. It's like someone took the best physical features of the parents, popped them into a cocktail shaker and poured out the daughter. I wonder if the same could be said about me.

Three gulls are sidling up the beach to watch me eat. Guys, flying would be quicker. They stop at a respectful distance, cocking their heads right and left, keeping one eye on me, or on my pizza anyway, and the other on the competition. I throw a crust so it lands bang in the middle of their triangle. The biggest, whitest one gets to it first, and there's a metaphor for life right there.

The stoning family packs up and leaves, taking their cup with them, so I set up my empty soda can, pushing a few of the smaller stones in through the sip hole to weigh it down. I guess the game's more fun with more than one person, but it's not so bad alone.

Down at the water's edge there's a guy with a baby. The baby is old enough to walk but is still wearing a diaper. (And nothing else – that's how I know; I don't have X-ray vision.) The guy is throwing stones into the sea, making these fancy cricket bowler moves with his arms (Thomas loves cricket; I get that it's better than baseball, but that's all I get about it) and the kid is copying him, but he doesn't understand what he's doing so does his fancy arm stuff as a separate movement to the throw. It's hard to describe but it kind of goes arm waggle, pause, toss, arm waggle, pause, toss. The dad is so engrossed in showing off his own throwing-rocks-into-the-water skills, he hasn't even noticed what the kid is doing. I want to run down the beach and yell at him to pay attention to his son. *Look!* See how cute your kid is? Get over yourself and your fancy arm shit and watch how cute your kid's being. But I don't. It might not even be that guy's kid. The guy might be really embarrassed that some stranger's kid is copying him. Instead I scramble over the stones and head back towards Kemp Town, through a stinking haze of barbecue smoke blowing in from the beach. Somewhere in the midst of it all is Marsha Ray and her party so I hurry along in case she's looking out for me.

I miss the Great Dudini; he'd snap her hand off if she tried to touch me. We could take it to a taxidermist and use it as a door handle.

When I get back to the Avalon, I text Marsha, tell her some lie about having to go to London, then switch off my phone.

Andrew's Limp #1

I'm on the train to Scotland, checking out the photos Ruth gave me. The one of Andrew and you and me, I figure was taken right after I was born. I mean minutes after. Someone has written the date, 6 *June 1992*, on the back of the picture and pressed too hard on the pen because the letters have embossed the front, right across your knees. I'm there but I'm not really visible, I'm just a bundle of yellow comforter in the crook of Andrew's arm. You are sitting next to us, in a chair, your face turned away as if you're listening to someone talking behind you, or maybe you're already looking for an escape route. Andrew is standing, leaning a little, with one hand on your shoulder, holding you back. He seems tall in that picture. He's tall in my memory too, but last time I saw him I was five years old so I guess most people were tall to me then. Tall and thin with orange hair – that much detail I don't remember but get from the photo – and his smile looks sad, but I guess he's happy. (How could he not be, right?) Looking at that picture, anybody would think Andrew was my dad.

It's bizarre (new favourite word, overheard at London Euston) how people from the distant past look familiar even though all you remember about them is not so much their physical presence, but more the things they did with you, like singing you a song as they push you on the swing (him), or being pissed at you for getting dirt on your clean sweater (you).

Yet another picture of you and my dad when you're first pregnant, with you both dressed in white tunics and pants with your bare toes poking out the end and my dad with a bush of a beard that's so big it looks fake. Your me-bump doesn't show yet and I can't see if you're happy or sad because you're looking down at my dad's hand on your belly like you're thinking, *Why does that creepy, weird guy have his hand on my belly?* He isn't looking at you, though, he's standing straight but not so tall, staring directly into the camera, not smiling. I never could tell if he was happy, even if he was smiling. He has this facial expression, like he's challenging the person taking the picture, like if he had a sword in his hand, his next words would be *En garde!* I totally get why you ran away from him.

I stash Ruth's photos in the folder with the ones Thomas gave me – yay, another envelope trashed!

When I was a kid I thought about death a lot. All the time. Anything I did, I imagined a million possible violent death scenarios that could result from that one ordinary action: dribbling the ball towards goal would end in me smashing my brains out on a goalpost; crossing PCH to go to the store, I would be flattened on to the pavement by an imbecile running the red light; standing on the beach, I would see the tide suck all the way out then turn back as a mega-tsunami. I guess these fantasies were the daytime versions of my night scenes. They stopped happening so much when I hit twelve/ thirteen, mainly because who needs to fantasise about it when the road you're on will lead you to a certain death?

Andrew is waiting trackside when I get off the train. That weird feeling I talked about that you get looking at a picture of someone you knew before you can remember? It's double weird when you meet them in person. As if you've known them your whole life, and have never met them before ever, all at the same time. Kind of confusing, if you think about it too much.

He is still tall. Taller than me. And super-thin, but healthy thin not junkie thin. His hair is cut short but there's a lot of it and it's not orange any more like it is in the photos but the whitest shade of grey, and that's the only sign he got older. With his serious face he's kind of cool-looking. Inscrutable. Ruth and Mrs C's first impressions of me showed in their faces, but I get the feeling Andrew doesn't form a first impression EVER. About anyone. He's a wait-and-see kind of

guy. We shake hands and I want to say *nice to meet you* but that would
be wrong because he was there at my birth so I make do with, 'Hey.'
As he shows me the way to his car, which is way too small for a man
of his height and he has to fold himself into it, I wonder if he always
walked with a limp.

In the car, he asks me polite questions about my trip. Am I jet-
lagged? Is this my first time in the UK since… (incomplete question)?
And I'm relieved that if I concentrate his accent is pretty easy to
understand. He's surprised by how many places I've already been,
tells me I've covered a lot of ground in a short time, and I tell him
that where I come from a couple hundred miles is considered a short
trip and then realise that's probably not what he meant. And from
his point of view Redondo Beach is not where I come from, either.
It's one of those conversations where you'd like to keep talking but
neither of you knows what to say because you're both scared of saying
the wrong thing. I guess I could ask if he has another family, stuff like
that, but I don't think of it until afterwards. I kind of hope he doesn't.
Guess I'll find out soon enough.

'This is Drongnock,' he says, slowing the car down as we pass a
couple houses, and I'm thinking one of them must be his house when
he says, 'Do you want to see your first school?'

'Sure.' I'm not sure I'm ready yet to paint myself into this picture,
but by the time I realise that, he's made a sharp turn to the left and
pulled up across the street from a building that's poking up like a
pyramid from behind a grey stone wall, like it's peeking over at us. A
sign at the gate says *St Mary's First School*. The huge front window is
stuck with papercuts of all different colours and sizes.

I wait for the memories to come flooding back in. They don't.

'Did I like this school?'

'Well, you were only here for a couple of months, but you seemed
to like it well enough. The village has had to fight to keep it open;
the council keeps trying to close it down and make the local children
travel to the school in Ayr. It's shut for the holidays now but I'm sure
if you wanted to take a look inside, it could be arranged. I know the
headmistress quite well, she was a teacher when you were here, and
I'm sure she'd like to see you.'

'Yeah, okay,' I say. 'That could be cool.'

'I'll phone her tomorrow. Almost home now. I expect you're tired.'

Home. From Andrew's point of view, this is my home.

Andrew says he'll take me to see the house he rented with you, where we all lived, but he doesn't live there any more. I'm going to be staying with him in his new house. Drongnock is not exactly a metropolis so I guess we won't have to travel far to see anything I want to see.

Andrew has to duck to go through his own front door; it's amazing that his shoulders aren't permanently hunched into a residential and transportational posture. Inside, the layout is similar to Mrs C's house, only without all the crap and the yap and the old-lady smells. In this country, the first thing everyone does when they bring you into their home is offer you a hot beverage of some description. Andrew is no exception. While we wait for the water to heat up, he shows me around: sitting room (TV, sofa, chair, fireplace, books), his office (desk, chair, computer, fireplace, books), his bedroom (bed, closet, books), my bedroom (*my bedroom*: bed, closet, books, nothing that's actually mine), bathroom (toilet, bathtub, shower, more books). It's over in a few minutes.

'Dude, I guess you like to read.'

Andrew laughs. 'Not a lot else to do around here. It's pretty quiet, besides the pub, though the locals are a friendly enough bunch.'

I can't help wondering how friendly they can be if he still refers to them as *the locals* after twenty years. I don't say that, I say, 'How do I sound to you – do I sound like an American? Back home, people tell me I speak like a Brit.'

He laughs again. 'Aye, that you do. Well, somewhere in between. You've no trace of your Scottish accent left, that's sure enough.'

'I had a Scottish accent? Like yours? How cool. Maybe that's why I can understand you so well.'

'You certainly did. I have a wee video of you at your fifth birthday party all set up ready to go. D'you want to watch it now, hear your accent for yourself?'

'Yeeeaah, maybe later.' (I'm guessing you'll be in the video too. One step at a time.) I'm standing behind him in the kitchen now, talking to his back.

He turns and gives me my beverage: tea. 'You having trouble making yourself understood, then?'

'Not so much that way around,' I say.

'Ah, I see. Do you fancy a wee walk after tea, to stretch your legs after your journey?'

Andrew's house is a mile or so from the ocean, and we walk there on a narrow trail that follows the course of a narrow stream. I ask him if it's a desire line and he says, 'Aye, it is, if you're a sheep.'

The landscape is super-flat and you can see all the way to the sea. It's not beautiful. A few hills or trees would break up the homeliness, stop you seeing it all at once. If landscapes can be described as homely. Flies everywhere. Andrew breaks a long, thin stick off a tree, demonstrates how to flick it around to keep them away and passes it to me. While we're walking, he starts to tell me about my childhood. I've left my phone charging at his house but I figure it would be impolite to ask him to hold off until I can record what he's saying. In the end, it seems better to just listen.

He begins by asking me if I have any memory of *that day* and I admit that most of my childhood before California is a blur, that I have no memories of anything much before Brazil and even Brazil is sketchy. I have no idea which day in particular he means.

There's a sheep stopped sideways on the trail, staring at nothing. Andrew claps his hands at it and it straightens up and trots ahead of us. We walk at sheep speed for a while until the sheep turns his woolly ass through a hole in the fence and trots over to join his homies in the field. By which time Andrew has set the scene of a regular school day: up at seven, breakfast, me in the wheelbarrow for the walk to school. I tell him I have a photo of me in a wheelbarrow and he smiles a sad little smile.

'You loved that bloody wheelbarrow. The buggy we bought you was a complete waste of money. As soon as you could sit up unsupported you wanted to go everywhere in the barrow. You'd ride to and from the allotment with all the spuds rattling around you. I thought you'd grow out of it by the time you started school, but no, you insisted on being pushed up the road on your first day. I sat you on a clean sheet to stop the dirt getting on your uniform. You don't remember?'

It feels like I do because of the photo, but honestly I don't in any real sensory way. But hey, how cool was I? 'I don't remember anything,' I say, 'but man, that would be dope. If I ever have kids, they're riding to school in a wheelbarrow.'

'Do you remember your mother?'

'Not so much. I mean, I think I'd remember her if I met her again. Now I've met you, I kind of remember you.'

'You haven't seen her, then?'

'No. Have you?'

'No. Not since.'

(That word *since* again. Since what? I guess it could be Scottish for *for a while*.)

'What's an allotment?'

'It's a wee plot of land for growing vegetables, fruit, flowers, that kind of thing, a hangover from the war. Ours was pretty basic – spuds, cabbages, onions, you know. You used to bring your bucket along and would spend hours shovelling dirt and stones or worms or woodlice into it with your wee spade, or anything you could pull out of the ground really.'

Now I get a sensory flashback, of an earthworm writhing in the palm of my muddy hand, tickling my skin. It could be a meth flashback or it could be nothing so I keep it to myself. We walk on in silence and I get the impression Andrew is thinking about what to say next.

'Our house was a bit further away from the school than most,' he says. 'I'll show you later. It was down a lane with no pavement so we had to walk on the road.'

I'm confused for two seconds then I remember sidewalk and pavement are false friends.

'When you started school you wanted us to let you walk to school alone. In those days, no one thought twice about letting the younger kids walk to and from school on their own. The older ones would look out for them and there was practically no traffic. But your mum said no, categorically, you were too small. She had her reasons, but I thought she was being overprotective.

'Any road, you and I made a sneaky agreement that on the days I picked you up, which was most days because your mother couldn't cope too well with the wheelbarrow, you could walk the first few yards of the journey home, just to where the pavement ran out. I knew it was wrong to overrule your mum, but I didn't see what harm you could come to.

'So, anyway, that day, the day I was talking about, it was Wednesday, 22 October, I was there waiting as usual at two-forty-five. The school bell rang at ten to. Followed by the usual chucking-out-time racket. We'd been through the routine often enough by then for me to know without counting exactly how long it would take you to get from the school gate to me. There were only thirty or so pupils in the whole school so it took no time for everyone to clear out. At first, when you didn't come, I thought maybe you'd gone to a friend's house for tea, because it'd happened before that your mother had accepted an invitation over the phone and forgotten to tell me, or told me and I'd forgotten. I stuck my head around the corner for a look. Nothing out of the ordinary was going on, besides you not being there of course, but then I noticed a camper van, parked down the side of the school, just a bit further along. Even that wasn't so unusual: we get our fair share of tourists, passing through on their way to Ayr or Troon or just lost or in need of a toilet. But then I see this wee white face smiling at me from the back window of the van, and a little hand waving, and I realise it's you.

'I ditch the wheelbarrow and start to run and the van engine starts up and my legs won't go fast enough, like in one of those dreadful dreams. I see the gun poke out of the driver's window and instinctively turn my body away even though I don't quite believe it's real. Next thing I know there's a bang and I'm falling face-down on the tarmac. It all happens in slow motion. The pain in my leg is excruciating. When I look up, the camper is gone, and you are nowhere to be seen.'

'What, so I was kidnapped?'

'Yes. And I was shot in the back of the knee by an air rifle to keep me from getting to you. I dragged myself along the road towards the school but an ambulance came before I even got there.'

"What happened after that?'

'Not a lot. I was in hospital for a week and the police came and took statements and what have you. I'd reported an incident with your father a month or so before, so everyone drew the obvious conclusion: that you'd been abducted by him. Or a professional hired by him.

Whoever shot me was a crack shot all right, and it was unlikely your father would know one end of a gun from another.'

An alarm is ringing in my head. I ignore it.

'And as far as we knew he couldn't drive. Your photo and your father's were on the front page of the newspapers for a day or two but apart from the usual nutters there was a poor response from the general public. It would have been easy enough for your father to not look like his picture. A shave and some normal clothes and hey presto, the perfect disguise.'

'That incident you mentioned. What kind of an incident?'

'Och, well, your father had come to the house late one night, demanding to see you, and we'd refused to let him in. We tried to explain that you were asleep and that to wake you up then would confuse you, and that it would be better to introduce you gradually with some explanation from us beforehand about who he was. You already knew I wasn't your natural father – your sperm father as your mother used to say. Anyway, that set him off shouting, about not needing to be formally introduced to his own son. We shut the door then, but he carried on, screaming at us through the letterbox, giving the door the occasional kick, calling your mother a whore and me a loser, so I called the police. Of course he'd gone by the time they arrived. You slept through it all, didn't stir.'

'I'm no different now,' I say. 'I sleep through earthquakes all the time at home. When did you say this happened?'

'About a month before you disappeared. Your father wasn't long out of prison.'

Are you thinking what I'm thinking? Thomas can drive. And he's had an intimate relationship with guns, right?

'I'm sorry, Sonny, I was stupid enough to think that visit would probably be the end of it. It was naïve to think in this day and age that a few hundred miles would keep someone like your father away. According to him, you were his property, and he was always going to come and claim you.'

By now we've climbed the low scrubby dunes above the beach, looked out over the oily grey sea and turned back to follow the same trail home. The sun's going down and our surroundings are disappearing into the gloom.

'Did you think I was dead? What about my mom? He took me to Brazil, you know.'

'Aye, it felt like you'd died all right. The police said it was possible but not likely, given that they hadn't found a body. They couldn't find your father either so him smuggling you out of the country was the most likely scenario. I didn't know you'd gone to Brazil until Thomas called the first time. As for your mother, when I came out of the hospital she'd gone too and I've never seen her since. I assumed she'd gone back to Brighton or London, but no one we knew down there had seen her. I thought it was possible she was with you and your dad and the police agreed. You know, we never were a couple in the traditional sense. And you called me Andrew, not Daddy.'

He gives me this weird look, kind of apologetic and sad. The same look Philip gives Shaun in SOTD when they're in the Jag and Philip's about to die and transform into a zombie. I think maybe I should smile and nod like Shaun does and show him I understand that despite all that's happened he loves me like his own son, but he's cool, he doesn't need me to do that; he just keeps talking.

'A year or so afterwards a letter came from your mother. In it she said she had made a decision to start a new life. She'd gone back to London and met an American man there, married him and was going to live over there.'

'She went to live in the US?'

'I didn't know for certain, the letter was posted in England and I never heard from her again. I was relieved she wasn't with your dad, but it made me more worried for you. Thomas said he had been trying to track her down. I thought you might know where she is.

'I still have all your things, you know, all your toys and clothes. Up in the attic if you want to see them?'

I'm on the floor in Andrew's sitting room, next to a pile of kids' crap that he's tipped out of a box: a tambourine; a few stuffed animals (none of these has an eye missing or a stitched-up stomach like they do in the movies; they all look pretty new, as if I never touched them); an entire plastic zoo in miniature, zookeepers and all, but no two-headed snakes. I tell Andrew about my two-headed-snake phase. Seriously, it went on for months. Most weekends Thomas drove me to

LA zoo so I could stand in front of the vivarium where the two-headed albino corn snake lived, while he sat drinking coffee from a flask and staring at nothing. Thomas can sit and stare for hours. The notice on the tank said: *This snake has two brains and one stomach. It wouldn't survive long in the wild because having two brains restricts its ability to move quickly to escape predators.* I guess I was hoping to be there the day it ripped itself in two. I guess that was my transition phase from Brazil to Redondo. We stopped going to the zoo when I joined the Galaxy U12s and all my weekends got taken up with football.

So I'm sitting there surrounded by all this shit, and the shit and I are surrounded by sections of racetrack. The racetrack I remember. Now.

Andrew goes out to the store to buy new batteries for the controls and to pick up Indian food. When he asks if he can get me a beer or anything while he's out I tell him I'm straight edge and he says he doesn't drink either. Andrew doesn't consider it in any way abnormal to be straight edge, I guess because he did the whole LifeForce thing when he was young.

While he's gone I set up the track, clicking the sections together like he showed me. I build it so it runs under all the chairs, transforming the entire room into a Grand Prix circuit. A simple oval, no fancy figures of eight like the pictures on the box. When he gets back I ask Andrew if he thinks Shaun and Ed might have had a racetrack when they were kids in the days before computer games and he knows exactly what I'm talking about. He has *SOTD* on DVD.

My car is red and Andrew's is blue. We speed around the bends and the cars shoot off and smash into the baseboards or roll into the central island where I'm sitting with my toys and my chicken tikka masala. And I must have felt real safe with Andrew as a kid because I feel real safe with him now. That's why I tell him about me. About the Galaxy and how I fucked it all up with the drugs and everything. I assume, living where he does, that maybe he doesn't know about crystal meth, but he's seen every episode of *Breaking Bad*. We don't watch it at the House of Reformation for obvious reasons. Our zombie viewing embraces the undead and avoids the soon-to-be-dead.

He wants the whole story so I tell him, about that first sleepover in Palos Verdes, about selling Thomas's computer, about failing the drugs test at the Galaxy, all of it. Andrew says drugs are a universal problem. It's worse in these small places where there's nothing to do, and even if there were stuff to do there's no money to do it with because there's no much work (not a typo, that's how he says it), people are depressed and the winters are long. And drugs are cheap as drink. Familiar stories, different people. Not so much of the overprivileged cohort coming down from the belief that they don't have the brains to be the next Steve Jobs or Beyoncé, despite what Mommy and Daddy have told them their whole lives, and realising that the only way to maintain the delusion of feeling different and special is the getting high scenario. (That's not me, by the way; I always knew I wouldn't be the next Lionel Messi and Thomas never gave me any of that pushy bullshit. I'm just a straight-down-the-line fuck-up, thanks to you and my dad.) As we're talking, I kind of get the impression Andrew already knows about me. It's just a hunch.

'When did Thomas contact you? The first time, I mean.'

Andrew puts down his car controller and leans back against the sofa. Looks me straight in the eye. 'Well, I don't know if the first time counts, because I didn't know the contact was from Thomas. A private detective came to the door one day, looking for information about your mother. I was still at the old house so it would have been twelve or so years ago now. He wouldn't tell me who'd employed him so I assumed it was your father, maybe looking to send you home. I had nothing to tell him anyway besides what I just told you, about her writing to say she was marrying an American. Do you not know about this? Thomas said he was going to tell you.'

'He wrote me a letter. I guess it's in there, I didn't read it all yet.' I don't tell him why I didn't read it all yet.

'Ah, right. Well, the next time was a phone call from Thomas himself, completely out of the blue. In 2009. The conversation got a bit heated, or my side of it anyway, but Thomas just kept apologising, over and over until I ran out of steam.'

I think I already know the answer to this question but I ask anyway. 'What was he apologising for?'

'It's tricky, Sonny; I don't know what's for me to tell you or what you should hear direct from Thomas. I thought you'd know all of his side of the story by the time you got here.'

'So you've spoken to each other since 2009?'

'We've kept in touch. I'd say we've become friends, albeit at a distance. He's told me everything.'

'Right, so he's told you he's a murderer?' I guess I'm pissed that I've been kept out of it.

Andrew uncrosses his legs, crosses them back the other way. Scratches his nose. Tries to appear calm. 'No, I can't say he's mentioned that. Who did he murder?'

'Tell me what he was apologising for and I'll tell you who he killed.'

'Okay,' he says, looking unsure. 'He apologised for two things: for taking you away, and for shooting me in the leg. He said he was following orders from your father. He wasn't all bad, Sonny. The reason the ambulance came so fast was because he had stopped at the telephone box and dialled 999.'

Fuck. I knew it. I fucking knew it.

I guess I'm just sitting there staring because Andrew says, 'That's my side of the deal – now tell me who he murdered.' So, I tell him about the other guru guy and then we both sit there a while not speaking. I break the deadlock.

'So how come you became friends with him? Why didn't you tell him to go fuck himself?'

'Because he needed help, with you. He was trying to deal with you and your problems and on top of that he'd had a letter from your mother saying your grandmother on your father's side had died and that at the age of twenty-one you were to inherit whatever was left of the family fortune. He needed your birth certificate and I still had the original.'

'So he's been in touch with my mom? She knew where I was?'

'Well, she wrote to him about that. But Sonny, it's after midnight, and it's been a long day. Let's get some sleep and talk about it tomorrow.'

Thomas always told me he was a liar and a cheat, and when someone tells you that stuff about themself it makes them honest, right? It makes you trust them. I can't sleep. I can't even close my eyes. I lie in bed in the dark listening to Andrew brushing his teeth in the bathroom. I hear him moving around in his room until eventually the noises stop and his snores come fluttering through the wall like clouds of glassywing moths. I work out what the time is in Redondo and imagine myself calling Thomas, forcing him to tell me the truth, what he knows about you. But I'm an emotional coward, I can't do confrontation, and I don't want to wake Andrew. I'm done talking.

I sit up and look out the window at the stars. The moon isn't full but it's big and bright enough that I can see its reflection on the ocean in the distance. There's no other light and weirdly this reminds me of Brazil before the commune, of going with Maria to visit her family by the sea and sitting on the beach with her at night all snuggled up in her arms and listening to her made-up stories about the stars.

I switch on the light and rip open Thomas's next letter.

Things We Can't Undo #3

Sonny, do you remember how stories about the Surubim-rei
gave you terrible nightmares?

Sure I do, but, in case you don't know, the Surubim-rei is a huge,
malevolent amphibian, a bit like the oarfish that Thomas and I saw
washed up on Catalina Island, only it lives in rivers – the São Francisco
river in Brazil to be precise. And it's mythological. The Truka people,
who live in Cabrobó, believe it attacks their fishermen in their boats
and winds itself around the legs of cattle at the water's edge and drags
them into the river. Cool, right? They sing songs about it and sit huge
carved wooden figures in the prow of their boats to frighten it away.

When they found Guru Mehdi floating face-down in the river,
they assumed he was a victim of the Surubim-rei. I'd never
heard the stories at that point so when a delegation brought his
body to Ken's clinic, shouting about the Surubim, I misheard
it as your father's name, Guru Bim. I genuinely believed they
had somehow divined the truth and, thinking my number was
up, was all ready to confess, but Ken explained what was going
on just in time.
    There'd been a couple of deaths in the commune since
my arrival, neither suspicious, one of old age, the other the
result of a lengthy illness. In both cases funerals were held the
day after the death, with the body buried in a kind of wicker

*coffin in a small graveyard on the periphery of the commune.
Mehdi's death was dealt with in the same way, although his
funeral was a much bigger deal, and the wailing and carrying
on continued for days. Meanwhile I was planning my next
step, which was to bring your father to Quilombo Novo and
restore my lifestyle to its former state of degradation.*

*Once a fortnight, the boy with the cart, Fabio, came by
to drive Ken to the clinic in Salgueiro to stock up on medical
supplies. When he was next due I waited out on the road to
give him a letter to post in the town and slipped him fifty reals
to ensure his errand was kept secret, especially from Ken. The
letter was addressed to your father in Olinda, telling him to
come exactly one month later.*

I should explain why I was so much in your father's thrall.

*I wouldn't say your father kept himself to himself in prison,
but he gave nothing away, only told you what he wanted you
to know in order to get what he wanted. He made no apologies
for himself, introduced himself as Guru Bim right from the off,
and in the end that's what got him through, nothing to do with
me. Despite the way he came across he was in no way soft. He
didn't need me to earn his privileges for him and he certainly
didn't need my protection.*

*He could switch on the charm when it suited him, but he
never made the mistake I've always made: he never ingratiated
himself to anyone, always managed to arrange his business
so that any sense of obligation fell to whoever he was dealing
with. He was the master of the transaction – you do this for me
and I'll give you that in return, but only as long as it benefits
me – he should have been a Wall Street trader, or a politician.*

Basically any one of those guys who makes your life really shit, pushes
you down so low that you believe them when they say they're going to
make it all better.

*Please don't misread this as an attempt to demonise your father
and underplay my own wrongdoing – far from it. Despite the
differences in our upbringing – me the overprivileged waster,*

him the poor orphaned manipulator, or so I believed – we were equals in so many ways.

He taught me how to meditate (a handy short-term fallback when drugs were scarce, albeit a poor substitute) and before long he was teaching meditation to the hard men, even some of the screws. It was down to him that we both served minimum sentences.

When I got out I found us a big old house to rent in the Lake District, near Keswick, chosen partly for its proximity to a recommended dealer. Then I went about finding out where you were living with your mother. I hadn't bargained on Andrew; it was typical of your father to only give half the story, the half that would inspire me to do his bidding and miss out the information that might make me think twice.

The day he got out of prison, I picked him up in my old car and drove him to a garage in north London that sold camper vans on behalf of Aussie travellers going home. He picked the one he liked, told the salesman we would part-ex my car, handed over the difference in cash and we were on our way. He thrust your mother's address, which I'd sent him a few weeks before, under my nose and told me to drive him to Scotland – via Torquay – which, you may realise by now, is something of a roundabout route. He had money in Torquay, stashed in an old lady's house. When I asked where the money came from, he said Father Christmas. It wasn't funny but I laughed because it was the first (and last) time I'd heard him make any attempt at anything resembling a joke.

The journey to Scotland took a long time. Maybe even days. When you've done a stretch in prison the value of time changes, slows down, expands. We didn't rush in any case, stopping for meal breaks at pubs off the motorway, cigarette breaks, pee breaks, meditation breaks. I would sit and smoke a couple of hours away while your father meditated at the top of a hill. We arrived in Drongnock after dark. The house was a bit off the beaten track so I couldn't get the van close enough and your father tore me off a strip for not having driven up to stake it out in advance. Eventually I parked up in a layby up the road and he ordered me to wait inside the van. Secretly I think he relished the added drama of seeming to have walked all the way from the Isle of Sheppey, as if on some kind of pilgrimage. He certainly looked and smelled as if he had. I'm sure I did too.

So he trotted off and I got out of the van for a smoke in the fresh air. There were no streetlights or houses nearby and it was a beautiful clear night, so I stood there blowing smoke rings up at the stars and didn't really register the shouting. And then I heard him come running down the road behind me. 'Get in the fucking van,' he screamed, 'they're calling the fucking police.' I'd never heard him swear before or seen him run and, what with that and the dope, I started giggling. He completely lost it then, started kicking the tyres and screaming at me to unlock his door when it wasn't even locked. A right tantrum. I told him to calm down or I'd leave him behind.

Back on the road he explained that he was upset because your mother had refused to let you see him and he suspected she was planning to renege on a deal they'd made when she was pregnant, which was, apparently, that from the age of five you would go and live with him. I found out later that was a lie. I tried to reason with him that he couldn't exactly blame her for changing her mind about giving her child up to a convicted criminal, but he stonewalled me by closing his eyes, the meditative equivalent of putting his fingers in his ears and la-la-la-ing. So I shut up and drove us to Keswick and not another word was spoken on the subject for a couple of weeks, until one day he told me that he'd somehow received a message from your mother and, as expected, she'd rescinded on their agreement. He had a back-up plan. This entailed me driving to Glasgow to get a copy of your birth certificate, which he then used to have you added to his passport. It was pretty easy in those days – he didn't even need a photograph. I was too away with the fairies to twig what the overall plan was.

Marsha Ray – or Mrs F as he called her – arrived around the same time. I didn't really understand why she'd come until we were on our way to Brazil. Until then I presumed she was there to keep house. I also assumed they were sleeping together.

*He'd always gone on about how meditation increased your
sexual energy and it made sense to my addled brain that she
might be his outlet for that. To be honest I didn't really care as
long as her presence helped to keep him off my case. As much
as your father liked to pretend he was incapable of executing
even the most mundane task himself, he somehow managed to
book the trip to Brazil without my or Mrs F's involvement and
seemingly without once leaving his room.*

*The spiritual retreat in Keswick plan was all nonsense, of
course – a ruse. No one in their right mind would have paid
to stay in that dump of a house with a bunch of oddballs like
us, but naturally I went along with it without questioning
anything. What the Norwegians say about prison is true, you
know. The removal of a man's liberty is punishment enough. I
was so happy just to be able to walk out of the front door any
time I liked that I would have bought anything he sold me as
long as I had access to drugs and a roof over my head. Mine
was a shameless life in those days, Sonny, shamelessly lived.*

*Which brings me to Confession Number Two. It was me
who kidnapped you. Me who took you away from Andrew
and your mother. Me who lured you into a camper van on
the promise of meeting your sperm father – as you called him.
Me who shot Andrew in the leg. And when I was driving you
to Keswick it was me who stopped you screaming by blowing
heroin smoke into your mouth and giving you Temazepam
to knock you out. All the ills in your life have been caused by
me. I am a monster and this is my pathetic attempt at making
amends for everything I've done to you. That I was doing your
father's bidding only makes it worse. Sonny, what can I say
except that I am unimaginably sorry. Sometimes we look back
at the life we've rolled out and see that it amounts to little
more than a sequence of things we can't undo.*

*That's the end of my wrongdoing, but please keep reading;
there is more you need to know.*

Seriously. What the fuck?

Andrew's Limp #2

I have a question I need to ask Andrew, but the words are all coagulated at the back of my throat and stuck there like a solid lump of phlegm. We're in the village pub waiting for our order of Sunday roast. Between us on the table sit two glasses of sparkling water.

People are looking at us. At me. Not directly – in quick turns of the head. The word *missing* is repeating over and over like a billion lawn sprinklers starting up. As in, 'Is that the wee boy who went misssssssssing?'

'How far is Keswick from here?' I say to block out the noise. That's not the important question, just an opener. I pronounce it Kez-wick.

'You mean Kezzick,' says Andrew, 'in the Lake District? It's a good few hours away on the train, or I could take you if you like, it's a gorgeous drive. You aren't thinking about leaving today, are you?'

'No, not today, but I might go there next. It's where Thomas and my dad were staying when they kidnapped me.'

'Oh, right. Just your average sightseeing trip, then.'

Our food arrives. It looks and smells delicious but I have no appetite. To be honest, if I were home in RB now I'd be in my room, lying on my bed, with the door shut tight. Andrew's looking at me with a worried expression on his face and I put some energy into cutting up the chicken on my plate.

'How do you feel about going to look at the school today?'

'Um, I think I'd rather wait, if that's okay. It kind of feels like a next-visit thing.'

'Sonny, that's fine. It's great just having you here. Looks like the sun's coming out. How about a walk after lunch?'

But after lunch we're too stuffed full of food to walk, so we go back to the house and sit in the room with the racetrack, groaning and holding our stomachs.

'We could watch the video of your fifth birthday party.'

What can I say? My resistance is low and I say yes, forgetting that it's not the hard things in life that get to you; the hard things bring out the fight. It's the soft things that dig their way in: birds, kittens, moving images of your own five-year-old self.

He turns it on and within seconds I get to see your face full-frontal for the first time. I ask Andrew to go back and freeze it a few seconds.

I always had this secret worry that without realising it I might be attracted to women who look like you. It's none of your business to know if that's true or not. I will say that you were beautiful, just like Ruth said. In fact if I had to pick you out in a police line-up I wouldn't have said you were my mother. Not that I don't look like you in some ways, I probably do, but because I don't feel any connection to you at all. But that's not what gets to me. What gets to me is watching that happy little kid with the squeaky voice, whose words I cannot understand even though it's my mouth they're coming out of, playing with his little friends, hitting a kiddie drum with a plastic stick, smiling up at the camera. Actually smiling up higher than that, at the person holding the camera, Andrew. That happy little kid, who had no idea what he had coming. And I start blubbing like that five-year-old would have if only he knew. I can't stop myself. I can't stop. The snot and the tears and the Sunday roast that feels like it's going to vomit right up. I'm lying foetal on the floor in the middle of the racetrack and I can't stop any of it. I even blame Andrew. 'Why didn't you come get me? Why didn't you even look?' I wail. And Andrew is sobbing too hard to answer.

Later, he tells me he didn't know where to go or what to do, so in the end he thought the best thing was to stay home, and wait, and hope that one day either the police would bring me back or I'd find him. He had no claim on me, you were my legal parent, and so far as he knew you were out there with your new husband, looking for me, so what could he do?

'But once you knew where I was, why didn't you come then? It might have helped me, didn't you think of that?'

'Yes, of course. It might have helped, but equally it could have tipped you over the edge. You were already on suicide watch. We couldn't risk upsetting a balance that was already precarious.'

'We? You and Thomas? It didn't concern you that I was living with a murdering kidnapping junkie? You didn't think that would tip me over the edge?' I know I'm venting my anger at the wrong person here, but when this shit starts coming there's no holding it back.

'Sonny, Thomas turned his whole life around to take care of you. He knew what he'd done and he was dead set on making it better. If I'd shown up, you wouldn't have known me from Adam. I thought, given the six thousand miles between us, that the best thing I could do would be to support Thomas and keep him strong so he could help you.'

'What do you mean by support – money? You gave Thomas money?'

'Yes, some money, but mainly just moral support. We talked on the phone. He had nobody, Sonny, just you.'

He gets up then to go to make us a beverage and when he comes back we sit there in silence drinking our tea.

'We could still take that walk if you fancy it,' says Andrew. 'The moon is almost full and we're not long past midsummer so it won't be getting dark tonight.'

Little Man and the Zombies

There's no railroad station at Keswick, so the final stage of my journey into the town is a bus ride. Sometimes in RB I ride the bus, if I've cycled a long way and don't have the energy to cycle home. Our buses have these neat racks in front for carrying bikes, so it's a breeze. There's no rack on this bus so I guess people don't use bikes so much. It's kind of hilly. There's one other person on board, a woman who's been somewhere else to do her shopping so I guess Keswick is small.

It's a pretty ride. The grey sky and the low cloud hanging over the mountains remind me of standing on the cliff edge at Big Sur when the fog rolls in off the Pacific Ocean and the cloud is below you and the sound of the waves below that.

The woman gets off the bus somewhere I don't notice, so by the time we hit Keswick it's just me and the driver, who has maybe forgotten I'm here because he's singing some kind of hymn real loud.

First impressions? This is England but it looks more like Scotland than London or Torquay. And nobody here wears normal everyday apparel; everyone is dressed for hiking, and for rain. That's the best I can do when I'm starving and tired.

GPS gets me from the bus stop to the Hedgehog Bed & Breakfast, which I chose mainly for its cool name. I forgot this when I was with Andrew but my first memory of living with my dad is crying for my Sonic the Hedgehog video and my Sonic the Hedgehog PJs. I wonder if I even knew hedgehogs were real creatures, and if I had would I have thought they were blue? In SoCal we have possums, skunks, raccoons, squirrels, bears, coyotes, snakes and mountain lions and all kinds of creepy critturs. Driving through Manhattan Beach at night the whole place stinks of skunk, though not always because of the animal. No hedgehogs though. Once, a possum died under our house and man, the stink was so strong you could taste it. You wouldn't want to be the poor guy who has to earn a buck taking those things away. That guy should be the multi-milly-anna, not me.

I have a hard time understanding the woman who shows me to my room. I don't want to appear ill-mannered by asking her to repeat everything twenty gazillion times, so after the second time of not understanding I switch to listening out for key words in hopes of piecing them together. I make out the word *breakfast* so I smile and nod and she smiles right back so I guess we're okay and that somehow some way I'll get something to eat the next morning. Which reminds me how hungry I am right now. I throw my backpack on to my bed, stuff T's next letter into my pocket and follow my nose to the nearest fish and chip shop. Chippie. It's eight-thirty at night and it should be dark, but it isn't, the sun's only just come out. This perpetual daylight is screwing with my jet-lag.

Keswick is located close to a lake, Derwentwater. I check out the distance from the town then go sit on a bench by the water to eat my fish and chips and try to figure out which of the houses at the top of the lake is the one Thomas occupied with my father. There aren't so many and they all look like regular rich people's homes. I guess it's the same here as in SoCal: rich people don't like to live too close to poor people, just close enough to have them come cut the grass and deal with the sprinklers. The lake is still and glassy and I take a photo of it on my phone then scroll back through my photo album. I stop at an old sneaky over-the-wall picture of Ike and Milly-Anna dancing in their yard. Milly-Anna's up on the deck and Ike's on the grass looking up at her. It's easy to see which song they're dancing to because Milly-Anna's lips are all puckered up doing the oo-hoo-hoos. In any case I have never known them to dance to anything else. Milly-Anna's watched *Grease* more times than I've seen *SOTD*, but then she has decades of viewing time on me.

I'm just thinking how far away they all seem and how peaceful it is here when these two kids, a girl and a boy, probably about my age, possibly younger, come stomping along. At least, the girl is stomping. She has her arms folded across her chest and is wearing a really tight short skirt that shows off her fat white thighs, and those thighs are marching a few feet ahead of the guy as if she's making a show of walking away but slow enough to notice if he doesn't follow. Looks to me as if he's in two minds about catching her up. Looks to me like he wants to drink his whole six-pack of beer in peace. He mumbles something that I assume she's expected to hear, then changes direction to come sit at the other end of my bench. The thighs keep on marching. I wonder if she thinks she looks like Beyoncé in that skirt, because she sure as hell doesn't. Bitch, those legs ain't never seen the sun.

The guy looks at me and lifts his chin so I say hey and my next chip falls off of my tiny wooden fork. I put it down and start eating with my fingers like you're supposed to. The guy cracks open a can. I look away but the only way to escape the smell of his beer would be to stand up and walk, which would be ill-mannered, right? Beyoncé's realised he's not following any more and has slowed down, but she doesn't look back to see where he is. In fact she doesn't look anywhere other than down at her own elbows and I wonder if she's always so fixated by them. The sound of the guy sucking and swallowing his beer triggers my misophonia, makes me twitch. I should go but I'm scared he's the kind of guy to take offence and express it verbally or even physically. I sit it out, try to focus my attention on other sounds. The lapping of the water. Lakes sound different from oceans. Oceans sound different from streams. I think about wading across the icy stream at Andrew Molera State Park when the bridge is out. That kills your feet. The water's so cold you don't feel the pain of the stones under them, that's for sure. A stream sounds different from a dripping tap. That's another of my trigger sounds. Man, I'm tense.

The guy mumbles something that I realise is directed at me and I look at him and say, 'I'm sorry, dude, I'm finding it hard to tune in to the accent here – would you mind saying that again?'

He shrugs and instead of trying to make me understand with more words he lifts up the five remaining cans in his six-pack and jiggles them in the air.

'No, thanks, dude,' I say. 'Good of you to offer.'

He shrugs again and we both sit and stare at a lone black bird floating on the water. It has a big red splodge on the front of its face as if its been shot in the head. He crushes his can in one hand, drops it on the ground and cracks open another.

Girlfriend is leaning against a wall about fifty feet away, facing the water but not looking at it or us, still inspecting those elbows; worse, she's picking at the skin on them, and, now I've seen that, I can hear it. Her pale thighs are luminous in the weird summer night. Man, this place is not relaxing. I need to get out of the electrical force-field that's crackling between Justin Timberlake and Cameron Diaz here. I scrunch up my fish and chip wrappers and at the same time there's a sudden burst of activity from them. Cameron has stomped back our way and directed a sulky question at the ground behind our bench. Loverboy sighs and gets to his feet like a reluctant ninety-year-old man and enunciates, 'See. Ya. Mate. Enjoy. Your. Holidays.' The accent is still thick as oil, but I appreciate that he's made an effort to be understood and it actually feels good to make contact. I guess you can't judge a man by the way his woman treats him.

'Thanks, skip,' I say. 'Good to meet you. See you around.' *Skip*? Where the fuck did that come from? I have never called anyone *skip* in my life before, and if anyone dared call me that I'd spit in his face.

They slouch off to wherever it is they're headed, her up front, him behind, as if they never stopped. As if they never even met yet, and I wonder if they'll still be working the same routine in twenty years.

I stay a few minutes more, long enough to toss my chip paper into the trash can (three attempts; I'm better at kicking than throwing), long enough to let the air settle. I toss his discarded can into the trash too and head back townwards.

I wake up too late for breakfast. Turns out that yesterday the woman was telling me breakfast finishes at nine. Somehow this morning I understand every word she says. My ears must have adjusted their tuning overnight. She asks me if I'm planning to go to the pencil museum and when I say no, that I want to get across to the other side of the lake, she's a little surprised – what right-thinking twenty-one-year-old male wouldn't want to gen up on the history of the pencil, right? – but tells me I can take a ferry on a tour of the lake which will drop me wherever I want to go. The sky is actually blue this morning, which makes the town look prettier, the grey and the green and the blue with wispy white clouds being blown around like the feathers of a giant bird that's been ripped apart by an airplane. When I get to the pier though it's kind of crowded with people eating ice-creams and potato chips, so on account of the inevitable chorus of mouth noises I decide to walk the trail around the edge of the lake instead.

Everyone I pass says *hello*. It's okay for them, they only have to say it once; I'm the only person headed this way. The trail is flat and not so muddy. Birds are singing. A couple times I think I see a deer's ass flashing at me through the trees. I wish I'd bought a Cornetto.

When I checked the house out online it showed on the satellite as a large plot, surrounded by trees except for where it opens on to the lake on one side. In real life it's been converted into a hotel and I guess it's kind of exclusive. The guy on the front desk looks at me all snooty when I ask to use the restroom. I am not impolite. When I come back from the bathroom, I go right up and tell him I lived in this house before it was a hotel, even though I don't know for sure that I did, I just want to make him feel bad. He's not affected by that in any way, so I think about telling him I have enough money to buy the hotel outright and that I might just do it, just so I can fire him. I guess I still have some anger, right?

Waiting at the little pier for the ferry to pick me up I compare the landscape in front of me to the map on my phone. The mountain behind the town has kind of an American Indian-sounding name, Skiddaw. The hill next to it is Little Man. When I see that it nearly blows my mind. My dad used to call me Little Man. I forgot that. Now I recall saying over and over, *my name is Sonny, my name is Sonny*, in that irritating way little kids repeat and repeat and repeat until finally someone tells them to shut up already. I guess he named me for the hill. Why not the mountain? Aim higher, right? (Skiddaw Agelaste-Bim.) I picture myself hiking up there. I read somewhere that if you think hard enough about exercise it has the same effect on your muscles as actually doing it. Personally I think that's a mountain of BS.

Skiddaw is awesome. The top of it is over three thousand feet high
but the trail to the top is easy going, grassy and wide, I have to run
in places to make it harder. Again everyone else seems to be walking
in the opposite direction to me and we do the whole *hellohellohello*
thing again, although this time it's more like *good evening* because
I've started out pretty late. I figure they all have followed a different
trail up and are coming down the easy route. Closer to the top I can
see they are all just turning right around and coming down the same
way they went up. There is no trail that I can see going down the
other side, just a steep downhill slide made of flat purple stones. I
stop for a while to admire the view. I swear I can see the ocean in
the distance. Thomas says that in England you don't get nature on
the same scale as you do in America and I wonder how he can have
lived here and say that. I guess he was too stoned to notice. I take a
panorama shot on my phone to prove how wrong he is.

I take the quick route down. My sneakers have no traction on
the stones, which stream down around me like water as I put to good
use the jump-and-turn jump-and-turn ski techniques I learned at Big
Bear. Oh my gosh, is that ever a fun way to get down a mountain!
At the bottom I sit on a rock, gasping for breath. I send Andrew my
panorama from the top of Skiddaw and he messages back, *Glad you
arrived safely,* and *Wow*. No exclamation point. My kind of person.

I smuggle my fish and chips and soda into the bed-and-breakfast,
breaking the no-food-in-bedrooms rule. While my veins are still
loaded with adrenaline, I get out my dad's tapes.

The Grace of Guru Bim #3

One two, one two… cough… There are no accidents, only destiny. Whatever has come to me in my life has come for a reason. My betrayal by Ruth Williams led me to my calling on the Isle of Sheppey. Nothing I said in the courtroom would have made any difference in the face of such prejudice. I was called, as I had been before and would be again. The Universe doesn't always send us to places we would choose to go. Meditation is a simple, easy and essential tool for the incarcerated man and, by extending my grace to the lives of those less fortunate, I was able to encourage my fellow inmates to follow a healthier path. Thomas Hardiker was sent by the Universe to assist me and guide others towards me. To help me through the suffering of separation from my newborn son. One by one the holes in Thomas's aura were repaired. It was a long, hard five years but my calling and meditation got me through. The earthbound human will always favour the word of the likes of Ruth Williams; only spirit recognises a higher purpose. I am no stranger to hardship and incarceration. I was raised by fools and educated by idiots. Only in the realm of spirit have I been the richest man alive. And my spiritual privilege has enabled me to get through all the long, dark days to touch the lives of others with my grace and my words. There is no convention in spirit, there is only healing.

I stop the tape and eject it. Only two more tapes left.

Tape Number Four:

> *One two, one two… cough… The title of this autobiography*
> *shall be* The Grace of Guru Bim. *It is dedicated to my son,*
> *Sonny Agelaste-Bim, aka Little Man. These past few years in*
> *Brazil with my son have been my happiest; we have grown so*
> *close. He is my spiritual equal in every sense and teaches me*
> *something new every day.*

Oh, come *on.*
   If I had a dollar for the gazillions of times I've heard all this crap.
   Oh, I *do*, right?
   I toss all the tapes and the stupid little machine into the trash.
Only a moron would carry so much junk around.

Things We Can't Undo #4 & #5

I head back to London to work out where to go next. I could get used to travelling first class. The complimentary beverages. The quiet, the comforting rock of the coach.

I try to remember my life in Brazil. None of my memories feature my father or Marsha Ray. All of them feature Maria and our life in Olinda, but I guess after we moved to Quilombo Novo I even forgot about her, like I forgot about Andrew in Scotland, and you wherever you were. Maybe I gave up on ever seeing you all again or maybe I just assumed I would and got on with my life in the meantime. Who knows how kids make sense of the weird stuff that happens?

At Quilombo Novo I became obsessive about football – playing not watching; there was no TV. Me and the other kids, we played barefoot, Brazilian style. Crazy, right? But that's how I learned to play well enough to get into the Galaxy. It wasn't so great after my dad stopped the local kids coming to the commune, but we kept on playing.

As I recall, classes there were given in English, but I don't remember the local kids speaking any English ever so maybe that's a false memory or I'm mixing up the time before and after they left. Most of the adults living at the commune were from places like Holland and Germany and England – cold places basically – and most of their kids had been born in Brazil. Most people spoke a mix of perfect English and patchy Portuguese and that's how we got by. I still have a few words of Portuguese, mostly football-related: *pé* (foot), *falta!* (foul!), *impedido!* (offside!), *toque de mão!* (handball!).

The shaking my dad made us all do was kind of fun, especially when the whole commune did it together. Every day before lunch we quit school to go shake with the adults. The best part was falling on to the floor at the end and rolling around in the dirt moaning and groaning; we considered it part of our football training. Kids gave each other points for the most dramatic dive. (*Ele amarelou!*) Every single one of us could keep goal. We were sure as hell not scared to throw ourselves into the path of a speeding ball.

Early mornings, before school, we helped in the vegetable gardens, picking the corn, rolling the squash and pulling the manioc. Only the older kids got to strip the manioc too because that meant using knives. I was just at the age to move up to this job when we left, and that, besides leaving my homies, was the only aspect of leaving I was pissed about.

We had these showers set up in the trees. We took turns to pump the water through while the rest of us chased each other around in the water. Showers were only for bedtime though so during the day we mostly cooled off by swimming in the river, jumping and pushing each other in off the rocks. Since the other guru guy died, a safe swimming area had been marked out with large rocks in the shallows.

The Brazilian kids were scared of my dad; they called him the Surubim. I stayed away from the house where he and Marsha Ray lived because I hated them by then. Mostly I hung out and slept at the other kids' homes where it was cosy and noisy and there was no Marsha Ray to boss me around.

Sometimes I ate lunch or dinner with Thomas and Ken. Ken was cool; he used to talk about fixing a date to take me and all the other kids to see Salgueiro Atlético play and sometimes he would stop what he was doing in the clinic and come kick a ball with us. If I ever had a problem, like we needed a new football – I can't think now what other problems were even possible – I went to Thomas. Thomas had a reputation as the man who could get anything; everybody's go-to guy. Obviously I didn't pick up on the full meaning of that then. And that's it, the total contents of my memory.

But Thomas has more:

The day you arrived at the commune, Ken and I were away
on one of our trips to Salgueiro to pick up medical supplies as
planned. When we were introduced later, you screamed and
hid behind Mrs F That stung, but it lent greater credibility to
the new guru's spiritual prowess in the eyes of the residents.
He explained that he'd bestowed upon you the power of auric
interpretation, and that the proliferation of bottomless black
holes in my aura had terrified you.

The communists – your father's name for the other residents
– seemed reasonably won over and excited and talk circulated
of a welcome party. I was sent to 'borrow' a PA system from
Fabio senior, the chap who ran the bar in Cabrobó I'd stayed
at that first night and who had since become a good friend,
and not just in the junkie sense of the word. The inverted
commas are because after the party I was sent back with a
wad of money to tell him we were keeping his PA. Your father
wanted the equipment set up on the verandah so that he could
use the microphone to address everyone. I might add that this
was quite unnecessary; if he'd raised his voice a little, everyone
could have heard him well enough.

The 'party' – there was no music – consisted of him making
a speech about how the great universal spiritual powers had
told him that standards of spirituality at Quilombo Novo had
been eroded and sent him to set everyone back on the path to
enlightenment. Mrs F stood up there next to him, nodding
away at his every word, until he ordered her to shake, right
there in front of everyone, to demonstrate what we'd all be
doing together every day. Then we all had to have a go. It
wasn't easy to keep a straight face through Mrs F's solo, let
me tell you, but the other communists took it all much more
seriously than I would have expected. Even Ken joined in,
albeit with one eyebrow aloft. Good to keep one eye open at all
times, he used to say. If there was a saviour living in our midst
at that commune, it was Ken.

I was shocked by how much your father's paranoia had
escalated in the few months since I'd left you all in Recife.
At first I put it down to the anxiety of parental responsibility,

*exacerbated by the difficulty of living in a foreign country. It
soon became apparent that that couldn't be the reason. At
best his parental style was hands-off; he delegated everything
to Mrs F., whom you clearly had the measure of and who
was able to assert no authority over you whatsoever. Within
weeks of arriving you were running wild, sleeping wherever you
happened to doze off at bedtime and eating with whoever put
food in front of you at mealtimes, usually within the commune
but sometimes at the home of a friend outside. You had a
bedroom in your father's house but I'm sure you never slept in it.*

*You weren't badly behaved, just independent, if not
completely detached. You were pretty fluent in Portuguese
when you arrived at QN. On top of that, you had more or
less rejected your mother tongue. Anyone who could speak to
you in Portuguese had a distinct advantage over those who
couldn't and the fact that your father and Mrs F had struggled
to learn even a few words between them sealed their exclusion.
That your father could allow you this level of independence
somehow elevated him even higher in the communists'
estimation; nobody recognised it for the neglect it was. People
were flattered to be included in your group of adopted elders.
For me it was an absolute honour, especially given our tricky
start, if that isn't too gross an understatement.*

*I was instructed to continue living and working alongside
Ken, undercover, like a neighbourhood spy in East Berlin,
which was fine by me because we were good friends by then.*

*Everything tootled along nicely for a few months. The
daily regime under Guru Bim, at first anyway, consisted of
two group meditations – first thing in the morning and in the
afternoon after the siesta – to raise new upward energy; plus
two communal shakes, before siesta and at bedtime, to clear
out any excess energy. My job was to report any complaints
to Marsha Ray, but I never heard even a mutter of dissent. In
fact I was surprised by how happily everyone embraced the new
routine and seemed to trust your father.*

*On the subject of trust, do you know what, or I should say
who, finally inspired me to get clean? It was you. The more*

time I spent with you and the more trusting you became of
me, the more I reflected on your kidnapping and wondered if
in some perverse way that event was the glue of our growing
attachment. To put it in less wishy-washy terms, I wondered
if the reason you hadn't rejected me in the same way you had
clearly rejected your father and Mrs F was because I was the
perpetrator of that kidnapping. I like to believe that kids are
quite logical in their thinking or at least in their behaviour.
Maybe somewhere in your subconscious you believed that if
you stayed close to me I might also be the person to take you
home again. A kind of Stockholm Syndrome with knobs on.

Anyway, as life in the commune got more difficult I began
to feel protective towards another person – you – for the first
time in my life. I mean truly protective, not just protective
in exchange for money. I found myself wanting to take
responsibility for your welfare. I went to Ken and told him
I wanted to be off all of it, even methadone, even the drink,
and for good this time. I asked for his help and naturally, Ken
being Ken, he gave it willingly.

Around the time I was rejoining the world of sobriety, in
the summer of 2002, life on the commune took a sinister turn.
Your father issued a ruling that from then on only herbal
medicines could be used in the commune and only Mrs F was
allowed to administer them. Ken was furious, but he toed the
line, outwardly at least. Even when he was ordered to move
out of the clinic and into the house to treat your father, who
had diagnosed himself with an unspecified serious illness.
This may be my own paranoia but I suspected the real agenda
was to separate Ken and me. Mrs F didn't like Ken and I was
sure she had told your father he and I were lovers. As you
know, he didn't recognise homosexuality. Naturally that led
me to wonder if he might be gay himself – he was certainly a
misogynist. Either way Ken was too popular and we were too
close and your father's preferred MO was always to divide and
rule.

While I was detoxing more new rules were introduced.
The first was a complete ban on alcohol (the cachaça still

behind the clinic was dismantled, albeit so it could be easily reassembled), followed by a ban on the use of all recreational drugs (most of the marijuana field was dug up and re-planted with Mrs F's herbs – I say most because a small section was fenced off for your father's own medicinal needs). Needless to say, none of this went down too well, and I sensed some of the blame was targeted at me for having brought my addictions into the community and generally lowering the spiritual tone.

And then he banned sex outside marriage. While the first two rules had been reluctantly accepted, this one almost sparked a revolution. The commune had been established in the age of free love and people were accustomed to sleeping with whoever they wanted. Your father quelled the protest by revealing that a message had come from the Universe that AIDS was spreading like wildfire throughout Brazil; if anyone at QN was HIV positive, he wanted to reduce the possibility of it spreading. Needless to say, the Universe had it all wrong, AIDS was no longer a big problem in Brazil – clearly he was counting on the fact that the communists had been cut off for too long to know any better. He was right: they all went along with it. As a sweetener he offered to temporarily extend his grace to any couple wishing to marry and to conduct those marriages personally. Your father's manipulative skills were not to be underestimated. This was all part of a bigger plan, playing the AIDS card here set him up to use it again later.

So the clinic was taken over by Mrs F and her herbs and Ken was reassigned to the sole care of your father, whose health was failing, according to the Universe, due to his overexpenditure of energy in maintaining the spiritual health of the commune. In the light of this, the Universe decreed that he alone had the right to continue using pharmaceuticals, but this wasn't made common knowledge and Ken was sworn to strict secrecy. I suppose your father presumed that if Ken told anyone it would be me first and that I would report it back to him. He was deluded enough to believe he still had my loyalty. (By the way, there was never anything wrong with your father; he was the healthiest person in Brazil. All those

*drips and medications were mostly placebos to placate his
hypochondria.)*

*Good old Ken always saw the positive in everything. At
least his new role allowed him continuing access to proper
medicine, and your father's assumption that everyone did as
he told them enabled Ken to continue treating others on the
side. We set up a system for smuggling medicine out to those
who really needed it, using me as intermediary, which was a
poor substitute for Ken's presence in the clinic, but it was better
than nothing.*

Nothing, aka Marsha Ray and her herbs.

*The people who really lost out were those out in the villages,
whose access to him was reduced to the few hours he could
salvage from our now monthly trips to Salgueiro.*

*The effects of the switch were masked at first by an
improvement of the general health of the commune –
presumably due to the reduction in alcohol and drug use – for
which Mrs F took all the credit. Unfortunately your father
interpreted this as proof that his regime was working and saw
fit to take another more dangerous step and do away with all
conventional methods of medical diagnosis. Instead, diagnosis
was to be by auric interpretation only, which only the guru was
qualified to perform, and then only when he was strong enough
to be in the company of the sick. He discovered a renewed
interest in you at this point and hauled you in to assist and
confirm his diagnoses. You were ten years old. You objected of
course, on the grounds that it would reduce your football time.*

*In early 2003 Ken's weight dropped dramatically.
Your father diagnosed AIDS and after an inspection of
the communal aura declared a state of emergency in the
commune: he diagnosed the majority of residents as being HIV
positive.*

*Under a new diktat, all trade with local farmers and
fishermen ceased and the school and clinic closed to local
children. The gates to Quilombo Novo closed and the*

*commune tipped into a speedy decline. Food productivity
dropped as people became weaker. People became
malnourished from the lack of protein, and anyone who got
seriously ill was denied proper treatment.*

*When Ken finally diagnosed himself with the real reason
for his weight loss – pancreatic cancer – I tried to persuade
him to leave and seek treatment, but he knew he didn't have
long and he wanted to stay. People with perfectly curable
illnesses were at risk of dying because of your father's stupid
rules and beliefs. I even suggested a plan to kill your father,
it would have been easy enough to do, but he insisted I
concentrate on getting you away, not because of your father's
fictional HIV and AIDS diagnoses, but to protect you from
him. Ken reassured me he could handle the rest.*

*Do you remember our escape, Sonny? Crawling through
that water pipe with a football stuck up the back of your shirt?
You have always been such a good egg.*

I guess, right?

You know how sometimes you can be told about an event you
were present at and you don't remember at first, but then someone
says 'you know, chocolate and strawberry' and suddenly it all comes
back. Truth is, I don't remember any of that, none of the bad stuff,
not even with all the information Thomas has given me. I don't even
remember how we got to Redondo. We lived in Brazil then we lived
in RB, with nothing in between.

I can't relax. All the complimentary first-class coffee's buzzed me
up and I'm determined to arrive in London knowing how this story
ends. I man right up and open envelope number five:

*I'll begin with the sad news. I wrote to Ken, care of Fabio
senior, to let him know we'd landed safely in the US. A year
later, I got his reply, along with a note from Fabio saying
Ken had died peacefully at the clinic in Salgueiro a few
weeks before and that they'd found a letter addressed to me in
amongst his belongings.*

I won't go into all the detail but, soon after we escaped,

your father hatched a plan and was mentally defective enough
to believe Ken would carry it out. He made a pronouncement
from the verandah that the ban on pharmaceutical use was to
be temporarily set aside so that every man, woman and child
there was to be injected, at great expense, with drugs to prevent
the onset of AIDS. Meanwhile, Ken was ordered to procure
sufficient insulin supplies to inject them all – your father, Ken
and Marsha being the only exceptions – with a lethal dose.

Talk about drug of choice, right? I can't wait to tell Ruth.

Ken knew he needed to act quickly, not least because his own
days were numbered. Instead of the insulin he ordered large
quantities of injectable multivitamins. He did order some
insulin, but just enough to first convince your father that he'd
carried out his instructions, and then kill him. Everyone else
was given the vitamins. In the end it was Marsha who injected
your father, but she had no idea what she was giving him.

Oh My Gosh. Marsha Ray killed my dad and doesn't know? This
is turning into a fucking Greek drama. With dramatic irony and
everything. With knobs on, as Thomas would say. I wish I'd known
this before I went to her house. Imagine if I'd interrupted her when
she put on that fake dreamy voice and pulled the fake sad face and
yelled, IS THAT WHY YOU KILLED HIM? Oh My Gosh, can you
imagine? Her face would be Blue Steel to the power of a gazillion.
Fuck fuck fuck. I think I'm going to die of overstimulation, right here
on the train.

I'll be honest, my motives for getting out of there weren't
entirely unselfish. The only real way I was going to maintain
my sobriety was by assuaging my guilt and returning you to
your mother. One night before we left, Ken helped me sneak
out to Fabio's bar to call an old private investigator contact in
the UK. He tracked Andrew down, which was easy – thankfully
he hadn't moved – and he gave us enough information to pass
on to a friend of Ken's in San Francisco who was a computer

whizz. I'm not sure it would have been so easy to trace her if
her husband had been less well known.

I'll get to the point.

Sonny, I have met your mother, once, here in LA. She lives
in Pacific Palisades…

WHAT?! That's so close to RB. I've been hiking up there like a
million times. With Thomas. Fuck.

… and is married to a Christian Evangelist preacher, one of
those guys with their own TV channel.

Fuck. I guess you have a type, right?

She's had three more children with him, two girls and a boy.
The eldest, one of the girls, is a few years younger than you.
That's all I know about them.

I imagined it would all go like clockwork. I'd bring you to
California where I could arrange a mother–son reunion, hand
you over and be on my way. As you're well aware, that's not
how it worked out. But Sonny, I promise, I really tried.

You may remember, or more likely not, that when we first
arrived in LA we stayed in a motel in Santa Monica and I
hired an agency babysitter to take you down to the beach to
play for a few hours every day. That was so I could spend time
trying to contact your mother. I won't bore you with the details
but eventually I went up to her home. They live in one of those
fortress-like villas up in the hills there, all bougainvillea, razor
wire and ocean views. We've actually walked past it a number
of times to go hiking and each time I've fantasised about your
mother seeing us, relenting, and taking you in.

Anyway, the day I went to the house, I rang the buzzer at
the gate and asked to speak to her. As soon as I told her why I
was there she cut me off and I stood there waiting, imagining
her rushing out of the house in a state of excitement to come
and let me in personally. After ten minutes, I buzzed again
and was told your mother wasn't available. I had to say I would

*pitch a tent outside the gate and buzz every three minutes
of every day before she would speak to me again. Finally she
came out to the gate, but it wasn't good news, Sonny, as I'm
sure you've guessed. She told me that she'd never told anyone
about you, not her husband and definitely not her other
children, your half-siblings. As far as she was concerned your
father was evil personified and your soul was contaminated. In
short, she wanted nothing to do with you, and no amount of
reasoning could change her mind.*

Fuck you, bitch. *Contaminated*?!

*I rented the house in Redondo so we would be close, or close
enough, that if she relented we could be at her door before she
had time to change her mind. I wrote her a letter giving her
our address, and repeated that there was no pressure, that she
could meet you without you knowing who she was, convinced
that once she met you all her religious prejudices would
crumble. I said that if we moved on I'd be sure to tell her where
we were going. All I got by way of reply, a few weeks later, was
the handful of photographs I've since passed on to you, no note
or anything. And that was the last I heard from her until she
forwarded the letter about your inheritance.*

    *Sonny, here is her address. Yours to do what you want with.
I'm sorry I didn't give it to you sooner.*

I change my mind about staying in London. I'm up for a fight, and
the only person I have access to that I have ammunition against is
Marsha Ray. I'm not proud of the impulse, but when my train arrives
at Euston I get straight on the tube and take the next train to Hove.

Listen to Your Heart, Right? #2

I don't call, I just show up. She's delighted to see me, and I'm kind of delighted to see her too, now I'm seeing her in a whole different light. Obviously it's twisted to find it funny that someone you don't like killed your dad, so let's just say I am appreciative of the irony. It's like everything he ever said about Karma packaged up in a neat metaphor.

I wouldn't say I have a long game in mind, but I'm definitely not about to come straight out with it. I even get into chit-chatting a little, while she makes us tea. She's overjoyed I went to Keswick, practically misty-eyed, like it's her spiritual home or some shit and that my going there was a pilgrimage to the founding seat of our relationship.

She suggests we go sit out on the verandah, and as we walk through her garden I have a sudden realisation about Marsha Ray, which for a fleeting moment makes me sad. If I could have met Marsha Ray's garden before I met her, or, better still, *instead* of meeting her, I think I might have formed a whole different opinion. There's no doubt that, when it comes to knowing which flowers to put where, she is an artist. I think even Thomas would have liked her if he'd seen her garden. Some people are best appreciated through their art, through what they produce. Everyone has a redeeming feature, right? Hers kind of takes the zip out of my excitement about telling her she killed my dad.

I tell her I need to know exactly what went down in Brazil, and for once she drops the performance and gives me what I need.

'We took a taxi from Recife airport to one of those big tourist hotels at the beach. It was either still being built or half-falling down, I couldn't tell. I was so exhausted. Robin had told Thomas at Manchester airport to pretend he didn't know us until we got to Recife. I had to carry you everywhere. You'd been asleep since Thomas brought you to the lake house, so I assumed that junkie had given you something to knock you out and was really cross that no one had asked my advice.

'The next thing I knew, I was being bounced up and down in my bed. I opened my eyes and squinted at this pale shape that was you jumping up and down next to me, reciting in your funny little voice that also jumped up and down as you bounced: *Way-cup-a-mungry, way-cup-a-mungry*. Like one of Robin's mantras. I'd been told you were called Little Man so I said, "Little Man, please stop jumping." And you said, in your sweet little Scottish accent, "You're not my mother." I sat up then and you stopped jumping and we peered at each other in the gloom. The curtains were shut but they were glowing orange so I knew the sun was up. It hadn't occurred to me that you would have an accent. It did occur to me that your father wouldn't like it, especially as Andrew was Scottish. "No," I said, "I'm not your mother, but I'm a very good friend of your father, and I used to be friends with your mother before she went to live in Scotland." I'll never forget what you said next. "Do you know my sperm father or my Andrew father?" That did make me laugh. Like all bright children you didn't wait for an answer but kept firing more questions. "What's my mother's name, then?" "Suki," I said. And you said, "That's wrong. You don't know her. You're a liar. She's called Sarah." I didn't know she'd changed her name. "Suki was her special name," I said, guessing what had happened. I'm a quick-thinker like that. "You ask her next time you see her. How long have you been awake?"'

Just as I'm warming to her she goes and fakes a Scottish accent.

'"All the time. I'm hungry. Are we on holiday? Why's there a swimming pool? What's your name? Marsha? That's the same as my granny's name. I can't have two Granny Marshas." You started bouncing again, so I suggested you jump over to the other bed so that I could get up and dressed and take you to find some breakfast. I had no idea what the time was, but if a child's been asleep and then woken up, the meal should always be breakfast.

'"Then can we go to the swimming pool? Pleeeeeeeeeeeeeeeez?" You put your little hands together as if to pray, with a funny little smile on your face, then you bowed and my heart melted. I had to laugh. You inherited your father's charm all right. I didn't know yet what Robin had planned for us so I told you to wait and see what he had to say. You perked right up then. "Is my father here? My sperm father? The bad man said I would meet my sperm father."

'It wasn't even six a.m., they didn't start serving breakfast until seven, so we went and sat by the pool and naturally you wanted to go in the water and had stripped down to your underpants and jumped in before I could stop you. You were a remarkable swimmer for your age; you said Andrew had taught you when you were a babby, and you could dive before you could stand on your own two feet.'

Do I still like to swim? It was my favourite thing to do when I was fucked-up. I haven't done it in a while.

'We ate breakfast out there by the pool. You mixed four different cereals together in one bowl and ate them dry because there was no soya milk. I wrapped you up in a towel so you didn't have to put your dirty clothes back on and we went up to our room.

'You were sitting watching TV when Robin poked his head round our door. You were engrossed in a cartoon, not bothered at all that it was in a strange language. Robin stepped back so you couldn't see him and put his finger to his lips. He was obviously furious about something and I assumed Thomas had upset him, but that wasn't it. "You allowed the boy to swim without my permission," he whispered. "Don't do that again." I supposed he had seen us from his window. To get him off the subject I asked him for your bag so I could dress you in clean clothes. He handed me a bundle of notes. "The boy's mother gave us nothing. Take him out and buy him new clothes. And some dye to lighten his hair. Get enough for both of us." "There's no need to dye it," I said, "it'll soon lighten up in the sunshine." Your hair was dark as it is now, and I knew it'd only go yellow or orange if we bleached it. "Get the dye," he said. "He looks too much like her. And from now on you are his mother and he is to call you by that name, so make sure you tell him." I protested at that, but he was adamant. "Any woman can be mother to any child," he said. "He'll soon forget her." Well I knew that to be true, so I stopped arguing.

'We stayed one more night at that hotel then went by taxi to Olinda. I was delighted to hear that Thomas had been sent on ahead to the commune. He gave me the creeps, always being around and me always having to speak to your father through him. I hoped it would be more like the old days with him gone. I hoped we'd seen the last of him. Robin had rented a beautiful fuschia-pink house halfway up a steep, narrow cobbled street, with an incredible view from the back garden all the way to Recife. Olinda was lovely, with its colourful houses and music playing everywhere, but unfortunately you had nowhere to swim because the reef there attracted sharks.

'The first thing you said when we arrived was, "Is Andrew and Mummy here?" and Robin flashed me such a look, as if it was my fault you were missing your mother, but I knew he only wanted you to be happy. To be honest, I was surprised we didn't hear from her, but your father said she'd given you up for good. I didn't know how she could have given you up, poor little mite.

'I had terrible trouble adjusting to the heat over there, and the humidity was unbearable. But you were extremely well behaved, polite towards your father and me. You made for a funny picture, the two of you, both with your bright yellow hair and your father in his pink outfits. I'd accidentally dyed all his whites pink by washing them with the new red underpants I'd bought him in Recife. He was so gracious about it, said he actually preferred them pink.

'We had a live-in maid, who came with the house. I don't remember her name –'

The reason she doesn't remember Maria's name now is because she didn't take the trouble to learn it then, even though it was Maria's home we were living in.

'– an overweight black girl who dressed every day in the same tight black cycling shorts and horrible, tight fluorescent vests with sequins spattered across her enormous breasts. I have a photograph upstairs of the two of you together.'

'Really?' Finally, a photograph I actually want to see.

She 'nips to the loo' and returns with photos, which she instructs me to hold by the corners so the chemicals in my fingers don't damage the picture or some shit like that. She passes me the first one and says it's not for me to keep. I'm only interested in the photo of Maria, but she insists on handing them to me one at a time.

Me and my dad at Quilombo Novo. I almost don't recognise him, he's so hunched over. But he's wearing his pinks so it can only be him. I'm not exactly healthy-looking either. I guess I'm seven or eight, weird-looking and skinny. It's not so much a photo of us together as a photo of us standing next to each other. The photograph is of him; I just happen to be there. I'm happy to give it back.

The next one, the one I want, she says I can keep. Five-year-old Sonny. My hair is daffodil yellow, and I'm wearing a white dress shirt and long pants and sitting side by side on a step under a palm with a short stocky teenager. Maria! One of her spread thighs is wider than my entire body. All the more to love. Her beautiful young face is just all smile. She's wearing a tight tank the exact same yellow as my hair. We are turned to face one another, each holding up a green coconut shell, bigger than my head, raised in a toast to our mutual affection. And I instantly recall how much it hurt to leave her.

Never mind what Thomas did, my dad and Marsha Ray were the real kidnappers. Or at least Marsha Ray was my dad's enabler. To take me away from Andrew and from you. And then from Maria. Anyone who loved me had to go. All to make him feel better about himself.

Marsha is yakking on…

'Those were lazy days, I spent a lot of time out in the garden, sitting in the shade reading about and learning the names of all the unfamiliar plants. I couldn't believe how quickly everything grew there. Robin suggested I plant medicinal herbs and learn their uses. We didn't have the internet then of course and it was difficult to get hold of the books I needed, but there was a good bookshop in Recife and I'd send you and the girl off on the bus to pick them up for me.

'You didn't go to school, but Robin taught you how to meditate out in the garden, so it wasn't as if you weren't learning anything.'

Yeah, now I remember him yelling at me for fidgeting.

'Robin said there was plenty of time for you to learn the boring stuff, and that children in civilised countries didn't even start to learn how to read and write until the age of seven. You picked the language up really quickly and after a few weeks you were able to translate for the maid in your funny Scotuguese, and the atmosphere between me and her became a little less fractious.

'When the time came I didn't want to leave Olinda. I tried to persuade Robin to stay and teach meditation there, but he couldn't be budged from his calling no matter how idyllic our life had become. You had settled in nicely with us, so you took the next move completely in your stride.'

That's not how I remember it. What I remember is being dragged to the car clinging to Maria's thigh with both arms, my head against that luscious pillow of an ass. I'm screaming and Maria is crying, '*Meu lindo, meu lindo,*' as my arms are wrenched apart and I'm shoved, all kicking legs and octopus arms, in the back of the car.

No wonder I don't like car journeys, right?

'The journey to the commune was unbelievably long and hot. You and Robin both slept on and off, him in the front seat, sitting bolt upright, you sprawled across me in the back. We were on the road for at least eight hours. Robin had taken a sleeping pill, and when you were awake you'd sit up chatting to the driver but mostly you slept. I didn't sleep a wink, I was so terrified the driver would doze off and kill us all. He only made two stops and one of those wasn't even a proper stop, just him slowing down enough to buy a bag of oranges from a roadside seller who trotted alongside the car. He peeled his oranges with both hands off the wheel and only half an eye on the road. I was a nervous wreck. And then, when we got there, Robin insisted we walk the last half-mile or so into the commune. I was so exhausted. He was fresh as a daisy. He marched up to the first person we saw and said, "I am Guru Bim and I have been sent to continue Guru Mehdi's work."

'I don't know what I'd been expecting. I think I'd imagined a large house with a few families living together in it, sharing meals and chores and what have you, but this was a complete village, with wattle-and-daub huts built willy-nilly in amongst the trees, a school, a clinic, a farm, the lot. I say huts because some of them were no bigger than garden sheds, while others were more rambling, as if new sections were built on as families grew larger. Everyone had their doors and window shutters open, with colourful curtains pulled across them to keep out the insects. Hammocks were slung between the huts, tied to the trees. Each hut had its own little garden. It was very pretty.

'After a bit of negotiation Robin waved us over and we were
taken to the main house, a single-storey, whitewashed stucco affair,
quite Greek-looking, I thought. The rooms were large, with ceiling
fans to keep them cool, which were powered by a row of huge
solar panels, lined up along the back of the house. Out front was a
full-width verandah, which was in the shade for most of the day. I
wouldn't go so far as to say it felt like home, but it did remind me of
my summerhouse.

'The residents threw a welcome party. They set up a microphone
and amplifier on the front porch and people crowded round, eager to
hear Robin speak. Hundreds of them if you included all the children.
Robin was on cracking form, insightful and kind and funny; he stood
and talked for two hours, praising the good work Guru Mehdi had
done, explaining that the Universe had summoned him to help them
all along the path towards enlightenment so they might be reunited
with Guru Mehdi in spirit. He talked to them about meditation and
shaking and after a short demonstration by me he said, "Listen to your
heart," and left the front porch to massive applause.

'Things rolled along nicely. I set up a medicinal herb garden
using cuttings I'd brought from Olinda. Eventually I took over the
clinic and became community nurse, treating people with my herbal
medicines. It was a huge responsibility but Robin convinced me I was
equal to the challenge. Before we'd arrived, the clinic had been run by
a doctor chappie called Ken. Poor man had AIDS but we didn't find
that out until later. When I took over the clinic, Ken became Robin's
personal doctor. I don't think Robin had thought through what a
drain it would be on him physically to care for the spiritual health of
so many others and over those first few years he became quite poorly.
Meditation, shaking and herbs really can heal most things, you know,
but the stress of having responsibility for other people can take its toll.
Not that he would have let that stop him.'

Seriously? She still believes all that crap?

'Running the clinic alone wasn't easy, but Robin was always
encouraging. When one new mother got an attack of mastitis that no
amount of cabbage and fenugreek compresses would shift, the poor
woman was so tired and run-down, I put in a request for antibiotics as
a special case. Robin refused but promised to meditate on the problem

and send her his grace. The next day, her mastitis had improved and within a week she was completely back to normal.'

This is my opportunity to tell her Ken probably treated it in secret, but I'm not ready to burst her bubble yet.

'One of the kids went down with measles, and I discovered none of the youngest children in the commune had been vaccinated so I warned Robin that an epidemic would be disastrous. He shooed me away, saying it would take seven years to see the effects of our work and that it was ridiculous to expect overnight results. He said the only epidemic to concern us was AIDS, which he said had spread way beyond the homosexual communities and was infecting women and children.

'I knew about AIDS of course, but didn't know enough, and at the commune we were so cut off, even from events in Recife. One thing we did have plenty of was garlic so I had everyone eat a raw clove every day to boost their immunity. I was frightened. Everyone was. I asked Robin if I could order HIV testing kits from the hospital in Recife, but he said not to panic, that we didn't need kits, and instead had me organise everyone into a long queue at the verandah so that he, with you as his assistant, could read everyone's aura to divine if anyone was HIV positive. To my horror, he diagnosed almost everyone with HIV. Ken had AIDS. He also discovered two previously undetected cases of cancer, both at an advanced stage, and showing no real outward symptoms besides weight loss, which was affecting us all by then so they had gone unnoticed.'

Long sigh.

'Those last couple of years there were tough. There was never enough food to go around. Fewer babies were being born, which helped, and we'd lost a few others to infections, etcetera. I found myself treating more and more people for anxiety and depression. I had bunches of valerian drying out all over the clinic, stinking the place out.

'Robin's constant encouragement, his assurance that the benefits of my endeavours would be spiritual first and physical second, kept me going. He was adamant that on a spiritual plane we were well and truly winning. I'll admit there were times when even my faith in his methods was tested, but I put my trust in his vision and consolidated my faith in my meditation and it got me through.'

Jeez.

'Then you and Thomas disappeared. No one knew where. Robin said you'd been sent on a special mission, but what the mission was and when you'd be back he refused to say. I just had to hope that whatever it was you were doing was part of his plan to restore health to the commune, but as time went on I suspected that Robin knew as little about your disappearance as I did. Meanwhile, things got worse. A few adults with other chronic illnesses contracted pneumonia and died. Everyone was hungry; some were starving. People had no energy to work the vegetable plots so less food was being produced at a time when even a full yield would have been insufficient to feed us all. After much pleading on my part, Robin agreed to allow those in the worst health to reduce the number of hours they spent working, as long as they maintained their daily shaking practice along with everyone else. I made little badges out of old cardboard boxes for those people to wear. Nobody developed AIDS, though, besides Ken, and for that we were grateful, but the commune was no longer a happy place to be.

'At last, Robin gave Ken permission to order essential medication for everyone. It had to be administered on a specific date given by the Universe, and he spent the weeks it took Ken to get all the supplies together making detailed astrological and numerological calculations. The date changed a few times, but when it all lined up at last everyone was given a holiday from all duties and ordered to spend the day resting in their homes.

'It was a long day. Ken and I went from hut to hut, made sure no one was missed. At the end of the day there were just two syringes left in the fridge, mine and Ken's. Robin's was in the fridge in his room with all his other meds.

'I injected Ken in the kitchen and sent him off to bed. Poor man was on his last legs. I was more than capable of injecting myself.'

She lifts her right butt cheek off the chair, slaps it.

'Robin was sitting up in bed, reading one of his spiritual books. A cannula was already fixed into his vein. He put his book down and patted the bedcovers for me to sit beside him. "Come and sit," he said. "It's been an exhausting day for us all."

'Tired as I was, I was grateful for a few moments of intimacy after

many months of little contact. Since you'd failed to return, his health
had deteriorated considerably.'

Wow, is she going to blame me for his death?

"'Is everyone resting?" he said. I told him they were and that I'd
never known the place so quiet, even during meditation sessions when
there was always someone coughing or a baby crying. "Excellent," he
said. "And Ken?"

"'He's gone to his room," I said. "I don't suppose he'll be up before
midday tomorrow, he looks completely washed out."

"'Good. Well, let's get me done so that you can go off and get
some rest."

As I pushed the syringe plunger slowly in, he said, "You and I will
be leaving tomorrow, so make sure you get a good night's sleep." I was
too tired to ask questions or even to think about whether what he was
saying was true, so I said I would, threw the empty syringe into the bin
and wished him goodnight. The last thing he said to me was, "Listen
to your heart."

'I can say in all honesty that the next day was the worst day of my
life. I woke up some time after eleven with a blinding headache. The
heat in my room was suffocating. I had fallen asleep in my clothes. I
went to fetch a glass of water from the kitchen. Someone, I presumed
Ken, it couldn't have been Robin, had made coffee even though
coffee had been banned. I'm putting off getting to the point. It was
so dreadful.'

She blinks and bravely bites her bottom lip. I don't feel like
laughing as much as I thought I would.

'I went out on the verandah. People were out and about as usual,
still weak and moving slowly in the heat. Nobody waved over to me
or even looked up, but then they generally didn't by then. Nobody
looked any the better for their shots and long rest but I supposed it
would take time. That's when I remembered what your father had
said about us leaving that day. The horrible thought occurred that
he'd been sitting around waiting for me the whole morning and given
up and gone off on his own, or, worse, with Ken. I rushed back inside
and knocked on his door. When there was no answer I panicked. I
knew he wouldn't have thought to leave me a note, he would just
expect me to find him wherever he had gone. I knocked louder

and called his name then Ken's door opened and he stuck his head out to ask if everything was okay. "Have you been in to see him this morning?" I said.

"'Not yet," he said, "I only woke up half an hour ago. Thought I'd have a drop of coffee to get myself going first. I expect he's still asleep. Want me to look in and check?"

"'It's okay," I said. "I'll pop my head around the door." I don't know why I said that; it was absolutely forbidden to enter Robin's room without an invitation. Maybe I thought the intimacy of our little conversation the night before had promoted me over Ken. But I knocked again out of respect for the rules and waited a few seconds before opening the door.

'Despite his huge spiritual presence, your father was a slight man physically. Even so, lying there that morning he seemed to have shrunk even more overnight. I had seen enough death in my career to know instantly that he was gone. Then everything went red and Ken's voice came echoing as if through a tunnel and the next thing I knew I was in my own room, propped up on the bed, with an electric fan trained on my face and Ken asking me to tell him my name.

'The rest of that day I just lay on my bed, turning our last conversation over and over in my mind, searching for a deeper message. I meditated, hoping to make contact with his departing soul, but his soul had been united with the Universe years before. It was my own that was earthbound and trapped inside this useless shell.'

Taps herself on the chest.

'I became obsessed with the idea that he had meant me to go with him and decided that if I meditated long and hard enough he would reach down from wherever he was and drag me up. I even tied my hair into a little ponytail like the Hare Krishnas to make it easier for him. But the next morning I was still there. In the end I understood that when he'd said we'd both be leaving, he meant that I was to return to England and continue his work here.

'The funeral was held that evening. Deaths were always dealt with quickly because of the heat, you know. It was a quiet affair – we were all in shock. Ken asked me to say a few words but I couldn't do it. Nobody in my position could have. Instead the whole commune honoured his passing by shaking together in silence through the night, like one of those silent discos they have down on the beach sometimes. What a blessing it was that you weren't there.

'When I thought no one would notice I took myself off to my room to pack a few essentials, clothes I hadn't worn since my arrival because they hung off me, I had lost so much weight. I've put it all back on again now. Then I sat there all night in the dark, waiting, listening for his voice.

'Just before sunrise, when the air was still cool, and everyone had gone to their beds, I set off to walk the few miles to Cabrobó. From there I went by taxi to Recife. My credit card had expired so I was stuck there for the few days it took for a new one to be delivered to the bank. Those days were torture. Nobody spoke English and I felt conspicuous and threatened even during the day. So I shut myself in my room and meditated until it was time to leave. I wasn't used to the noise of the traffic, the oily traffic fumes and the smell of the river that wafted up through my hotel room window. The people out on the streets scared me. I'd been away from home for six years.'

Sad Blue Steel.

Okay, so now I'm stunned at how someone can be so ignorant. Not just her, me too. I was there, for some of it anyway, but I had no idea. At least I have the excuse I was a kid and I can honestly say I never fell into the trap of thinking the sun shone out my dad's ass. I do feel kind of sorry for Marsha, though, for how pathetic she is and how deluded.

I can't do it, I can't tell her. Not so much because I don't think she should know but because I don't want to witness her reaction.

I tell her I need to be on my own to process everything she's told me. I even manage not to fight back when she throws her arms around me and says, 'So wise at such a young age, so like your father.'

I make for the side gate, but she follows, begs me to go through the house. She has something to give me and tries one last time to persuade me to see my dad's old room. I want to see it even less now than before, but she's upset so I lie and say I'll come back and see it another day.

On the window ledge by her front door is a pile of postcards. She picks one off and gives it to me. At first I assume it's another old card from the Trembling Leaves days because it has a photo of my dad on the back, sitting cross-legged in Marsha Ray's garden in the sunshine, the summerhouse behind him. But I'm wrong about that.

'It's just a little meditation group we've started,' says Marsha. 'We meditate on the Grace of Guru Bim. Perhaps you'd like to join us tomorrow evening as our guest of honour.'

All that nice stuff I said just now, about feeling sorry for her and all? Forget it, she's an idiot.

I walk real slow down towards the water. I head over to the pizza joint to pick up a latte and then go sit on the same beach where I saw the cool family in hopes they might be there again.

This one day, right, I was sitting on the beach at Redondo, watching the surfer dudes, when a pod of dolphins came in, wheeling around in the waves alongside them. Six or eight of them, doing their usual stuff, looping around so that after a while you're so mesmerised you forget you're even watching them. Then, right when my brain had switched off, four of them shot up out of the ocean like guided missiles, getting some serious air, then flipped over backwards to all four points of the compass. It was like they'd been rehearsing it for days out there in the ocean and had come in to the shore to try it out on an audience for the first time. You've seen them do that stuff, right? Man, that shit changes your life. I wasn't even high. I expected the whole beach to burst into applause, but only me and this one other guy saw it. Fucking zombies will applaud a routine plane landing, but not even notice an Olympic-standard act of marine life spontaneity. Everyone else on the beach was looking the other way, throwing balls or taking pictures of themselves kissing their boyfriends. I have to look away when I see that, but once I've seen it I can hear the mouth noises, even if the kissers are too far away for that to be humanly possible. I guess that's why me and the Great Dudini can relate – we both have supernatural hearing. And why I will probably never find another girlfriend. Not that I'd ever date another SoCal girl; they all speak like they're choking on a fishbone.

Once, in school, I had the brilliant idea of wearing earplugs while making out. Man, that made it worse – the noises were louder than ever. My experiment got me dumped and my dumpee told her girlfriends I was weird so I haven't so much as made out since, never mind getting laid. I need help with that, or I'ma wind up A.L.O.N.E.

I look around for the stone-throwing Taliban family, but it's the middle of the day and the middle of the week and I guess the kid's at school and her parents are working. Normal stuff. The atmosphere is chilled: a woman tanning an elephantine ass there, a guy reading a newspaper here, sharing a spliff with his pal. I guess they don't have jobs. For the first time I really notice the weather got warm and take off my jacket and sweater. I grab a handful of stones and toss one, hard as I can towards the sea. Some guy sitting closer to the water turns and shows me his warning face so I put the other stones down and pull the leaflet Marsha Ray gave me out of my pocket and sit there pretending to read it.

It's clear now why Thomas and Andrew thought I should make this trip, but I've only just really woken up to why I went along with it. I didn't have anything better to do, that's for sure, and I was stoked at the opportunity to see where Shaun and Ed hung out and to find out what my life was like before Redondo, who my parents were, all that. But I've been kidding myself that those were my reasons for leaving RB, deluding myself about the real reason, which is the same reason I've always done things, the reason I went along with everything my dad threw at me, the reason I pinned my fate to Thomas's ticket. The reason I joined the Galaxy, the reason I took drugs. The truth is, I wanted to make myself so big, bad and dangerous, so visible that you would see me, would come find me out and love me no matter how great or how pathetic I really was. My real reason for coming to the UK was to find you.

Walking along the boardwalk, I call Andrew to tell him what I've found out about you from Thomas and he tells me more. Turns out you never wanted me. From the second you saw my dad having sex with another woman in Marsha Ray's summer house, you wanted an abortion. Andrew persuaded you to go through with the pregnancy and when you rejected me as a baby he raised me as his own. Which I guess makes Andrew my dad. My other dad. No way does Thomas get to check out now, junkie-kidnapping-murderer or not. Plenty of kids these days have two dads and no mom, right?

Then I call Ruth to ask her if she'll be my gran. And it makes me unbelievably happy when she says yes. Better than being high. Who knew how great that would feel?

I guess it's weird how I never really thought about family before. I knew I didn't have one in the same way most other people do, but it never really bothered me. Thomas was enough. Probably the truth is it was too scary to think about and that's why I did all the bad stuff. Who knows. But what is clear as I walk over to the Avalon B&B is that all those people you and my dad chewed up and spat out are my real family. Even Marsha Ray is the aunt nobody likes much but will call on now and again for gardening tips, to make her happy and keep the gifts coming in on birthdays and Christmas.

What I've learned is that having no family can be a huge advantage in life. You get to assemble your own, or at least you get to choose people and ask if they wouldn't mind being assembled. And what I also realise now is that, if I could choose who my mother was, it sure as fuck would not be you.

What, you think I should be devastated by your rejection? Let me tell you what I know. I know that a kid can fail big-time. I know that character can reform (just not yours or my dad's, right?). I know that Thomas had to fall for me to rise and vice versa, just as Philip had to die for Shaun to realise he loved him and Ed had to turn into a zombie so that Shaun could be a proper responsible boyfriend to Liz.

When I tell the guys at the Avalon B&B I'll be leaving the next morning they fuss over me more than ever, saying I've been the perfect guest and how they'll be sorry to see me leave and that they will always find space for me whenever I want to come stay again. When they ask me where I'm headed next, I say Brazil, without even having thought about it. Yeah, *fungible* is still my favourite word after all. And that's where I'm going now, to Porto de Galinhas to be precise. To find Maria and ask her if she'll be my big sister. And, from tomorrow, my name will be Sonny Harrison Hardiker. Cool, right?

There's a short version of this letter. It goes something like this:

Dear Mom,
Fuck You.

Acknowledgements

This novel was written on the move, during which time I was the unworthy and supremely grateful recipient of extreme levels of hospitality and generosity from friends old and new: in Redondo Beach, Mike Mena and Ileana, Michael and Eric Landon; in Hove, Dawn Wills, Brett Lomas, Sue Forrest, John Davison, Heather Gratton and Rob Mockett; in Brighton, Lisa Jansen and Andrew, Phoebe and Jay Springham; in Paris, Peter Wilberforce-Jones, Philippe Bien and Marina Gigova; in Auvers-sur-Oise, Nicolas Hervais and Régis Cocault; in NYC and PA, Lenny and Stephanie Kaye; in London, Alan Pell, Sarah Barron, Clare Grady and Paul Fennelly; in Manchester, Kate Engineer; in Villefranche-sur-Mer, Michaela Morgan. Thanks also to everyone at the Albergue Canto dos Artistas in Olinda and the Pousada Capitães de Areia in Porto de Galinhas.

There's no place like home, right?

Huge thanks to Philippa Brewster and Linda McQueen for their superlative editorial input and ongoing support. Also to Mathew Clayton, Phil Connor, Jimmy Leach and everyone at Unbound. Thanks too to Daniel Burke for the video and Kaspar Forrest for help with social media.

Thanks also to those who offered time and expertise to help with research: Dr Rob Mockett for advice on all matters medical; Frazer

Bradshaw and Anna Hendry for advising on and checking legal accuracy; and Clare Gabriel for invaluable insights into life within a spiritual community. Also to Ben, Michael, Eric, Mike and Ileana in the US and Fabio J. Benez Secanho in Brazil for help with the finer points of vocabulary. I take full credit for any mistakes in that department.

Also to those who took the time to read and feed back on early drafts: Jeff Skellon, Astrid Williamson, Joel Sayers, Alex Green. And especially to Liz Garner for recommending it for publication.

The following books were also invaluable: Dr Anthony Storr, *Feet of Clay: Saints, Sinners and Madmen: A Study of Gurus*; Peter Robb, *A Death in Brazil: A Book of Omissions*; Deborah Layton, *Seductive Poison: A Jonestown Survivor's Tale of Life and Death in the People's Temple*; Russell Miller, *Bare-Faced Messiah: The True Story of L. Ron Hubbard*; William Shaw, *Spying in Guru Land*; Susan Cain, *Quiet*.

Extra special thanks to Eric Landon for entrusting me with his diaries. To Sixto Rodriguez for permission to use his brilliant lyrics, and of course for the music. To Redondo Beach Public Library for providing a great place to write and research and to Catalina Coffee House in Redondo for the best iced teas and lattes anywhere.

Last, but by no imaginable means least, I send heaps of gratitude to everyone who supported me at the crowdfunding stage. This book would not be seeing the light of day without your investment, and having your support means more to me even than seeing the book in print, so thank you again, I really appreciate it.

Supporters

Unbound is a new kind of publishing house. Our books are funded directly by readers. This was a very popular idea during the late eighteenth and nineteenth centuries. Now we have revived it for the internet age. It allows authors to write the books they really want to write and readers to support the writing they would most like to see published.

The names listed below are of readers who have pledged their support and made this book happen. If you'd like to join them, visit: www.unbound.com.

Ethan Abraham
Leila Abu El Hawa
Nigel Adams
Dinah Alan-Smith
Jo Alderson
Camelia (Maddi) Alexa
Sarah Bailey
Debbie Ball
Karen Barratt
Jenny Barrett
Sarah Barron
Frances Barron-Pell
Paul Bassett Davies
John Baxter
Stephen Beagrie
Charlotte Beck
Gael Beddoes
Katja Bell
Deanne Bennett
Devon Bennett
Janine Bennett
David Best
Philippe Bien
Clémentine Blue
Al Boorman
Ben McDonagh-Booth
Penny Booth
Maureen Bowes
Louise Bradford

Philippa Brewster
CafeBookClub Brighton
Bob Brown
Johny Brown
Moira Brown
Maria Burberry
Joe Butler
Louise Byrne
Sue Campayne
John Carroll
Kate Chapman
Jacqueline Chnéour
Andy Cliff
Michael Cohen
Rose Collis
Catherine Connor
David Cooper
Conor Corkrum
Steven Crowther
Chris Davies
Martin Davies
John Davison
Les Dennis
Celia Dickinson
Kay Dickinson
Heidi Dilworth
Tracey Dodd
Paul Douglas
Niamh Dowling

Adrian Driscoll
Keith Dunbar
Chris Ellis
Fleur Emery
Lizzie Enfield
Zarina Engineer
Jennie Ensor
Therese Eyres
Paul Fennelly
Jelles Ffonk
Pete Fij
Krzysztof Fijalkowski
Dymphna Flynn
Kaspar Forrest
Nick Fowler
Lindy Fretwell
Annabel Gaskell
Marina Gigova
Claire Gilliver
Bernice Gonzalez De
   Torres
Clare Grady
Peter Gray
Alex Green
Paul Guiver
Matthew Hainsby
Deborah Hall
Pippa Harris-Burland
Catherine Harrison

David Hebblethwaite
Steve Herring
Trisha Hext
Brian Hibbert
Lisa Holloway
Peter Howe
Dylan Howitt
Sarah Hughes
Sarah Ivinson
Mick Jackson
Lisa Jansen
Ralf Jeutter
Jon & Mari
Susanna Jones
Stella Kane
Colin Kennedy
Dan Kieran
Jannet King
Peter Knell
Rebecca Labram
Candida Lacey
Stephanie Lam
Jane Lawson
Natalie Le Bouedec
Jimmy Leach
Anna Lewis
Steve Lewis
David Lidz
Brett Lomas
Zachary Loofs
Julia Lyon
Ben McDonagh-Booth
Lee Madgwick
Toyin Manley
Richard Manners
Dean Marsh
Stephen May
Sadie Mayne
Jonathan McAneney
Scott McCready
Carol McDonagh
Jo McDonagh & Rocio
    Maruny

Stephen McGowan
Graham McPhail
Linda McQueen
Mike Mena
Nina Mer
Anne Middleton
John Mitchinson
Kyoko Miyake
Rob Mockett
John Moore
Michaela Morgan
Anthony Mulryan
Charlie Myatt
Carlo Navato
Emma Nuttall
Georgia Odd
John O'Donoghue
Maria Olsson
David Oselton
KP Parker
Gary Parnell
Corinne Pearlman
Deborah Pearson
Keiren Phelan
Catherine Pierce
Justin Pollard
Sophie Pratt
Yvonne Prinz
Susan Purvis-Mold
Tony Reynolds
Phyllis Richardson
Mark Ridgway
Tiffany Robinson
Rachel Rooney
Domenica Rosa
Sammy Rubin
Helen Saelensminde
Miguel Salvador
Joel Sayers
Gil Schalom
William Shaw
Christopher Shevlin
Colin Short

Wade Shotter
Matthew Sigley
Ian Skewis
Tim Slack
Ed Smith
Jenny Smith
Justin Smith
Mimi Solis
Soapy Soutar
Susan Soutar
Jay Springham
David Steele
Kimberley Stephenson
Lisa Stevens
Dave Swann
Julian Tardo
Lesley Thomson
Marina Todd
Ioanni Tsakalis
Debbie Tutty
Mr Vast
Mark Vent
Hannah Vincent
Tim Waters
Charlotte Watmore
Frances Wetherilt
Rachel Wexler
Helen Wheatley
Peter Wilberforce
Tim Wild
Astrid Williamson
Dawn Wills
Rita Willson
Sue Woods
Karen Zelin